T0150826

ALSO BY ROCH CARRIER IN TRANSLATION

La Guerre, Yes Sir! (1970)
Floralie, Where Are You? (1971)
Lady With Chains (1991)
The Hockey Sweater and Other Stories (2012)

ROCH CARRIER'S LA GUERRE TRILOGY

ROCH CARRIER

TRANSLATED BY
SHEILA FISCHMAN

La Guerre, Yes Sir! first published in French in 1968 by Editions du Jour, Montreal. First published in English in 1970 by House of Anansi Press Ltd.

Floralie Where Are You? first published in French in 1969 as *Floralie, ou est tu?* by Editions du Jour, Montreal. First published in English in 1971 by House of Anansi Press Ltd.

Is it the Sun, Philibert? first published in French in 1970 as *Il est par là, la soleil* by Editions du Jour, Montreal. First published in English in 1972 by House of Anansi Press Ltd.

This edition published in 2013 by
House of Anansi Press Inc.
110 Spadina Avenue, Suite 801
Toronto, ON, M5V 2K4
Tel. 416-363-4343
Fax 416-363-1017
www.houseofanansi.com

Distributed in Canada by
HarperCollins Canada Ltd.
1995 Markham Road
Scarborough, ON, M1B 5M8
Toll free tel. 1-800-387-0117

Distributed in the United States by
Publishers Group West
1700 Fourth Street
Berkeley, CA 94710
Toll free tel. 1-800-788-3123

House of Anansi Press is committed to protecting our natural environment. As part of our efforts, the interior of this book is printed on paper that contains 30% post-consumer recycled fibres, is acid-free, and is processed chlorine-free.

17 16 15 14 13   1 2 3 4 5

Library and Archives Canada Cataloguing in Publication

Carrier, Roch, 1937–
[Novels. Selections. English]
Roch Carrier's La guerre trilogy / Roch Carrier ; translated by Sheila Fischman.

Translated from the French.
"La Guerre, Yes Sir! first published in French in 1968 by Editions du Jour, Montreal first published in English in 1970 by House of Anansi Press Ltd; Floralie Where Are You? first published in French in 1969 as Floralie, ou est tu? by Editions du Jour, Montreal. First published in English in 1971 by House of Anansi Press Ltd; Is It the Sun, Philibert? first published in French in 1970 as Il est par là, la soleil by Editions du Jour, Montreal. First published in English in 1972 by House of Anansi Press Ltd" – Title page verso.

Contents: La guerre, yes sir! – Floralie, where are you? – Is it the sun, Philibert?
Issued in print and electronic formats.
ISBN 978-1-77089-373-3 (pbk.). — ISBN 978-1-77089-378-8 (html)

I. Fischman, Sheila, translator II. Title. III. Title: La guerre trilogy.

PS8505.A77A6 2013   C843'.54   C2013-903506-0
C2013-903507-9

Library of Congress Control Number: 2013909834

Cover design: Brian Morgan | Cover illustration: Jillian Tamaki
Typesetting: Laura Brady

We acknowledge for their financial support of our publishing program the Canada Council for the Arts, the Ontario Arts Council, and the Government of Canada through the Canada Book Fund. We acknowledge the financial support of the Government of Canada through the National Translation Program for Book Publishing, for our translation activities.

Printed and bound in Canada

ROCH CARRIER'S
LA GUERRE TRILOGY

INTRODUCTION
by Noah Richler

COLLECTED HERE FOR the first time — not in the order in which they were written but according to the chronology of their events — is Roch Carrier's extraordinary La Guerre Trilogy, a master work of Canadian invention. In this triptych of stories, the Québécois literary icon, celebrated in English-speaking Canada most of all for his classic children's tale, *The Hockey Sweater* (1979), creates an unforgettable portrait of a colonized people coming to terms with an oppressive church and a military conflict to which it feels no great commitment. But, even more so, these stories tell of a community's slow movement away from isolation and toward the twentieth century and its dubious gifts of progress — atheism, war, the city.

The setting of *Floralie, Where Are You?*, the first novel in this loose generational saga (though the second to be published), is a lush boreal forest that is threatening but also compelling and fantastic. The countryside in which Anthyme and Floralie marry, part, and are reunited is elemental and mythic, a place of mystery, delirium, spirits, serpents, and dark invocations.

"The road will be rough," says Floralie's mother, ominously, of the journey ahead. The wedding dress that her daughter, not an innocent, is wearing as the horse-drawn cart leaves the village for the woods where she will be married is, unusually, black. Her husband Anthyme has only consummation on his mind and drives the buggy so impossibly fast that it careens on two wheels, and Floralie wonders, with foreboding, "Who would come to rescue her in the forest, where she would not have the strength to shout?"

Men, she tells herself, "go crazy on their wedding night."

As readers, we are not quite sure where we are. The village is unnamed, though we are most certainly in the Québec countryside and living close to the turn of the twentieth century. The novel, one could say, is surrealist, though to describe it this way is to resort to a label of convenience that suggests the story's vivid reality, its fabular world bending the rules of our apparently more rational experience, is apparently less credible than our own. Who can be so certain? It makes more sense to think of the myth world of the author's first episode as *pre*-realist, if we intend for the dubious term "real" to describe those more contemporary circumstances of struggle and humiliation at the hands of unjust *human* powers that Carrier's fictional progeny comes to know in the grim city of *Is it the Sun, Philibert?*, one of the author's fictional progeny will ultimately come to know. Montreal, in that final episode, is certainly a more recognizable place than the fiercely animated woods of Carrier's first episode are, but the city is also where prior realities are so successfully and easily distorted — where lights and heat and habitations allow a man to ignore nature and the myth world with which Anthyme and Floralie must contend. The modern age has made humankind powerful enough to obscure the natural world, foolish enough to believe he controls it.

Not so in *Floralie, Where Are You?*, in which flight through the forest puts Floralie in terrifying touch with spirits and daemons even as Carrier lets us know that life as she knows it will soon be upturned. Floralie's world is "mythic" because there are no borders of being in it — no science to tell her that what she imagines may or may not be *ipso facto*, "real." But a new means of transportation is auguring in a new, technological future. A railway is connecting Carrier's community of innocents "who doubted the train's existence until it actually arrived," and is about to put an end to their rural — and intellectual — isolation even as a politician, not quite as backward as he sounds, cautions that the railway will sow "seeds of sadness that we will harvest some day soon." We are in the last moments of an anxious age in which all the couple's encounters and fears exacerbated by the pitiless grip of an intimidating faith are ones that we, in our enlightenment, may confidently determine to be reveries, hallucinations, moments of possession. But to Floralie, the frightened world of her wedding night is absolutely real; an awesome, terrible confusion of kindness and cruelty, love and obedience, light and dark.

Floralie's fiancé, Anthyme, who, with his dark hair and stubble resembles her father, is but another presence in the dark forest of her wedding night. For all intents and purposes, the groom, as was the father, is simply *man*. He reminds her of the angry horses "with their manes ablaze" that, as a child, she remembers having seen run amok through the streets of the village, ramming other horses and breaking wagons and sending "all kinds of things" rolling. He is but one of the constant elements in the natural order, and that by which she will be bedded, first on the spring's open ground — her tears of apprehension met with Anthyme's agitated order, "Don't cry, *Hostie*! This is the happiest day of your life" — and then in the horse-drawn cart in which she'd sought to flee the brutal moment. The memory of another man to whom Floralie was more viscerally attracted, a labourer working on the locomotive line who was an emblem of possibility to a young woman incarcerated by custom, is crushing. Obedience trumps love, cruelty, kindness, and dark the light, for the time being.

Floralie's intoxicated myth world is filled with unbridled passions and temper, and the hell the new bride imagines she deserves is mediaeval in its punishment. She runs through the forest hoping to outpace her religious fright, her whirling sense of guilt, but cannot. First, she lands in the company of a mysterious and affirming spirit, "Néron, son of the Almouchiquois," an Eros figure promising that her "soul will be blossoming with love," and then a bevy of actors performing as the seven deadly sins. "Lust" sidles up to her like the snake in the spruce where she and her husband lay short moments earlier. "Pride" suggests she play a virgin. The comedy of the licentious Father Nombrillet, a priest taking advantage, follows. This is Carrier at his most colourfully fantastic.

Anthyme, too, is consumed. Suspicious of his betrothed, he multiplies the number of her sins in an exponentially maddening affront to his manhood and the purpose of his wedding night. Quickly, he is derailed, damning and then beating his wife before wandering the primaeval forest in his own Dantean fever, his heart black as the night. It is so black, says a less sympathetic Néron, that his blood is black and — we are living a nightmare of the time — that his children "will be niggers." The horse the pair has lost is the locomotive of their passions, aspirations and prejudices for a moment run loose. Their *guerre* is, on the one hand, with existential mystery — with wonder, lust, and the body — and, on the other, with a fierce church that uses its dogma to keep the soaring spirits of its flock tidily reined in. It is a church that teaches, as Father Nombrillet does, that "all women are sinners" and that "man corrupts everything he touches." But, come the dawn, the dark night of the soul is done. The lovers come to their senses before villagers that "danced around the couple, swearing to show how happy they really were, to express the beauty of a man and a woman entwined in the grass."

*   *   *   *

With *La Guerre, Yes Sir!* the effectively pagan world of *Floralie, Where are You?* has receded and the fright Carrier conjures is political rather than religious in its fabrication. The village of primitive yearnings and appetites is now a more guarded, agitated society, one defending itself against other men, not spirits. We are situated in a particular age, and it is winter. The threat at the margins is the second war in Europe, one distantly fought and, for that reason, barely understood.

But the conflict is not so far away that villagers have been able to avoid conscription, or the train that brings the greater world and returning soldiers back into their lives. As the first book's politician warned, the seeds of sadness that the railway has sown are being harvested. Amid the locomotive's cargo of groceries, booze, and Eaton's catalogue mail order stuff is the body of Corriveau, son of Anthyme and Floralie. A further insult, the soldiers bringing the local son home are English-Canadians.

Corriveau has come home a war hero — which is to say, dead. Says the stationmaster, "he died in his soldier suit and far away from the village; that must mean something."

Corriveau was "one of the little guys," likely to have been opening and shutting doors for the big guys, *les maudits Anglais.* His irritated pallbearers are a part of that bunch, trudging from the station to the village through the snow. The military cortège is followed — Carrier has a knack for marvellously quixotic and meaningful tableaux — by the Newfoundlander Molly in a bridal gown, this time white.

The village is married to the package of the war but not quite sure of what is in it, this second *guerre* as much with English Canada as with Germany. With Corriveau's return, the war has hit home. It is close enough that no quarter of the village is untouched in Carrier's mischievously comic, bawdy and irreverent tale. In the fields, a terrified Joseph cuts off his own hand rather than — as he fears soldiers are in the village to make happen — be called up. And in the bedroom, impressive Amélie shares her bed very methodically with two men knowing their place — with Arthur, who has absconded from the war and settled comfortably into her home, and her husband Henri, who returns from the war unexpectedly.

"Who's going to fight the Germans while you're here?" she asks. "Two men in a house is too much for one woman."

But Henri (reconciled to Arthur's presence) would rather not fight again. The world is all a kilter. The "big sun, round as an orange," that previously caressed his face is "a mirage, a poor thought that would not revive the dead earth beneath the ice and snow," held on a wire and threatening to "swallow the whole world."

As it nearly does.

The day of Corriveau's wake is a maelstrom of drink, excess, and confusion, egged on by villagers and soldiers unable to comprehend the other's language and customs. The English-speaking soldiers ask, "What kind of animals *were* these French-Canadians?" They see the *habitants* as "pigs in a pigpen" and conclude, "Give them something to eat and a place to shit and we'll have peace in the country." The villagers, meanwhile, think of the offending soldiers as not even "real Anglais," but ones who "came to Canada because the real Anglais in England wanted to get rid of them." The insults flying back and forth are inadvertent, natural, and immediate. To wit: when the soldiers bring the coffin into the family's home, Mother Corriveau, the aged Floralie, says, "Tell them to take away the cover; our little boy is going to be too hot in there."

The soldiers gave Mother Corriveau a withering look. How dare she refer to the British flag as a "cover"! The old lady had no idea she had offended England; she would have been astounded if someone had told her that this "cover" was the flag her son had died for.

Quickly the intended funeral goes awry. The procession that started with the libidinous Molly in pursuit becomes a drunken wake in which her husband viciously beats the gravedigger Arsène, the French-Canadians are booted out of the Corriveau house, their allegorical home, and an English soldier is killed. But let not the power of *La Guerre, Yes Sir!* as political allegory obscure its outrageous humour, its dark sense of the ridiculous and its understanding of the absurdity of not just the French-Canadian *guerre* but of war in general. "There are people who say if there was a God he wouldn't be allowing this war," says one old man, grieving (to a point). "But there have always been wars, or it seems like it," says a companion. "Then that means maybe there's no God," concludes another.

*   *   *   *

Philibert, son and apprentice of the gravedigger Arsène, hints at such atheist understanding early on. The professional experience of mortality that has the father, in *La Guerre, Yes Sir!*, ruminating about the soldiers' easy distance from the kill is, to young Philibert, budding proof of God's impossibility. Says Philibert to his father, "Every time I see a pig laid out like that I can't help thinking of Christ on Calvary." The son's sacrilege is a harbinger not only of his disbelief but of a desire to leave the village and a swift boot in the arse from the more penitent father follows. The boy asks himself, "Was this what life was all about? Was this why a child was supposed to honour his father all the days of his life?"

In *Is it the Sun, Philibert?*, the concluding episode of Carrier's

Guerre trilogy (and the last of the three books to be written), there is nothing Philibert can do but leave. The way out that was a dreamily imagined road to the United States in *Floralie, Where Are You?* and then a place of nasty *mores* in *La Guerre, Yes Sir!* is the city of Montreal, real and named. Accordingly, Carrier abandons the animated spirits and delicious, ironic comedy of the first two novels for grim tones and new, acidic ways of seeing. His imagery is still fantastic — the quacking heads of thirty-nine ducks frozen in a river, a procession of crippled children pushed in wheelbarrows in the village left behind — but the mood and portrayal of the city, by contrast, is dark and austere and godless.

Deprived of gaiety and colour, the Montreal of *Is it the Sun, Philibert?* is all mud and grey and steel, a kindred wasteland to that which T. S. Eliot conceived of in the wake of a prior conflagration. The snow of the city is brown, too dirty to eat, the wind smells of ashes, and the houses are built so close that they appear as if "ten villages had been thrown down, piled on top of each other." Philibert wanders the winter streets like an Odysseus — but unknowing, incensed, and purposeless, not wily — and carrying a shovel, not an oar. The English language he does not speak stymies him until he finds shelter with a sympathetic woman who gives him a bath and then beds him under perfumed, embroidered sheets, and to whom he might have returned had he known how to note an address amid the strange houses, bafflingly alike. For too brief a moment, Montreal is a city that might have been called "Bonheur. Happiness."

But the *guerre* of the third novel is Philibert's with alienation. The city is a hostile place. It is a "quiet nightmare" of destitution, criminality, deranged religious belief, and tragicomic spouses sunk into depravity. He is a man perennially unsatisfied — with the church, the war, but also the government, the bank, the newspapers and factories. For Philbert, it is *authority* that will not do, and Carrier has a grizzled factory worker reiterate the hapless complaint of *La Guerre, Yes Sir!*

> *"The guy that's responsible," said the old man, "is the good Lord. He made the world the way he wanted. With rich guys and poor guys. With little guys like us and the big guys."*

But Carrier's little guy has come out swinging. Philibert cavorts with drunken soldiers and — *The Hockey Sweater* for adults — attends a Montreal Canadiens match at which he scrambles onto the ice to deck the Toronto Maple Leafs player who has hooked the folkloric hero, Maurice Richard. He finds humdrum jobs — carting groceries and then, working for the city, "digging his own grave down the middle of Ste-Catherine Street." He tells himself, "Life should be beautiful," though it is as strange and grotesque as the circus, never more so than when Philibert stumbles upon Boris Rataploffsky, "the Ninth Wonder of the World," and makes himself the giant's manager. "You are a good boy, don't forget," says Rataploffsky to his unlikely friend. And then it all unravels. Montreal, in Philibert's darkness, is "a funeral wreath placed on the ground," and Carrier, pulling the strings but not defending the raging Philibert, lets him lapse into anti-Semitism, be bloodied by another's death, and squander his unexpected good fortune before "the untouchable black vault of the sky" hurtles down and consumes the unfortunate in a scene of mediaeval revelations such as the terrified young Floralie would have imagined.

We are who we are. Carrier's "big sun, round as an orange," has finally swallowed the world and poor Philibert can only run toward the salvation of its punishing light.

CONTENTS

FLORALIE, WHERE ARE YOU?

*I dedicate this story to those who sought the dawn
but found only night.*

R.C.

The translation is for John Glassco.

S.F.

TRANSLATOR'S FOREWORD

ROCH CARRIER'S SECOND novel, *Floralie, Where Are You?* is technically a sequel to *La Guerre, Yes Sir!* but it is possible that readers of *La Guerre* may not recognize in Anthyme Corriveau and his young bride Floralie the elderly couple whose dead son, his coffin draped in the British flag and carried by English soldiers, provided the occasion for an ironic confrontation with death during the long winter night of *La Guerre*. For the sequel takes us back some thirty years; the season is spring, not winter; and the occasion is a wedding night, not a wake. But just as death may ask what it is that joins us together, love may ask what it is that divides. Night again sets the scene for much of the action. It is the time when our inner life reveals itself best in dream or nightmare. So the night here separates and tests and discovers the characters, to themselves and to the reader. The result is a kind of medieval comedy dramatizing conflicts characteristic not only of the experience of Quebeckers of a generation past but of that perennial mixture of dream and reality we call life.

Floralie, Where Are You? indicates, perhaps more clearly than *La Guerre, Yes Sir!* that Roch Carrier is no sociologist. He is not a realist except in the sense that the classic folk tale, in its primitive and sometimes ribald action and in its delineation of essential types, is realistic. And he writes in a style that has something of the classic purity and simplicity of the tale. Thus, though some English-language reviewers have spoken of Carrier's use of "joual" in *La Guerre, Yes Sir!* they are mistaken. Some writers, like the poet Gerald Godin and the novelist Jacques Renaud, may employ "joual," partly to make a political statement. Carrier does not. He sees "joual" as a degradation of his language and, although his characters may *speak* that way, he leaves it to the reader to *hear* the accent and the mispronunciation. A real-life Anthyme may call his horse (cheval) a "joual," but that's not Roch Carrier's doing. (If he were writing in English he probably wouldn't write "hoss" either.)

The young Anthyme has not yet developed into the virtuoso blasphemer of *La Guerre, Yes Sir!* He directs a remarkable variation on a biblical harangue to an unresponsive deity, but his cursing is mostly limited to "hostie," the sacred host. Here, as in *La Guerre,* swear words have not been translated, and for the same reason.

The kind of Catholicism that was until not too long ago one of the strongest forces in Québec is very evident here. The name of the priest, Father Nombrillet, is significant. "Nombril" means navel, and the name might suggest the rather narrow range of much clerical contemplation of the time. Some readers will be troubled by what may seem to be an exaggerated preoccupation with images of hell and damnation, but to the Roman Catholic Québécois these are very real, an important part of their spiritual or, if you will, "folkloric" formation.

Ingmar Bergman is another artist who deals with specific religious concerns and uses his own northern landscape to make statements with universal relevance and appeal. Just as his films are not exclusively Swedish, so Carrier is not *exclusively* a Québec writer. Still it is Québec that gives to his work its particular flair. In any human society there will be those who see in change, the coming of the railway, a threat to the moral order, the work of the devil and of foreigners. But they will not all be like the local politician who unwittingly sees his fellow citizens as cows, stampeded by the train, and sees in the train the diabolical designs of the "maudits Anglais." It is the ironic incarnation of the type, the play of the novel and the conventional, in which the reader delights. And in this instance, perhaps no reader more than the *maudit Anglais* himself.

S.F.

THE HORSE WAS restless in its collar; the traces were irritating its flanks. It stomped, trying to pull the buggy whose four wheels were squealing on their axles. With one strong hand on the bridle, Anthyme Corriveau kept the horse from moving its head.

Shirts soaked, collars open, hair damp, the wedding guests looked happily at the departing couple.

"The horse farted," announced the idiot boy with a blissful grin.

"You hear that, daughter?" asked Ernest. "The horse is wishing you *bon voyage* too."

The wedding guests danced happily on their drunken legs, until their laughter was exhausted.

"Mama," Floralie complained, "I don't feel right in this dress. I wish you'd let me wear my white one. A black dress isn't a wedding dress. If I don't wear my wedding dress today I'll never get another chance."

"The road will be rough," replied her mother, in a voice that would not tolerate argument.

Anthyme climbed into the buggy. "Thanks a lot, father-in-law, for giving me your daughter. We'll come back in a few years with our children."

"May the good Lord help you!" Ernest prayed.

"None of that! The good Lord'll never set foot on my land to help me pull up stumps."

The wedding guests greeted this blasphemy with laughs that welled up from the depths of their being. The men laughed at their wives, who had been offended by the words, and swallowed great mouthfuls of a yellowish liquid swimming with dandelions, raisins and brownish apples.

"Two arms, it's a man; but God is God," Ernest pronounced in a reproachful tone.

Anthyme pulled hard on the reins, which he held in his left hand while his right whipped the animal's hindquarters. "Get moving!"

The wheels made practically no noise on the muddy road. Standing erect, with all the majesty of a man dominating a beast, Anthyme abused his horse. The end of his whip stung harder and harder. The family and guests watched as the buggy reached the top of the hill and then disappeared into a cloud of dust.

"He couldn't wait to see the last of us," said Ernest sadly.

"Don't talk like that. You know where words like that come from, but you don't know how far they travel."

"Floralie's always been hard. You saw — she didn't even cry."

The guests had turned their backs on the newlyweds and were going towards the grey wooden house. The women were all talking at once, all with the same sharp voice; as for the men, flask or glass in hand, they needed only laughter to understand each other.

"If I'd had the chance to marry Floralie," one of them said, "I wouldn't have waited till late afternoon to disappear into the woods."

Another, the only one who was still looking towards the top of the hill, said, "Floralie wasn't for us."

Waving his flask, a boy from the village shouted in a loud

voice which Floralie, however, could not hear, "I hope you'll be miserable with your foreigner from the mountains."

"It's true, you know, the land we come from's as flat as the palm of your hand," commented another.

Floralie's father came up to the one who had wished his daughter bad luck. He snatched away his bottle and turned it over, letting the drink gurgle out. As he replaced the empty bottle in the man's hand he said, "I hope my land never gets as dry as your heart."

Ernest rubbed his hands together as though to clean them, then went off towards the stable.

The cows, their udders heavy, were mooing, expecting to be milked. Ernest kicked one on the shin. "Shut up! I want to be able to hear myself think."

His footsteps resounded on the wood floor between the two rows of stalls. His Sunday shoes could not avoid the cow pies or the urine-soaked straw. He spat pensively.

"*Baptême!* I didn't even get a chance to talk to Floralie. Anyway, my girl, I'm going to tell you what I wanted to say. You aren't here, but you're my daughter, so you'll hear me just the same as if you were. So listen: Floralie, if your soul is clean like the nice cloth on your wedding table, and if you work like your mother Mathilda, and then if you don't forget that a man's got to eat and he needs his woman to look after him, and if your husband's a little bit like your father, I promise you'll be happy. Not like a fish in water maybe, but like a married woman. Then, don't count the children . . ."

Tears were coming to his rough wrinkled eyelids.

"*Baptême!* This stable sure stinks today."

As he left the stable Ernest was blinded by the light.

"I'm going to drink more than I ought to."

★ ★ ★ ★

Floralie did not turn her head to see the village getting farther away behind her. She said, "Anthyme, I'm scared."

She wanted him to ask her why, to say, "With me you don't need to be scared; I'm strong." But he was silent. His whip lashed out at the horse. Then, after a long silence, without turning towards her, he explained, "If we want to get there before night we're going to have to move faster than the sun. Giddyup!"

A little farther on he let himself fall onto the seat near his wife. The ashy smell of strong soap that had disgusted Floralie all day had disappeared under the stronger smell of a man. Anthyme's shirt was soaked from driving his horse so hard.

"Anthyme," she insisted, "I'm afraid to be going on my wedding trip in this black dress. Mama said it's because of the dust, but as far as I'm concerned you only wear a black dress when you're in mourning. And mourning, that goes against life."

"A man never looks at a dress, he looks at what's under it. *Hostie!*"

Anthyme began to laugh and he could not stop. He stood up, whipped the horse, sat down again, fastened the reins to the apron of the buggy and then roughly put his arm around his wife's shoulders, his fingers in her armpit. He spread his other hand on Floralie's bosom and pressed his hairy face against her cheek. His big brown fingers groped furiously at her firm flesh as though he were trying to put out a fire.

"Oh! That hurts!" she groaned.

As the horse galloped the wheels whined. Floralie listen to the noise but Anthyme heard nothing.

Floralie moved nervously, trying to dislodge her husband's hand. Its big fingers seemed to be embedded in her bosom.

"You're hurting me!"

Anthyme did not want to hear. Floralie put her soft hand on her husband's and dug her nails into it.

He loosened his embrace. The blood made four red lines.

"Blood! I don't like that!"

He got up and cracked his whip on the horse, which could not run any faster.

A road had been formed in the turf by the action of cart wheels repeatedly turning in the same place. First there was underbrush. Grass grew thickly, high and wild. Where the road was, the grass bent over, trampled down; it masked damp ground that had been torn up by wheels. There were ruts where horses had tramped heavily, trying to pull a buggy out of the mud. There were still large brown spots of mud under the grass. Then the road entered the forest, climbing among black spruce trees. Twisted and shaken by the bumpy turnings, Anthyme's buggy was complaining on all sides and Floralie was afraid it would break like an egg. Anthyme kept lashing out at the horse. At every turn they could see black spruce branches spread out ahead of them. Anthyme avoided them all by pulling on one rein or the other, with a cry that hurt Floralie's ears each time she heard it. When the buggy turned on two wheels she clutched the seat. At that speed Anthyme would not be able to avoid all the spruce trees spread out at every turn in the road; they would hit a tree. Then what would happen to the buggy? It would split open like a nut under a hammer, the horse would roll whinnying into the thicket, its legs crushed. What would happen to Anthyme? And who would come to rescue her in that forest, where she would not have the strength to shout? As a matter of fact, no one would be able to hear her at all: the too heavy silence would stifle her cries, the silent spruce would hold her voice in their black branches from which mute birds flew out.

Anthyme was breathing as noisily as his panic-stricken horse.

"Apparently," Floralie thought, "men go crazy on their wedding day."

★ ★ ★ ★

Because of the veil of branches over their heads Floralie saw the sky only as flashes of blue; it seemed to be swimming among the branches, appearing and then disappearing in a black cloud. She stopped looking at the horse and raised her eyes to the sky. As the wheels turned and the buggy jolted frantically along the road, Floralie felt the earth moving farther and farther away from the sky, the road sloping down so abruptly that she felt dizzy, as if someone were squeezing her throat.

Floralie had waited for this day so she could say, "I love you." She had waited until this day to light the little flame at the tip of her lips that would illumine her whole life. She had said it to herself, in a low voice, for herself alone, repeating it carefully so that she would learn to say it well when the time came to ignite the precious little flame that only death would extinguish. She had often repeated it as she repeated her prayers. Now that the day had come to say out loud, "I love you," the only words her lips could form were, "I'm scared, Anthyme."

How could he hear those stammered words that were lost among the grinding noise of the buggy, the cries of iron striking the pebbles, and the smothered sound of the horse's hooves pounding the ground? He was panting as if he were running in place of the animal.

Floralie looked down. She had no desire to say "I love you" to this man standing in front of her, his behind on a level with her face, his legs bent in his crumpled trousers.

She said nothing; she was dreaming about her parents' house with its good smell of hot milk. She was afraid. She held on to her seat so tightly that she almost tore the flesh of her little hand.

★ ★ ★ ★

She used to like the well-combed horses' manes. She used to amuse herself by putting flowers in them and saying, "You're beautiful;

you're the most beautiful of all" if it were a mare. But Floralie did not want to put flowers in the mane of Anthyme's horse. It was all standing up, tangled and shaking as the wind whipped it about. She would not have had the courage to put her hand in that furious mane.

Several times in her father's village she had seen horses with their manes ablaze. It often happened that an angry horse would rear up and bolt through the village like a streak of lightning. It would overturn everything, ramming and breaking other carriages and wagons. All kinds of things would roll through the streets — potatoes, jugs of molasses, jars of preserves, nails, rolls of fence-wire. The horse would overturn its own carriage and drag it along in a cloud of dust. It would snort, standing on its hind legs like a man, and drive its hooves into the white picket fence, neighing. The men would think that the horse was worn out; the braver ones would leave the women and children inside and appear silently on each side of the road. The horse would whirl round and round as though it wanted to tear out, with its teeth, the weight of the carriage behind it. Failing to do so it jumped, it leaped in the dust to trample its burden and suddenly it hurled itself against a house. The men swore and Floralie blushed because she had heard forbidden words. The carriage struck the horse, or a tree, like an enormous whip. Windows shattered and a wheel was always flung out into the middle of the road, slicing like a knife at first, then slowing down, hesitating, until eventually it flattened out against a wall. But the horse was still fleeing. It might leave the village to lose itself in the forest or, running away, it might strangle in its harness. Then a man detached himself from a group. The others were quiet; the old women murmured "Jesus." He moved along the road, his arms open so that the horse would understand that it would not be allowed to pass. The horse charged the man, rearing up and threatening him with its forefeet. The man slipped past, seized the bridle and pulled with all his might, tearing at the horse's mouth. The horse, whinnying, dragged the man along and little by little relented, giving in to the man at last. It stopped, glistening with sweat and panting. The man would put his hand in the horse's mane, patting the collar so the horse would know that it was forgiven. The men and children could approach and the women would beg them to be careful.

Once the horse had lunged at a man and trampled him. The man was supposed to get married the next day and the horse was the one he had rented for the wedding.

The mane of the horse that had brought the young man down was as furious as that of Anthyme's horse.

Anthyme controlled the horse very well, but Floralie was still afraid.

★ ★ ★ ★

Suddenly Anthyme pulled on the reins so hard that the horse's head was turned around. Its jaw, tortured by the bit, seemed like an open wound. The animal tried to resist. It reared up and tried to turn its head back into place. Anthyme, with another short pull on the reins, reminded him who was boss. The horse gave in, quietly. Anthyme released the reins. The head, then the collar, sank slowly towards the ground and the animal licked at the grass, seeking a little freshness. There was no sound from the motionless wheels. The earth no longer resounded under the hooves and the buggy stopped complaining. No sound could be heard except the horse's breathing. The whole forest, the whole earth seemed to be breathing through its lumgs. The trees were frozen in their silence. Despite the sweat, everything that Floralie saw seemed to be fixed in an invisible ice. She shivered in her thin black gown. The trip had tired her out, and it had barely begun. The buggy, jolting at too lively a pace, had shaken her so much that all her thoughts were in disarray. She could not even think. Even though the vehicle had stopped she felt as if the wheels were still turning over the bumps and potholes, as if the ground were trembling beneath her. She could think of nothing but that sensation. Although she could see the horse, crestfallen, its legs weak, its head hanging above the grass, rubbing its nose among the leaves, it really seemed as if it were still running.

Anthyme, seated, listened to his own breathing for a moment, saying nothing. With elaborate care he tied the reins to the apron of the buggy, then suddenly he jumped to the ground.

"Get down," he said.

She got down. When you marry a man you follow him and obey him. During the first weeks she would have to repeat to herself that women are made to obey; then, as she got used to it, she would obey without even thinking about it.

"Come with me," he ordered.

She followed him, her short steps following his long ones as he sank into the ferns. She stopped to put her finger on a touch-me-not, the tiny flower so bright and fragile in the shade.

"Are you coming?"

He knew where he was taking her. Under a very old spruce covered with grey moss, its branches spread out to form a roof, Anthyme turned towards Floralie.

"It's pretty here."

The spruce was redolent of all the freshness that had perfumed the Decembers of his childhood. The fallen needles formed a soft carpet.

"It's pretty," Floralie repeated.

"We'll be nice and comfortable."

"When we were little we used to make houses under the pine trees."

"This is a spruce."

"It's a tree."

"Now you're going to really be my wife."

He took off his jacket, spread it over the carpet of needles and pulled off his necktie. As he unbuttoned his shirt Floralie could see his white shoulders and hairy chest. She watched, saying nothing. Anthyme looked her up and down.

"What's the matter? Have you turned into a pillar of salt?"

A tear pricked at her eyelid, but she dared not move her hand to wipe it away. Such a gesture seemed to be forbidden by some strict law.

"Don't cry, *hostie!* This is the happiest day of your life."

Anthyme let down his trousers and, keeping his shoes on, freed first one leg, then the other. He put on his best smile. Then, the lower part of his body enclosed in long woollen underpants like Floralie had seen on her father, he came up to her, smelling strongly of horse.

"Floralie," he pleaded, "take off your dress. You know very well we can't do it with all our clothes on."

She realized how small she was in front of this man who was her husband. Her legs were pressed tightly together and her arms were crossed on her bosom. She would move only if she were forced.

"What's the matter?"

"I've got a stomach ache."

"I don't believe you. *Hostie!* We haven't made a baby yet."

"I ate too much molasses pie. I'll never be able to make them as good as my mother . . . so I wanted to eat as much as I could . . ."

He gathered her into his arms. Her ear stuck against his sweaty chest, Floralie could hear his heart galloping like a mad horse.

"Floralie . . . do you love me?"

"You're my husband, Anthyme."

He could hear only boredom in her voice.

"What's the matter with you? Are you my wife or aren't you?"
She did not reply. Anthyme expected a word at least.

"Anyway, I won't take off my underwear till you take off your dress."

He shaped his mouth, which had become sad, back into a smile.

"I can't wait to see you naked."

"Why?"

"Because you're my wife. And because I'm a man. And because the good Lord made men and women. And because the good Lord is perfect."

Anthyme had moved his hand from her shoulder down to her thigh in a reassuring caress, hoping to tame this nervous little animal that was his wife. She seemed to give in, to tolerate the hand which had become more insistent. Suddenly she disengaged herself, pushed Anthyme's hand away, stepped back a few paces and gave him a look in which he could feel her mistrust.

"As far as I'm concerned my eyes are staying shut. I don't want to see *you* naked."

If Floralie had been a man Anthyme would have replied with a fist in her face or a kick in her belly. That always paralyzes the enemy. But Floralie was a woman. How did you reply to a woman? Perhaps a gentle answer would be best. He said, in his most tender voice, "Sometimes us men, we talk a lot, we talk loud. But we don't always know as much as we say we do. I want you to know I've never seen a naked woman."

"Not even your sisters?"

"When they were babies."

Anthyme seized his wife again and pressed himself against her. "It's not me that made men and women, *hostie,* it's the good Lord!"

His arms were knotted on her back. Floralie was surrounded

by strong chains. Slowly, he bent his knees and let himself down to the ground without releasing his embrace. On the contrary, he tightened it, as though he were trying to drown Floralie in himself. She was silent. He had recovered his panting breath; his damp lips, circled by his coarse beard, covered Floralie's face.

"I'm going to get undressed because you want me to," she said finally.

Anthyme opened his arms and freed her. She brought her hands up to the high collar of her dress, unfastened the buttons, the long row of buttons, and slipped the dress off her shoulders. She emerged dazzling in silk and lace. She folded her dress, then looked for some grass to lay it on.

Anthyme looked at his wife with admiration. After a little resistance, which was quite understandable, she had given in to reason. It was a difficult moment.

"It's a moment a woman remembers: after birth and death, it's the most important moment of a woman's life. You can't remember being born, or dying either, probably, but a woman always remembers when she became a woman."

Floralie was submissive now. Under the petticoat that she lifted, the flesh of her thighs, her belly, her little breasts blossomed like a glorious flower. Anthyme had trouble keeping his eyes open. They were burning as if he had looked directly into the sun.

"Come on!" he said, patting the ground near him to indicate where he wanted her to sit.

She came like a good little dog. He started to take off his woollen drawers. Floralie stretched out on the carpet of dead needles that nibbled at her flesh.

Anthyme did not dare to touch her. Dazzled, he could not even brush this woman's flesh with his fingertip. He was afraid, like a person who doesn't dare touch a fascinating flame.

Floralie jumped to her feet, crying, "Anthyme, look!"

"Where?"

"There!"

She pointed towards the ground, but what could he see among the bushes and ferns in the undergrowth where everything was shaded in green?

"There, in the roots."

"There," grumbled Anthyme, "I don't know where 'there' is." He got up impatiently.

"A snake! Near that hump in the root. Can't you see it?"

"It's a tiny little garter snake. It can't hurt you."

"It's awful."

Floralie's face was crumpled with tears. "A garter snake is still a snake, and a snake is the devil."

Anthyme wanted to take her in his arms to pacify her. She pushed him away.

"It's a harmless little garter snake. The devil," he said teasing, "the devil has no business here. If we weren't married, sure; but are you my wife or aren't you?"

Floralie drew back to get away from the snake, which was rolled up, completely still. Its little tongue was flickering outside its mouth.

"It's looking at us!"

Anthyme advanced, avoiding the dead branches on the ground. He bent towards the creature, grabbed it by the tail and brought it up to the level of his eyes.

"It isn't the devil; it hasn't got any horns. It's a little green garter snake."

"You shouldn't have touched it."

Anthyme came out from under the branches. Still holding the snake by the tail he whirled it around and, with a great laugh that echoed through the forest, threw it over the top of the trees.

"See what I did with the devil?"

"You shouldn't have."

His wife's fear amused him. And because he was not afraid he felt strong, and proud to be a man.

"I'm so scared."

She was trembling. The more frightened she was the stronger he felt.

Suddenly Floralie grabbed up her clothes and raced away from their retreat.

*　★　★　★*

Not laughing like lovers enjoying themselves, but terrified, her clothes in her hands, panic-stricken, Floralie ran towards the buggy, oblivious to the sharp weeds that grew in the perpetual shadows, ignoring the bushes that scratched at her legs. She jumped into the carriage, untied the reins and struck out desperately at the horse, which took its time about responding to this feminine anger. She struck with all the strength of her fear, but the animal was unmoved.

Anthyme caught up with her, snatched away the reins and without a word began to strike the horse as though he wanted to engrave the marks of his whip on the horse's back forever. The carriage was yanked off the ground, fell back and then began once again to fly over the bumps and hollows, twisting and creaking on the road that seemed as if it would never end.

At such a speed the horse ran the risk of stumbling over a stone and being crushed under the buggy, but Anthyme did not stop whipping. When he judged that the horse had been beaten enough that it would no longer risk its life by stopping, Anthyme tied the reins to the apron, enjoying the sight of the animal trembling with fear. He glanced towards Floralie. His wife's eyes were no longer shining with fear: they were grey with regret.

"She won't put up a fight now." A smile spread on his lower lip.

Floralie closed her eyes. Anthyme swept her up and held her tightly in his arms. He had trouble breathing now. He began to groan. His legs were crossed behind Floralie's and their two bodies rolled together. In the buggy, shaking as if it were tumbling down a rocky hillside, Floralie became Anthyme's wife. In silence.

*   *   *   *

The horse dragged them along for a long time. They didn't talk. On the rough planks of the buggy's floor they didn't move. They lay united, cleaving to one another. She was scarcely breathing, while Anthyme was panting like an exhausted horse. They let themselves drift as the buggy continued along the dips and hollows of the road. Floralie opened her eyes. The branches hovered above her like great black birds and the sky was turning like a silent wheel. The buggy's shaking became more subdued, slower. Gradually it came to a stop. Without a word Anthyme freed her from his embrace and got up.

"No!" she begged.

She hadn't wanted to say it. The cry had burst from the bottom of her heart as her husband looked at her — with blazing eyes that she had never seen in him, the eyes of a stranger. She hid her bosom with her hand. Anthyme jumped down from the carriage and, patting the horse's rump, said, "You're a good animal."

Floralie did up her dress.

*   *   *   *

Anthyme came back to her.

"Get down. We're going to take a rest."

He went to rummage around in the back of the buggy and took a red blanket out of their baggage.

"Come on, it'll be nice."

He looked for a little clearing in the tall grass and prickly bushes. Floralie watched him unfold the red blanket and spread it on the ground. He lay down.

"Come on!"

He pointed to a spot close to him. She obeyed and lay down on her back. The big hand unfastened her buttons one by one. As the dress opened her breasts burst out, sparkling in the light. The hand climbed onto her bosom and rested there.

Floralie was thinking of nothing. She was no longer afraid. The stone that had been at the bottom of her heart had become a butterfly coursing through her blood. Her worry had been extinguished like a little fire in the depths of the night. The sun was flooding the universe and if they had not been protected by the vault of the branches the light would have been blinding.

Floralie forgot Anthyme, forgot that she was his wife. She no longer remembered the bumpy road or the horse's blazing mane. She gave herself up to the simple joy of breathing, even forgetting to breathe just as the river forgets that time is flowing through it. She looked absent-mindedly at the sky and no longer felt the earth beneath her body. The sky fled as the road had fled under the buggy-wheels, and farther away, beyond the sky, Floralie heard the music of distant wheels. She thought of a locomotive, but there are no locomotives behind the sky. From the depths of her memory the song of wheels on rails hammered more and more insistently. She heard them coming close, saw the smoke belching out, then she saw the locomotive itself, ready to burst with its power.

It was a day that time could never stain. The locomotive from far away had appeared in the field. Floralie was wearing her Sunday dress with its pink ribbons. For the rest of her life she would remember the frenzied people, the squealing children who doubted the train's existence until it actually arrived.

She would never forget the uproar, all through the spring and summer, of axes attacking the trees. When a tree was felled, with leafy murmurs and a dry crackling, axes sounded in the trunk to square it off. That spring and that summer had been more precious than all her childhood. She could think of no sound as beautiful as the sound of the axes in the wood, and of the steel mallets pounding in big nails. The wood from which the ties were made was young and the nails entered badly. The mallets trembled and stuck in the wood; the men swore and Floralie was afraid because they were so strong. She smiled at all the sounds singing in her memory.

Anthyme slept.

Some workers were boarding at her father's house: five or six to a room, in the beds, on the floor, head on a rolled-up pair of trousers that served as a pillow. Several slept in the barn too, to save the money they earned at their construction jobs. There were Italians who were always talking, stopping only when one of them brought out a knife. Then Floralie's mother would shout, "Floralie, I need you!" and the Italians would begin to laugh again. There were Poles too, who looked up at the sky as they listened to someone playing the accordion. And Ukrainians, with wide trousers, who were never happy. All of them used to work from the time the sun appeared over the horizon, stopping only when their eyes could no longer penetrate the shadows. All day long her mother prepared meals, sweating, gesticulating, jostling, complaining, trying to make herself understood with gestures. She stepped over the sleeping bodies on the floor, scolded those with mud on their feet, wakened the ones who had fallen asleep in a chair or with their heads on the table, waiting for their plates.

Finally it was the day for the train to arrive. Floralie had never seen a train. Everyone — the villagers, the Italians, the Poles, the Ukrainians, cousins from other villages — had come down into the alley. They seemed to get along well with each other;

everyone spoke together; the women and young girls wearing their prettiest dresses and the men their Sunday suits — except for the immigrants, who had only their work clothes. Suddenly, like a long, drawn-out peal of thunder from behind the mountain, the train surged into view. It was black and it belched black smoke, and it was faster than any horse. It was hard to believe that it was a real train.

A man got up on someone's shoulders so that he was higher than the others, and began to shout.

"As the official candidate for the opposition in this county I wish to express my undying opposition to this engine, this locomotive, this train that is already strewing material and moral disorder across our peaceful countryside and which today is sowing seeds of sadness that we will harvest some day soon. With this train going off to the cities do you think our children are going to stay in the country with us? Let us unite in opposition to the passage of this train on our land where it is sowing despair. Its cars are filled with misery. As the poet said, 'Farther fields are not as green as some people say they are.' Let us stay at home. Ladies, gentlemen, dear voters, look at the cows run away. They're afraid of the train. A cow that's afraid doesn't give milk; without milk we won't be able to feed our little French Canadians. Without little French Canadians, no more Canada. Without Canada, no little French Canadians. And when there aren't any more little French Canadians, what are you going to do then? There won't be anything left but *maudits Anglais.*"

Floralie remembered the man who had gesticulated with his raised fist. She heard again the music of the immigrants who greeted the train's arrival. Here and there among the crowd an accordion, a harmonica, a guitar and a violin began to play different tunes. Then gradually they united in the same song. Floralie would never forget their singing.

A young Italian who was staying at her place, a child almost, had come up to her. Soon his shoulder was grazing hers and a caress flashed through the young girl's body. He stretched his arm behind her, and his hand came to rest on her thigh. Floralie's legs trembled as though the ground had reverberated under her feet. She had never experienced such overpowering joy. He was handsome, with his black hair and his eyes that looked as though they were never in the wrong. She discovered the marvel of being alive, of having her blood maddened by a young man's look. The marvel of being a girl. When she was serving plates to the boarders between the tables in the dining room, from which the furniture had been removed, she often felt a hand on her bottom or an arm around her waist. Floralie pushed them away impatiently. She was afraid of virile hands, those five-footed beasts clambering over her. At the very moment when the train arrived in the valley, the Italian's arm, his hand nervous as a bird, changed her life. On that day a life began where nothing would ever again resemble what it had been before.

The labourers, the immigrants, the people from the village all ran towards the train and followed along after it. The train went on its way, making a mooing sound. Behind it men and women and children sang songs that made them laugh. Soon silence would return to the sleepy valley and the young Italian would go away to await the arrival of another train, somewhere else. Floralie would come back alone to see the train go by. Someday, perhaps, the Italian would be on the train, but she would never know.

Floralie began to walk with him, following. They climbed the hill. She let her head fall onto his shoulder. He spoke, but she didn't understand. She laughed, if she spoke he laughed too.

He let go of her waist and took her hand. She ran behind him in the oatfield, which was beautiful — brilliant, tall and thick. They plunged into it as if it were pure water, rolling against one another, embracing, their lips joined. It seemed to Floralie that they were very near the sun. They rolled, rolled together, and the sun rolled with them. Floralie's dress was open and the Italian was pressing his face against her breasts. He could not open his eyes, the sunlight was so blinding. Floralie thought she was drowning. She did not struggle. The young man pressed against her as though he wanted to mix his bones with Floralie's own. Suddenly a burning sensation tore at her belly. She yelled with pain. The young man's mouth blew vehemently against her ear. Then the valley became calm again, like gentle rain; they slept like tired children. When she woke up she smiled at him. The young man's eyes were sad. Her heart became calm. Floralie opened her mouth to cry out, with a voice that would fill the valley, "I love you! I love you! I love you!" but she saw Anthyme's face bending over her.

"How come you're smiling?"

"People don't always know why they're smiling."

"I don't like you smiling like that. I get the idea all you women do that. I don't like it."

Anthyme took his hand away from Floralie's bosom and turned his back to her.

She did up her dress.

She was shivering.

⋆　⋆　⋆　⋆

Anthyme stomped furiously through the pigweed. He was overcome by the desire to break something. He clutched at the branches of some bushes that were as sharp as the blade of a knife, pulling with all his might. The bush bent over, resisting, and Anthyme loosened his grip. The bush straightened up quivering.

"There wasn't any blood. I didn't see a single little drop of blood. That means it wasn't the first time she's had a man. *Hostie!*"

He attacked a thin stem with two leaves, a future maple,

winding it around his hand. The muscles in his arm contracted. He held his breath and the earth moved around the stem. The roots came loose, the maple came out and Anthyme waved it in the air like a precious trophy. He went back to stretch out on the red blanket. Hands clasped behind his neck, eyes questioning the blue of the sky, he reflected.

"She can say whatever she wants, but there's one thing I know for sure: there's a wall you have to break through. Not a stone wall, but a wall, a wall you've got to break through. I didn't find any wall. Maybe that means there wasn't one there? It can't be. So it must mean that somebody broke through the wall before me."

The ground was hard under his back; he turned over on his stomach.

"There wasn't any wall and there wasn't any blood. So I'm not Floralie's first man."

The rough spots on the ground were digging into his ribs, so he lay on his side.

"I'm not even a man, because I didn't give her a smash in the face. But I'd like to hit her. Maybe there was some blood and I didn't see it. Then I'd be sorry I hit her. But I didn't feel any wall."

The red blanket was as unbearable as a carpet of thistles. He sat up.

"Sometimes there's things you can't see. As a matter of fact, blood's a liquid like water. Maybe I didn't see it. But blood's like *coloured* water. And it's a colour that you've damn well got to see. You can't miss it. So now I know for sure that Floralie's had other men before me. *Hostie!*"

He swelled up with hatred.

A furious ox no bigger than his heart was being hysterical in his chest. Anthyme didn't dare look at his wife. He would not be able to resist the pleasure of jumping on her, feet together, and crushing her.

"If I'd felt a curtain . . . but I didn't even feel a curtain! It's hard to know . . . a wall? Maybe people exaggerate when they talk about a wall. But apparently there's at least a curtain that you've got to tear. But there wasn't any wall and there wasn't any curtain. The window was wide open. *Hostie!* She's had some man before me. And if she's had one she could have had dozens!"

It was impossible to go on sitting down.

His bones were twisting in his body; he could feel them, like the beams in a house on a night when it was too cold. It was not really summer for him now. He was shaking. Anthyme stretched out on his back.

"Me, I think it could be that this curtain or wall they talk about's nothing but a fairy-tale. Floralie couldn't have had anybody before me. She's an honest woman, she's no sinner. This curtain you've got to tear is likely something they've invented to make fun of newlyweds. So if the curtain's some fairy-tale, Floralie wasn't thinking about anybody but me when I got hold of her to make her my wife. For all the bother she gave me thinking about it, she deserves to get beaten up. I'm not a real man if I haven't got the courage to hit her and make her forget all about these other men, and bust up the pictures of them she's carrying around in her head. It's the good Lord that gave women this curtain. So if somebody gets her curtain torn by anybody but her husband she's a sinner. In the Bible they stoned sinners and Christ threw the first stone himself. But how can I tell if she's a sinner? I'm going to go and see the priest. He'll know if women have a wall or a curtain . . ."

The same thoughts kept coming back, tenacious as a saw that sank, grinding, into his head, his flesh, right down to the marrow of his bones.

"When I wanted to take her, make her my wife, show her I was her husband, she was pale. Didn't say a word. She was scared out of her wits because she thought I was going to find out her awful, shameful secret. She was scared I'd hit her when I found out about her sins. Then she started to smile and laugh and show all her teeth. She was glad I didn't notice she'd had other men before me."

Anthyme got up.

"She just kept quiet and me, I loved her, and I thought there's nothing as good as loving a woman. I was a little bit sad when I was thinking about all the years when I hadn't loved a woman and there she was comparing me to some other man! I was heavier on her than one of them, or I breathed louder in her ear than somebody else. She was making fun of me by keeping quiet. *Hostie! Tabernacle! Christ!*"

He swore without thinking about it. The words burst from the depths of his being, propelled by an enormous wrath.

The sky was inaccessible to his fist.

With all the weight of an unforgiving man he pounced on Floralie and hit her in the face. Then he buried his big fingers, like the teeth of a fork, in her face and shook her head as if he wanted to smash it on the ground.

"Whore!"

And the name-calling continued as he shook her.

"Anthyme!" Floralie begged.

"You've had every man in the parish!"

Holding Floralie's motionless body between his outspread knees, he struck her face, trying to tear away its mask of beauty and reveal the monster she really was.

"Anthyme!" she barely murmured his name as she turned her face away.

She thought she was shouting in a voice that could be heard far away, above the trees. And Anthyme's hand struck with much less force than he thought.

"Anthyme!" she said voicelessly. "My husband."

She raised both hands and her fingers brushed at her delirious face.

Blood was flowing on Floralie's lip. Anthyme grew calmer. He looked at the blood and smiled. He was overcome by a great feeling of peace. He loved his wife in spite of everything. He leaned over and touched his lips to her forehead. There was no woman he could have loved except Floralie. Since God created the world there had been a law which established that Floralie and Anthyme were created for one another, like the light for the day. He stretched out on her, placed his arms under her body (it was so light) and took her a second time. Inside her he found gentle fire, a fire with the softness of her hair.

He would have liked to go to sleep on Floralie's silky body, his face lost in her hair, but he was unable to accept the fact that other men before him had loved Floralie as he did.

He rose, dressed and spat on the ground.

"You're a fallen woman!"

He went away:

"You'll be damned!"

★   ★   ★   ★

Never again, as long as she lived, would Floralie say "I love you."

She did up her rumpled dress and touched the blood on her lip.

The sky was beautiful, smooth above the black trees, with foamy clouds like the ones in holy pictures. Perhaps there were archangels flying among them.

"Fallen woman!" a coarse voice repeated from the other side of the trees. "You'll be damned."

Floralie was damned, but she was alive. She was young, beautiful. She was damned, but she was smiling. Among the tangled branches a ray of sunlight broke through the shadow and spread itself out on the red blanket. Floralie moved, to offer her face to the sun. She opened her arms and surrendered to the caress of the light. She was damned. The sun breathed so gently. And it did not know that she was damned. In Hell, at the centre of the earth, underneath her body, another sun was blazing. It was not a caressing sun, but one that tore and devoured with jaws of raging flames, flames that killed like poisonous snakes. It was the sun of Hell that never sets, that is never hidden by rain, a sun of ravenous flames that gives off not light but shadow, stinking night, eternal shade. But Floralie was alive.

"You'll be damned! Damned!" she heard, as though her husband were very close.

The damned are not alive, she reasoned, because the sun of Hell preserves death just as the sun in Heaven makes things live.

The sun of Hell was very deep in the earth, under her feet, but perhaps its grey viscous rays extended, dying, as far as the roots of the grass.

A man from her village had gone far away to work in a mine. His wife and fifteen children had never seen him again. The miners dug tunnels under the ground, many miles under the trees. They dug in the rock and made roads like the ones you make in the fields. The man from the village was digging when suddenly a beam of light shone up from under his pick and changed the rock into dust. And that dust crushed the tunnels, the iron cars, the miners. The man from the village had been touched by a ray of sunlight from Hell. Men had gotten too close to Hell.

Floralie would stay on the ground. She wanted to smile at the sun that was illuminating the sky and the forest, to marvel at her new life that was beginning that day, but a coarse voice that was no longer Anthyme's was repeating, "Damned! Damned!"

As long as she could see the sun in Heaven light up the earth, as long as she could see the earth with its beautiful colours, like new dresses, Floralie was not afraid of that other sun, the fire of the Devil. The infernal sun was much farther away from her than the heavenly one.

But just as the heavenly sun kissed her body there in the clearing, so the other sun would take hold of her one day. Its rays would come to lick her body, so pale in its coffin. She would feel its bite. When someone touched her brow he would feel only the cold of death and no one except Floralie would know that the sun of Hell was devouring her already, each of its rays like a huge famished worm.

And Floralie's body, because of all her faults, would burn on the inside and invisible demons would come to dance in the walls of the house. Their claws would be heard scratching on the wood. Through the cracks in the walls and the ceiling they would laugh at the sight of Floralie's body as it burned. Their shadowy faces would be seen stuck to the windows and then slipping away because Floralie would burn in the infernal flames, as big as a sun. She would be consumed without smoke or ashes, consumed like a rotting fruit. No complaint, no tear would burst from her mouth, but in Hell her soul would shout, all at once, all the prayers and blasphemies it had learned on earth, spitting each word from her mouth like hot coals. Her soul would have the same mouth as her body, burned to a cinder under her white skin. Because she had sinned with her body her soul would spit out everything she knew of the world, everything she believed about Heaven, and when she no longer knew anything her soul would be nothing but a flaming, suffering rag that would not remember that it had once been a young girl. It would even forget its sin.

The forest was perfumed. Every tree had a good smell, like a flower that you bring up to your nose. The gentleness of the sun seemed eternal. Floralie was alive. Birds were singing in the branches, wild as schoolchildren, knowing nothing of the Hell that was under the earth, under Floralie's feet.

The Italian had left the same day the train arrived. Farther away another railroad was waiting to be built, a forest to be torn down, ties to be laid one after another like beads on a rosary. And all he knew how to do was build railways and play the harmonica. He also knew how to give happiness. He never came back.

"You shouldn't let yourself get attached to birds," said Floralie's mother, "because they don't get attached to you."

Would he have come back? Perhaps Floralie would eventually have chosen a local man instead, one who spoke the same French as she did, who heard the same masses as she, one who had learned the same things in school and seen the same people living and dying. But she would never forget the young Italian. Thanks to him her youth would not go up in smoke.

"Anthyme! Where are you?"

Behind the gently sloping branches the sky was a soft blue. It was the same sky Floralie had seen on the day she gave herself to the Italian. Afterwards the sky had been even more beautiful, above the tall oats that looked like an avalanche of pearls that had fallen on the young couple. She closed her eyes but the sky penetrated her, perfumed with blue. Floralie stretched out on the red blanket; the goodness of the sky mixed with the light had eased the little pains that were cutting at her face. The blood had dried under her nose.

"Anthyme, I forgive you for hitting me."

She said this without thinking, just as the sky was blue without any reflecting.

One day this whole forest would disappear. The road would be covered by overturned earth and torn-up roots; the villages too would disappear into the depths of the earth like a pebble flung into water. Heaven and Hell would collide and shatter like fragile plates. Then there would be the kingdom of night, the kingdom of Hell.

Anthyme had hit her, but if he wasn't a brute he wouldn't be a man. She called him.

"My husband!"

All the branches of the forest were mute. Nothing moved. She held her breath.

"Anthyme! I'm here!"

A sudden shadow, like a scythe, seemed to tilt the forest, which fell down on her. Floralie was alone and in the depths of her soul a coarse voice, Anthyme's, furious and desperate, was saying, "Damned woman!"

She was one of the slaves of Hell. No one could do anything for her now. She had been abandoned and there was nothing to protect her against the whips of remorse. Floralie was abandoned in the forest: every tree concealed demons, every corner of the shadow might be a doorway to Hell. The silence of the forest was no longer a terrestrial silence, where you can still hear the heart-beat of life, if a branch moved, a demon was climbing on it. The sun darkened. She was cold, so she went back to the red blanket, wrapping it around her like a cloak. Hell fire touched her heart; it burned. To keep her from getting away, needles from the under-brush clung to her dress, and their thousand claws held her back.

"Anthyme!"

She saw the Italian smile with his white teeth. He had long teeth and he was always laughing. The other immigrants didn't laugh like that, and neither did the men from the village. When the men were brawling, breaking wooden chairs, he kept laugh-ing; and he laughed when a knife blade gleamed in the hand of an angry man. He laughed as he played his harmonica, and you would have thought that ten harmonicas were vibrating when he made his own sing. He danced with the vigour of a man with seven lives. Floralie saw him in his sweat-soaked shirt, laughing: men didn't laugh like that.

Might it not be the demon that had taken hold of Floralie's soul in the oatfield?

"Anthyme!"

★   ★   ★   ★

Anthyme could not find his horse on the road. Many horseshoes had left their prints in the dried mud which was also marked by the passage of a number of wheels. He kept his eye on the freshest prints, which had probably been made by his horse. He saw some grass that had been trampled down by a wheel and several low branches that had been broken. Then the order of the forest and the road seemed undisturbed, as if the horse had flown away with the buggy. His horse was no bird.

"*Hostie d'hosties!*" he muttered between clenched teeth. He was dumbfounded by so much mystery. Nothing was moving in the foliage; light and shadow seemed made of wood.

Anthyme had thought that the fresh grass would keep his horse from straying off; but perhaps the creature wanted other things besides food. Anthyme should have tied him to a tree, but a man can't keep his mind on a horse and a woman at the same time. Perhaps a horse doesn't like his master to disappear into the underbrush with a woman; and perhaps the horse wanted to imitate his master and had gone off to look for a mare for himself. In that case, even if he had been tied up he would have taken off. There was no reason for Anthyme to blame himself for not tying up the horse. What had he done then to make the horse bolt off? A man whose own horse doesn't like him is no man.

"*Hostie d'hosties d'hosties!* Lose my horse on my wedding day! I'll remember this for the rest of my life."

Had the horse continued along the road? Had it turned back?

Had it gone deeper into the forest? There were no recent tracks. No one had passed that way for days. Nothing had flattened the tall weeds. Anthyme, walking like someone who has a long way to go, plunged ahead on the bumpy road. He had decided to walk all the way to his village, to go home alone. He would blame himself for this day for the rest of his life.

"Lose your horse on your wedding day and then find out your wife's a fallen woman! No wall, no curtain . . . it was an open door. My wife was a fallen woman. And to punish her my horse packs up."

Anthyme speeded up, stretching his legs out. He did not want Floralie to catch up with him. Women cling like weeds: they're always right when it comes to dealing with a man, and the husband gets caught like a fly in a spiderweb. Anthyme was anxious to get so far away from his wife that she wouldn't be able to catch up with him.

"When a woman gives herself to somebody once, or often — I don't know which — she can't give herself to somebody else afterwards. She's only on loan. Me, I don't like borrowing like that. I don't like leftovers."

Now he was running as though he were being pursued. How he wanted his horse! The buggy would have taken him a long way. But he felt capable of running to the end of the earth, where the sky meets the earth, to get away from Floralie. Had he heard a voice? He stopped and held his breath, his feet riveted to the ground like roots. He listened. Nothing. He began to run again.

This was nothing new. Horses, quietly grazing, had been known to disappear while their masters' backs were turned. Suddenly, no more horse. No more horse. Vanished like a soap bubble. He had known people who had suffered this misfortune. Where *was* that horse? No one would ever know because such horses never come back. There was no reason for him to have such bad luck.

Horses had disappeared, taking their carriages with them, even taking a plough once, as if the earth had swallowed them up like a huge mouth. Such things had happened in his part of the country.

Anthyme knew some farmers, like himself, who knew a traveller who had been the victim of such an accident. He was a peddler who charged too much for the old clothes he sold to poor people. And he used to take unfair advantage of the women, too, when their husbands had been away in the forest for too long and they were dying for a man.

The Devil had come for the peddler and dragged him off to Hell, because the horse wasn't really a horse, it was the Devil disguised as a horse.

Some people thought it wasn't the Devil. Not the Devil? But its hooves had left black marks; they had burned the gravel on the road. The horse's shoes were red from the fires of Hell. That was a curse that had punished an honest-to-goodness sinner, a public sinner, but Anthyme hadn't committed such grave sins. He didn't deserve that kind of punishment: he got drunk only rarely, he never took the name of the Lord in vain and Floralie, his wife, was the first woman he had had.

Something else had happened during his childhood that people were still talking about. A horse-trader was coming back to his village somewhere behind the mountains. There was a woman with him whom he passed off as his wife, but in fact she was a girl who had run away from the hotel in Cranborne. The horse-trader and the girl he referred to as "my wife" were sitting in the carriage, the man whipping his horse to urge all the strength from its muscles. All of a sudden it was no longer a horse that he was striking but a flame as big as the horse; it was no longer a horse pulling the carriage but a blazing crackling whirlwind that set fire to the branches of the spruce trees, turning them into trees of fire. Even the carriage was no longer made of wood, but of fire. The horse-trader and the loose woman with him were carried off by the Devil in a carriage of fire. The horse-trader never stopped whipping, as though he was not aware of the flames around him, and the girl laughed with all her might because she was not really a girl at all but a demon in disguise. The fiery harness devoured a path through the forest and little by little the flames diminished, the horse began to fade away, then the carriage. The devil sank into the earth, taking the horse-trader and the fallen woman, still alive, into his Hell.

Where had Anthyme's horse hidden itself?

*   *   *   *

Night was coming down on the forest like the foot of some large animal crushing the day. Floralie was trembling among the upright sleeping trees. She had not stopped walking, the red blanket rolled under her arm. The night would be cold. Floralie would make a bed of ferns and roll up in the woollen blanket. When she called Anthyme, in a tiny begging voice, the whole forest repeated, "Anthyme!" but her husband did not answer. Why didn't he speak? Was it a game? Anthyme would spring out all of a sudden from behind a tree, fold her in his big arms, put his hands on her breast and rub his big, bearded man's face against her cheek. She was silent. She would not call again.

Her feet followed the path. She did not know where she was going, but a path always leads somewhere.

The sun sank slowly into the forest. In the distance the black branches seemed to be aflame, but aflame with a gentle fire that instead of burning slipped like rain, sparkling, down the length of the trees. The leaves and grass became grey, the dirt on the path became black. Her hands were so pale under the red blanket. As she walked the pebbles made a noise like little gnawing animals. How could she have walked in the forest without this path?

If Anthyme had been against her at that moment perhaps she would have said, "I love you."

*   *   *   *

Like tranquil masts the spruce trees sank deeper and deeper into the night. Floralie's new shoes hurt her feet. Under the shadow, under the grass, in the rough spots and pebbles, the road seemed to take flight. When it was no longer visible Floralie would let herself fall and there in her red blanket, kneeling and praying to God, she would wait for the light to return.

The road faded from sight. She knelt and closed her eyes.

Suddenly there was a glorious burst of light. There were no more trees but, in their place, a golden field that was soft as a bed. From the end of the field, as silent as light itself, came joyful music, a tune she remembered: it was the Italian's harmonica.

Before her eyes, open again now, the night reappeared rooted solidly in the earth. The trees covered the earth like a vast night, their arms stretched out and their heads asleep in the sky.

Somebody really was playing the harmonica.

*   *   *   *

For a long time Anthyme had been running as if he thought he could escape the night, but now it had captured him, holding him in its claws. The spruce trees were closer together now, and their branches seemed thicker. You could no longer distinguish the road from the ground around it.

If he'd had his horse he could have been a good distance away by now. He could have been sleeping and dreaming between clean sheets. But he didn't have his horse. If he hadn't got married he wouldn't have lost his horse, and if he hadn't married a fallen woman he wouldn't be trudging alone through this forest where he was blinded by the night.

All his attention was concentrated on not straying off the road. Because men just as solid as him, just as strong, had not followed the paths, they had been forced to remain in the forest forever and lumberjacks had found their clean white skeletons in the green grass with flowers growing inside them. Other times the skeletons had fresh marks on them where wolves had gnawed at the bones.

Sometimes an old wheelmark appeared, then quickly disappeared again under the dark grass of the night, like a fish under water.

Anthyme had heard that a man can be swallowed up in swamps where the ferns, spruce and moss look very much like the kind that grow on solid earth.

"My one foot gets stuck in the mud; I move the other one ahead to pull out the first one and they both get stuck and then *I'm* stuck there like a tree. The mud is climbing up to my knees and I feel like a tree growing upside down — I'm growing down into the ground instead of up towards the sky. The earth can swallow a man the way a cat eats up a mouse. *Hostie!*"

Anthyme remained standing, his head raised towards the sky. He no longer had the courage to go on. It would be better to stay where he was, alive, than to go farther and drown in the earth or deposit a skeleton under the leaves.

The firmament was at his feet, rather than above his head. Anthyme wanted to plunge into the sky like a bird. Swaying on his feet, he closed his eyes.

"*Hostie!* I must be famished to be so crazy!"

He pulled up a handful of grass. It tasted good, fresh in his mouth. The forest was completely asleep; nothing seemed to be alive. The ground was solid under his heels.

A bird woke up on a branch somewhere and the whole forest was shaken by it. One minute it seemed to come tumbling down on top of him, then once again the spruce trees mingled with the night. Time passed among the trees like slightly stagnant water.

Anthyme would wait for the dawn without taking another step.

* * * *

In the middle of the night, somebody really was playing the harmonica. The music couldn't be a dream. Floralie's eyes were wide open to the night as she listened and her heart was pounding. The harmonica's song was as real as when she used to take refuge in the girls' bedroom, throwing herself onto a bed the better to hear the Italian playing in the next room.

"Floralie! Have you finished washing all the plates?" her mother would ask every time.

Or Floralie would go to the window and imagine her life, and her eyes would close on the oatfields that stretched out so far, and Floralie would live inside her head.

"Floralie!" her mother insisted.

Someone really was playing the harmonica in the forest. Someone was playing behind her. She turned around. The music seemed so close that she shuddered as if she had been brushed by a wing. Tiny flying flames approached her now — eyes, perhaps — and then the harmonica music. And Floralie heard the noise of grinding wheels and the little sounds of crushed pebbles.

"Anthyme!" she cried out, happy.

Only the little flames trembling before her were not swallowed by the night.

"Anthyme doesn't know how to play the harmonica," she reasoned.

A horse she hadn't seen before neighed behind her, and its

smell came to her face.

Afraid that the horse would step on her, Floralie threw herself off the road into the thicket, where her feet had trouble finding the ground. The animal didn't move. The carriage and the horse seemed to emanate from a yellowish spot of night. Vaguely lit by lanterns hooked onto the buggy, a man stood up. He was not alone. He addressed Floralie as though she were a crowd:

"Néron, son of Néron, son of the Almouchiquois, can talk to the moon and the sun. He knows the language of men too. Néron can find springs beneath the earth, awaken the rain, put suffering to sleep and stop toothaches. Néron makes women fertile, and also the fields. When Néron spreads his hands over a pain the forces of evil know they've been beaten. Néron, that's my name. Son of Néron. Have you got a cold? Drink the water that Néron has dipped in a holy bucket from under the ice of a stream at sunrise on Easter morning and bottled the following Good Friday at three o'clock in the afternoon. That water! I've sold barrels of it. Have you got rheumatism? Rub your joints with the skin of a frog that Néron has spit on three times while praying."

The man unfastened one of the lanterns and held it in front of him to see who he had been speaking to. The wavering motion brought the lantern close to his face, which seemed distinctly untouched by the night. His face looked like a bear's. On his head there was a feathered top hat. His hair hung down to his shoulders. Floralie felt his look weighing on her.

"Néron gives the love you've never had, and he gives back the love you've lost."

Children, hidden by the night, intoned:

Néron, Néron,
Is good
Néron, Néron

Is holy.
Néron, Néron
Is good
Néron is holy.

Néron added, in a supplicating cry, "O sun! O moon! O dead! Never cease to commune with Néron!"

He jumped down from the carriage and directed his steps towards Floralie, who was paralysed as though the night surrounding her were a black stone.

"Woman," he said, in a voice that was too tender, "tell me what causes you to suffer. Tell Néron your troubles."

The man's clothes could not be distinguished from the night. Only his face received a wan light from the lantern; it seemed to be unattached to a neck or a human body, but rather to fly like a bat. Floralie didn't have the strength to close her eyes, to keep from seeing any more.

"Woman of the forest, you need not speak; I can read what's in your soul. Your heart is a sterile land because your spirit wills it to be. The plant of love will never flower, because your heart says no to it. The plant of love is sick. Néron reads right through bodies. Give me your hands."

She made no movement; he seized her hands. Now a force was pulling at Floralie's hands as though her fingers were bound to the soil by roots.

"You know because I've told you, because Néron has said it — Néron, son of Néron. You know your soul is a desert and your heart is a stone."

She heard her mouth answer, "Yes."

"Néron can make barren lands fertile; he knows how to cure the pains of body and soul."

"Yes."

The two hands holding Floralie's fists were made of fire.

"Little daughter of the forest, do you want a river, a mighty river of love, to flow in your heart?"

Néron's lips moved soundlessly; it was Floralie who answered, "Yes."

Néron, Néron
Is good.
Néron, Néron
Is holy.
Néron, Néron
Is good
Néron is holy.

The refrain was raised again by the chorus of children, invisible in the night along with all the other little forest creatures.

"Close your eyes, little girl."

She obeyed. But she could still see him. What colour was his skin? Was it red? Yellow? Green? Were his long teeth black? Were they brown?

"Don't think about anything. Let the little voice deep down at the bottom of your head start to sing. Sing along with the voice in your head. That music is made by a river in the depths of the night, farther away than the moon, farther than the sun. Listen! the river is going to come right up to your soul. Your soul will drown in the river, so it can come to life again. Listen, child; listen to the song of the river that cradles and rocks you."

The river's voice grew stronger. Floralie saw the water whirling around like an eddy. The river's song became more and more strident as Néron danced around Floralie. The water was stirred up by a strong wind, a hurricane. The earth spun around Floralie the way it did when she danced too much. The water wrapped itself around her. It was useless to protect her ears with her hands: the music would have burst a stone wall. The ground gave way under her feet.

"Woman, the Dead Ancestors of Néron are dancing around us. They are speaking through my mouth and I am going to heal your soul."

The music subsided, the song became gentle, slow, long as passing time.

"Woman, pay attention to the flower of love springing up in your soul which is no longer arid like a desert. Look at the flower of love open its petals. Soon your entire soul will be blossoming with love."

"I see," murmured Floralie.

"You love! You love! You love!" Néron proclaimed. "O moon! O dead! O sun! You have helped Néron accomplish another miracle. You love! You love!"

Néron flung himself to his knees and seized Floralie's ankles, saying, "O dead!"

He slid his hands along her legs, her thighs, her hips, her belly. "O moon!"

The hands moved slowly along her bosom, her shoulders, her neck, ears and hair.

"O sun! O dead! O moon! We have created a woman!"

Taking her, so light, in his arms, he went further into the night and laid her down on the damp moss.

Her sleep was illuminated by the vast light of a sky beneath which she kept saying, "I love you" to a young man with black hair whose name and language she did not know. The words were as clear as the oats and the sun had been on that day.

"Open your eyes," Néron ordered. "Come."

She followed the rounded back, the long glistening hair that was adorned on top with bird-feathers stuck into a ribbon. Near the carriage Néron raised his lantern in order to fasten it. By the light it shed Floralie recognized Anthyme's horse, his harness and his buggy. Néron took her by the waist, lifted her and, without effort, hoisted her into the buggy filled with quarrelling children.

"Sit down."

He got up beside her.

"My late relatives the Almouchiquois made me a present of this awful beast. I'm going to sell it."

With one crack of his whip he took command of the horse, just as Anthyme had done. The animal set off reluctantly.

Floralie turned around to smile at the children piled in behind her.

"We made you a nice Christmas tree!" one of them announced.

The others began to laugh, too enthusiastically. Floralie turned her head farther so that she could see better through the darkness where the reflections of the lantern's little yellow flames were meandering. A cry of fright was caught in her throat, for she could not believe the horror of what she was witnessing.

The Christmas tree was a little spruce from whose branches were suspended, upside down and attached by their tails, dozens of mice that squealed and waved their little paws.

Néron had seen too.

"What have you done, you monstrous little brats out of diverse mothers?"

Briskly he brought the handle of his whip down on the heap of children, who tried to escape the blows by hiding under one another.

"Lousy brats with your worthless mothers!"

As the blows increased, instead of crying the children laughed as though it were all a game. Néron's anger abated.

"You'll be sorry if you lose my sacred mice."

"We'll catch you some more," a little voice jeered at him.

"In the schools," another shrill little voice went on.

"In the churches!"

"Up the girls' behinds!" said another voice, less innocent.

The whip cracked through the air.

"Shut up, you fruits of sin! Put the mice back in the trunk where you got them, if you lose Néron's mice "

"We'll catch you some more. Thousands! Millions!" one of the children assured him. "They're all over."

"In my mother's belly!"

"In the holy tabernacles!"

Néron stood up, whipped the horse, then turned back to the children.

"Stinking lousy brats! You haven't learned a thing about the beauties of the French language! I'll pound it into you in spite of yourselves."

Néron would never have whipped a recalcitrant horse with so much ardour. Fearless of the whip the children were jumping around in the buggy, which continued to roll along with all the strength the horse could muster. They jostled each other, choking with laughter. It was useless to hit them. Néron folded his arms. He had decided to use tenderness.

"If you let my mice loose," he implored, "how will Néron be able to sell mouse-skins for consumptives to rub against their chests? How will Néron be able to sell the mouse's eyes that you put under beds to find out their secrets?"

The children thought he was crying; not one of them was laughing now.

"Go on!" he ordered. "Put the mice back in the mouse-trunk. And don't let the frogs get out either!"

A little girl burst into tears.

"Papa, are you going to spoil my pretty Christmas tree? Why do you always ruin everything I make?"

"I can't refuse that one anything," Néron explained. "Is it because I love her or because I detest her?"

At the signal from the whip the horse picked up speed again and as it clattered and swayed along the bumpy road the carriage was a raft drifting through the night, with its three lanterns, the children piled around the Christmas tree, the trunks, Floralie with her eyes closed and Néron, who saw the road as though it were the middle of day.

Floralie's nerves were all on edge. She was so afraid that she would gladly have flung herself into the arms of this man who gave off a smell of muddy earth. She would have hidden her face in this man's chest, with his red or yellow skin; she would have put her forehead in his sticky hair. Fear took her voice away. In place of her lips she felt an icy ring. She couldn't jump from the buggy; her legs were too heavy. Néron put his arm around her and pressed her against him. She liked his warmth and she wanted to sleep.

The carriage jolted. Her head fell onto Néron's shoulder. She slept.

Behind them the children were singing around their Christmas tree, with its squealing decorations.

Néron, Néron
Is good.
Néron, Néron
Is holy.
Néron, Néron
Is good
Néron is holy.

In the forest, where night was taking root deep in the earth and spreading into the sky, the Indian declaimed,

"I am Néron, son of Néron, son of the Almouchiquois! O moon! O sun! O dead! Good people, give me your rheumatism and your phlegmy throats; give me your bellyaches and your troubles; give me your cut fingers and your broken legs. Women, give me your barren wombs. Give me your gangrenes and Néron will make flowers of life from them. O moon! O sun! O dead! Never abandon your Néron."

★   ★   ★   ★

To Anthyme, night had always seemed as unreal as the azure sky. This evening it had swallowed up the earth and he was in the depths of night like a pebble at the bottom of the sea. He no longer recognized the ground; his feet no longer knew how to place themselves, on ground transformed by the night. The earth was as mysterious as the pelagic deeps. Just as Anthyme had never seen the sea, so he had never seen the night before tonight.

He had lost his horse, he had lost his wife, and the night was stripping away the very road beneath his boots. Nailed to the earth, he could go no further. He waited, his eyes on the sky. Dawn was far away, on the other side of day. All the small animals taking advantage of the night to come to life and crawl about made him afraid to lie down. Soon his fatigue would overcome his fear — then he would fall to the ground. Thinking, his eyes open to the night, made him dizzy.

Anthyme could have asked God, who never sleeps in Heaven, to hurry the daybreak and light the earth and the road in the forest, but God would never have turned on the sun for a man like Anthyme. He lowered his gaze: salvation would not come from Heaven. He fixed his eyes on the earth, which the night had turned into hardened mud.

All doubt had vanished. When he took Floralie, no little wall, no curtain had resisted him. Floralie was a fallen woman.

Anthyme would have bet his right hand that his wife was nothing but a fallen woman, even though she looked like an honest one.

To wreck something, to give Floralie a thrashing, to beat his horse or smash his fist against a wall — that might have relieved his mind. That kind of violence would have liberated his heart, which was crushed in a vise. But he was alone in the middle of the night. He could not hurt the forest, nor make the silence sob. He contented himself with taking several steps, but he noticed that he was getting off the road. He came back. He would wait for the light.

He was alone in the heart of the forest and night had blotted out his whole life. Nothing existed now in this insuperable shadow. Neither his village nor his horse nor his marriage nor his wife, nor the deception she had practised on him. Because of this night, Anthyme could believe that he had never lived the day that had brought him to this place. The night had changed that day into thick, black smoke.

There was a loud clinking of carriage wheels; someone was moving, cautiously. He saw eyes glowing. A spot. It was the blaze on his horse's forehead. His horse was coming back. He saw it as if it were broad daylight.

"It can't get along without me!"

Anthyme was sceptical of this state of dependency, but he was delighted to find a buggy that would serve as transportation. He leaped up to take hold of the horse's bridle, and with the other hand to stroke the animal's neck and reassure it, but he found nothing except the night. Before him there was nothing but night, bristling with trees. No horse.

He looked around for the horse he had seen — his horse — which was on neither side of the road. It wasn't ahead of him or behind him either. Could he have seen a horse when there wasn't a horse to be seen?

Anthyme kept still, upright, fixed, his arms pressed tightly to his sides as the night and the forest were pressed around him — a black snow, cold and soft, that was sucking him down. The night pushed at his arms, pressed on the back of his neck, crushed his heart. Anthyme could barely breathe. He was choking. The night was drifting into his lungs like dry dust. He saw branches beating like the wings of birds. Each branch was a bird with a huge wing-span, flapping wings that were tipped with claws. The branches were whirling in a black eddy where the sky was sinking like a stone. The sweat pouring from his forehead burned his eyes. The black birds, after they had wandered vainly through the sky, would strike at him with loud hisses.

"Christ! Christ!" he called. "Don't leave me here all alone. Come and help me. Come down from your cross or your Heaven or wherever you are. Come and help me!"

He thought he had shouted these words loud enough to tear through the night, but his mouth had been silent.

The black birds stopped tearing at him. He remained prostrate, his face in the damp grass, while the noise of the wings moved away. When he no longer heard anything he opened his eyes. Everything had returned to its place in the universe: branches were attached to tree-trunks, trees were planted in tranquil soil and the sky was very high above the forest. The night, already less dense, had begun to allow him a glimpse of the firmament.

A big cloud moving slowly caught his attention. It was gliding through the sky, with a sound like a buggy going along a bad road at full speed. The shape he had thought to be a cloud was, he could see now, his buggy, drawn by his horse. His own buggy; his own horse.

When you see a carriage flying through the sky it is a sign that you are going to die soon: the carriage comes to look for the soul of the person who has seen it. Anthyme collapsed, to melt into the earth. He did not want to die. Life was stirring in his body, like a cat thrown into the river in a sack.

The buggy was no longer visible in the sky; it was approaching, coming towards him. The wheels were no longer rolling through the air, but along the road in the forest. The earth shook under the horse's hooves. The uproar of spinning wheels was shattering his eardrums. The buggy was destroying everything in its path. He tensed his muscles to make himself like a stone, but his whole body was trembling. The horse came to a stop. It was breathing down Anthyme's neck.

He should not have abandoned Floralie. It was the first time he had had a woman and he was no longer certain that he had not broken the little curtain that would prove she was an honest woman. To be fair, he should admit he had no proof that she had belonged to another man before him. Had he seen Floralie give herself to someone? And he, Anthyme, had he given Floralie any proof that he had never had a woman before her? After today he would never know anything as good as having a woman, but death was soon going to take him, capture his soul and carry him far from the earth in the buggy of death. His fingers clung to the earth he did not want to leave. It would take a lot of strength to drag away his soul, but who can conquer death when its carriage stops near you?

Anthyme fell asleep, the same warm sleep he had known on Floralie's body.

Suddenly an invisible hand grabbed his throat, another tore at his back, spreading his flesh as you would spread open a wall of bushes. His soul left him, abandoning his body to the wolves with cruel, mocking laughter. His head was as heavy as a sack of flour.

A voice that cut the night like a saw said, "Néron, son of Néron, son of the Almouchiquois, can find the sources of water, preserve the harvest from ants and frost, make hunchbacks straight, put out fires, fix broken bones, stop wounds from bleeding. Néron can read hearts and he can cure colds too."

The cord of the whip around Anthyme's throat was loosened and children's voices raised up a crystalline cry:

Néron, Néron
Is good.
Néron, Néron
Is holy.
Néron, Néron
Is good
Néron is holy.

"Néron can read secrets in onion skins. He knows when winter will begin. In the forest Néron knows which way is north and which way is south, if you're generous Néron will tell whoever is lost in the woods how to find his way."

Anthyme's eyes had begun to see again. He recognized Floralie sitting behind the man with the tall hat. She turned her head, hiding her face in the yellow shadow of the lanterns attached to the front of the buggy.

"I want my horse," said Anthyme.

The whip whistled above his head and knotted around his ankle.

He insisted. "I want my horse and I want it right now."

With a dry crack of the handle Néron flicked the whip back to himself. Anthyme's feet slid on the wet ground and he fell. The children, delighted at such a funny sight, twisted with laughter, applauded and danced.

Anthyme got up.

"I want my horse, *hostie!* My horse!"

The whip whistled and Anthyme felt something burn his cheek like an insect bite.

"Young man, Néron sees your heart and it's black, black, black as this night. Your heart is so black your blood is black too. The blood on your cheek is black."

Blood was flowing from the scratch. Anthyme put a finger to it and held it up to the lamplight. His blood was black.

"Young man, you're a coward. I can read it in your heart. You have a black heart, you have black blood and your heart is so black that if you made babies with a woman they'd have black skin. Your heart is so black it would be just as well if you never dared make babies at all. Néron gives you his word: they'll be niggers."

Anthyme was humiliated that Néron had succeeded in reading his mind so deeply. He was ashamed not to be able to look someone in the eye. He could live only by creeping and hiding like a snake.

"Your heart is so black even your horse refuses to recognize you."

"I always go to mass," he whined.

"Your heart is so black you obscure the night. What have you done that's so horrible? Néron will read your heart, and he'll know."

"I say my prayers three times a day and I don't even swear as often as that."

"Your heart is so rotten that when you talk a person would think he's standing beside a corpse. Why have you hurt another human being?"

"I don't love sin. I swear I don't love sin."

"You've committed a terrible sin because you've hurt a woman. I can read in your heart that you're not sorry."

The devil was breathing words into the ear of this man, who saw through every secret. Anthyme would rather have been facing a wolf.

"Come on, *hostie,* since you don't want to give me my horse I'm going to take my wife back."

Anthyme went towards the buggy. Floralie looked away.

"Come on, woman."

Néron said drily, "I won't let you take this woman even if you give me a horse in exchange. Your heart is so black you'd rape her and leave her under a tree."

"Woman, come here!"

"Giddyup!" Néron ordered the horse.

The whip clattered, this time on the horse, which had already set the buggy in motion. Every board was screaming at the violence of the takeoff.

Anthyme had been able to hold onto something that belonged to him — one of the lanterns, whose slender flame he brandished, shouting, *"Hostie d'hosties!"*

He wished his voice would shatter the night like a window: he wanted it to smash the trees and tear them up and hurt the sleeping animals. But the silence was deaf to his anger.

When the cries could no longer escape from his raw throat he threw the oil lamp as far as he could over the spruce trees, following the little flame with his eyes. It disappeared. He waited for the flame to burst out and smash the night, devouring the entire forest. He already regretted his action. His heart was truly black: it was the colour of a devastated forest where the blackened skeletons were dancing in the blue sky; it was as black as the earth where grass has been burned. Nothing exploded. The night remained black. The spruce trees were not turned into firebirds. The little flame in the lantern had gone out.

Anthyme was so happy he could have danced for joy.

Was his heart really as black as he had been told? The flame his hand had touched went out. This tree-filled night was like his heart: no light would penetrate it. He had refused to let Floralie's love enter it.

It had been good of God to keep him alive when his heart was so black.

"My God, who invented the light, I'm asking you not to squeeze my heart in your hand. My heart is so black it's possible you can't see what's in it, but that's no reason to punish me right away. Wait a while, God. Give me time to be converted. Then you can wipe me out."

From far away a choir of angels seemed to utter a celestial response to his prayer. But he soon recognized the words.

Néron, Néron
Is good.
Néron, Néron
Is holy.
Néron, Néron
Is good
Néron is holy

"When you've got a black heart it doesn't matter much where you go. You always take your black heart with you. I've been too wicked with my wife. Maybe she's an honest woman. I don't love sin. If I've got a black heart maybe I love sin. Or maybe it's sin that loves me."

*   *   *   *

On that night, when the face of the man seated close to her was as unknown, as removed from her as the moon, Floralie was sound asleep.

Néron briskly tightened the reins. The horse stopped as it felt the tearing in its mouth and Floralie was almost thrown out of the buggy.

"You see what's down there?" asked Néron.

"Where?" murmured Floralie, her eyes still full of sleep.

Néron pointed.

"There, in front of us. On the other side of the trees, the other side of the forest. Where the road stops there's another road that leads into town. At the end of that road is the United States. Look. There. That's the United States. You see?"

"All I can see is the night. Everywhere."

"Your eyes are bad. Look at the smoke coming out of the factory chimneys. When that smoke comes down to earth it falls in a rain of gold."

"I don't see anything."

"Néron sees everything. Listen. What do you hear?"

"Nothing."

"Those are machines singing. They bite into metal and spit out chunks of gold."

"I can't hear a thing."

"Come on, little forest girl, let's go to the United States."

"Let's go to the United States," a chorus of clear children's voices repeated.

"I don't see anything and I don't hear anything," Floralie insisted, her voice pleading.

"Woman, you've got blind eyes and deaf ears. I've read in your heart that you like gold. Néron's taking you where the gold grows like wild strawberries."

"No! I want to stay here!"

"Here! What does 'here' mean? 'Here' just means wherever you happen to be. When the gold comes raining down on us we'll say, 'Here it's raining gold.'"

"I want to get out of here."

"No. Néron knows that you like gold, even if you aren't acquainted with this marvel. You're poorer than one of my little mice and you like gold. I'm going to have a white hat and a gold watch and I'll buy you anything you want."

"Let's go to the United States!" insisted the children.

"Giddyup horsey!"

Painfully, the carriage was pulled out of the mud where it had stuck.

"Stop!" Floralie ordered.

Néron did not hear. In his mind gold was falling like a musical shower. Floralie, standing, was about to jump from the buggy.

"Stop! Stop!" she pleaded.

Néron had heard, but the rain of gold was singing louder and louder in his head. He had made up his mind to go to the land where the golden song would be wafted to him on the wind. He would have liked Floralie to come too, but she refused to go to the United States with him.

"When Néron works his wonders women kneel before him. They don't refuse him anything."

"Stop!"

Néron wouldn't stop her, this idiotic girl who was afraid to go to the land of gold.

"Go on and get lost in the night."

Néron pushed her scornfully. Floralie tumbled into the thick woods, which lashed at her face. She got up, dazed, astonished that she was unharmed.

The children opened the mouse-trunks and began to throw the maddened little creatures at Floralie. Instead of giving in to his first angry instinct at seeing the children waste his sacred mice, Néron stopped the buggy and encouraged the children to go on pelting Floralie.

At first Floralie thought they were throwing clumps of mud which flattened as they struck her. She protected her face with her hands, but when the mice began to run over her shoulders, their dripping little noses in her neck, when they caught hold of her hair and scurried among the folds of her dress, she was so frightened she could not breathe. She thought she would die of fright.

The projectiles came less frequently and the night grew calm, closing around her like a wall that nothing could open. From the other side, growing farther away, came the words of a well-known song:

Néron, Néron
Is good.
Néron, Néron
Is holy.
Néron, Néron
Is good
Néron is holy.

The very ground was made of night. It gave way under Floralie's weight. She was the last woman on earth. Her village, the men whose faces she remembered, the young men and their dances in their Sunday suits, the strangers who had come to build the railway, the Italian and Anthyme, all had been swallowed up by the night as it murmured beneath the trees, crackling under the branches. Only Floralie had escaped being buried alive. Floralie and Néron with his children. Néron with his bulging eyes. Néron, that toad.

Néron had taken her in his toad arms. He had looked at her with his toad eyes. Had he pressed his toad mouth, full of sticky spit, against hers?

The night had even invaded her memory, where an innocent toad smile prevailed behind a veil of heavy shadow.

Her stomach heaved.

She did not dare to move on.

She was alone.

Every step beyond the ones she had already taken could make her lose her way.

Who had brought her here?

She was hungry.

The forest was sumptuously perfumed.

She was hungry.

A young girl couldn't eat grass.

At each step her leg stretched out or pulled back, but too far, and she tripped.

A little water would have quenched the fire in her belly.

Cautiously, Floralie put one foot ahead of the other, without seeing. The weight of her body pulled her ahead. She was moving like a stream whose shores were the endless night. Floralie was lost already in a black sea; perhaps the channel that guided her steps would lead her to Hell, because her soul was so laden with sin.

How could she think otherwise?

At her birth God had given Floralie a pure white robe that it was her duty to keep immaculate. Tonight it was all stained with sins. Floralie had succumbed to the sin in which a man takes off his clothes, the better to be like an animal. God's anger must be terrible at the sight of this creature of his whose robe was as dirty as an old rag.

Why had her mother made her wear a black dress for the trip? Did she know that her daughter was mourning the innocence of her soul?

The road led down to Hell. Behind the bushes the eyes of amused little demons were shining. In the damp holes beneath the shrubs viscous little creatures were salivating in the shadows. They were following Floralie. At the end they would return to Hell.

Flee!

Floralie was walking so slowly.

Flee!

Floralie stopped completely. That way she would never arrive at the gate of Hell.

* * * *

Meanwhile, Anthyme was running downhill at a breathtaking speed, tripping on the overgrown path, running on his feet, his hands, stumbling over projecting roots, scraping his hands, catching on branches that were hemming him in on all sides.

He was no longer afraid.

It had been a mistake to remain standing, blind and angry. The village would not come to him. The village would not come on a buggy drawn by a horse: it would take too big a buggy and too many horses — immense horses, at least as big as the houses in the village, and that would have required stables so big the people in the village could not have built them because they could barely build normal-sized ones. The land was miserly; what it had most of to give was rocks, and horses like that would have devoured as much hay as a whole herd of cattle, and his cows — what was wrong with his cows, anyway? Why had they lost their appetite?

Anthyme hurried.

For the village to come to him a very wide road would have been needed, like the roads in the United States. The village would not come on its feet — it would take too many feet. So, on his own two feet, Anthyme set out for his village.

* * * *

Suddenly there was a peal of thunder behind Floralie, and the air stirred against her back, disturbing the shadows. Floralie threw herself off the road. The ball of thunder stopped beside her, like a carriage, with a sound like that of wheels crushing pebbles into the earth.

"What kind of animal is that?" a voice inquired.

"At this hour, in the middle of the forest, it's probably only the devil wandering around."

"It's a woman, unfortunately."

Floralie raised her head, but she kept her eyes lowered. She dusted off her dress with exaggerated care in order to reassure herself.

"It's the devil disguised as a woman," said a feminine voice.

"If you want my opinion, I'd rather have a woman disguised as a devil than a devil dressed up like a woman."

"If all the devils are made like that one, I say, 'Open up, gates of Hell.'"

Hearty laughter streamed out of the long cart, which was pulled by two horses. A garland of lanterns with dancing flames hung around the cart, where Floralie could read, painted in big letters: THE SEVEN DEADLY SINS, and in smaller letters: A Dramatic Comedy.

"Hell," said one of the voices jokingly, "doesn't open its doors to just anybody. Anybody can go to Heaven, but Hell is choosy. It only welcomes the nobility."

"When he opens his mouth it gives me shivers up my back," said a woman.

"Get up here with us, beautiful," said the one who was holding the reins.

"THE SEVEN DEADLY SINS, what does that mean?" asked Floralie.

She heard sudden laughter, like the cawing of a flock of crows.

"If there were eight sins the eighth one would be innocence."

"Seven is enough. I wouldn't want eight. I can barely keep seven actors alive. The public isn't very generous."

"It doesn't pay us much for all our sweat," said a woman.

"Seven sins is enough for one man!" said an actress.

They laughed like children, with sinister voices.

"Get up here with us, beautiful."

A hand was stretched out to her, and another, and Floralie held on. She placed her foot on the spoke of a wheel and they hoisted her up, very lightly, into the cart.

"Innocence," mocked one of the actors, "there's no such thing. Innocence doesn't exist. In the purest spring water you find bugs as big as spiders. And apparently there are some that are even more disgusting that you can't see. If water isn't pure, a woman . . . No, innocence is all a dream."

"Lust has spoken."

The man had read the truth in Floralie's body, as you can read a letter still in its envelope by holding it up to a candle. The man knew her as well as she knew herself. She hated him for it and assumed that he was horribly ugly there in the half-darkness.

"You'll be all right with us."

"It's the first time I've seen the Seven Deadly Sins in flesh and blood," she said.

"Let's go!" ordered the driver.

"Thank you for welcoming me."

"It wouldn't be Christian to let you walk when we have a cart."

"You're right! We'll find a way for her to repay the favour."

What did they mean? Their talk worried Floralie. What would they ask of her? They were quiet. What were they imagining in their silence?

"Anyway, I promise to help you if you ask me to do something honest."

In the cart Floralie could not distinguish the faces any better because of the trembling shadows they cast on one another.

"I've got a marvellous idea," announced Pride. "This child can play the Blessed Virgin. At the end of the performance she could crush the head of a paper serpent. People like the show better if the devil loses out in the end."

"And they pay more!"

"I protest!" said Wrath. "It's a wild idea. How can you offer a part to a young girl you pick up in the forest? Does she know anything about the art of the theatre? No. Does she know how to declaim her lines and make the rhythms ring out? No. Does she know how to improvise? No. You offer her the part of the Blessed Virgin. Is she even a virgin?"

"Are you a virgin?"

Floralie lowered her eyes and did not reply, crushed by the heat of their looks directed at her, which could read the undeniable reply. She should have continued to wander, refused to get into the cart.

"Passing yourself off as the Blessed Virgin when you're not a virgin — wouldn't that be a sin?" asked Envy.

She could not talk to these people who were tormenting her and she could not get away. She began to cry.

"Look at that — and you want to give her a part. She doesn't even know how to unclench her teeth," grumbled Wrath. "Tell us. Are you a virgin? We've got to know."

Terrified, Floralie hid her face in her hands and closed her eyes. Her gesture did not blot out the night, gliding behind her back like an endless serpent.

All around her, hands had caught hold of the bottom of her dress and were gently lifting it, looking avidly, in a silence where anything could happen.

Floralie opened her eyes as she felt the cotton slipping against her thigh. She saw eyes like atrocious mouths looking at her. Her arms slid along her body, hesitantly at first, then holding onto the skirt with more certainty. But the skirt, pulled in every direction, continued to climb. Floralie stopped resisting.

"She'll make a dazzling Blessed Virgin."

"But how do we know if she *is* a virgin? We've got to find out. I don't want to blaspheme the Blessed Virgin by giving her the body of a girl with loose morals . . ."

"We can find out."

Floralie saw the compassionate eyes of Lust approach her face.

"Get out, all of you!" he ordered.

The actors emptied the cart. Only Floralie and Lust were left. The actor took her hands and pressed them lightly, caressing her palms with his fingertips. His caress spread like a star in Floralie's hand and through her whole body the tide of her blood was set in motion by the insistent softness. Floralie could not pull away from Lust's piercing eyes.

He knew everything about her; he knew all her faults — Floralie could read it in his eyes, which did not shine in the night but had become part of it. His eyes had seemed ugly because she had wanted them to be. They were beautiful. She was afraid that she would lose herself in them as she had gone astray in the night.

Lust gathered her into his arms. Floralie's knees gave way and she clung to him to avoid falling.

"No!" she protested. "No!"

"You shouldn't say no to life," he said gently.

Heads surrounded the cart.

"Tell them to go away!"

"Now you can't even look where you want to!" complained one of the actors.

Without relaxing his embrace, and without being pushed away, Lust had stretched out on the floor of the cart.

"Floralie! Floralie!" cried a distant voice. "What are you doing? What are you *doing?*" cried her mother's voice. "Is that what we taught you?"

Her mother's voice came from as far away as childhood.

"Damned girl! Fallen woman!" came the distracted voice of Anthyme, who was not finding the road between the trees.

"Little fawn, little kitten, little nose, little mouth," whispered Lust, "little delight, little love."

He lay down against Floralie and his hand wandered deliciously in the hollows of the young woman's body.

"I'm not a wicked wolf," said Lust, "I'm a gentle little lamb that needs to be rocked like a tender little child."

A burning sensation zigzagged through her body like lightning and gave way to a calm and fragile dawn. Gradually a little sun rose in her. It spread out with immense petals which hid the earth. Her body was as vast as the vault of the sky. The sun had the taste of the most delicious fruit. Could Floralie's memory, at that instant, not remember?

"No! No!" she wept. "You're handsome but I don't want . . . No!"

"Sweet little animal."

"I beg you! No!"

She was a rabbit and a wolf had her by the stomach. Her hands and feet were moving desperately. But she did not want to scratch the young man or hurt him. His breath whispered past Floralie's shoulder and reached her heart.

She could no longer cry.

"You're handsome, but we mustn't."

Lust drew back his face and smiled.

"I might already have a child in my belly. If you're the devil he'll be born with big pointed ears and only one eye."

"And his body all covered with hair," mocked the actor.

"I can tell you really are the devil," she cried in a voice that was calling for help.

She began to fight again, biting, frantic. She could see only her tears.

"Is she a virgin?" asked a curious voice.

"Yes!" Lust replied.

Around the motionless cart shadows clapped their hands, happy.

"Bravo!"

"We've got our Blessed Virgin!"

"She's a virgin, all right," Lust insisted.

These words wounded Floralie more than an insult. The actors, laughing, got back into the cart.

"We'll put on a beautiful show!"

"The public will throw beautiful money!"

"Thank you, Blessed Virgin."

"I won't have to rob henhouses any more!"

"At least not so often."

"Thank you, Virgin Mary."

"When we've got together enough money we'll paint on the cart, THE SEVEN DEADLY SINS AND THE BLESSED VIRGIN – A Dramatic Comedy."

"We're late. Let's go."

★　★　★　★

When he moved ahead Anthyme felt as if he was staying in the same place, as if the earth was sticking to his feet, as if the very trees were following him like dogs and he could not escape.

"The good Lord makes men and the good Lord makes women. The good Lord made women for men and men for women. Men expect to be ready, they look around, they choose a woman. This woman follows her man: she's going to help him live his life. A man wants to clear out a bit of land in the forest: he cuts the trees, burns the branches, pulls up the stumps and goes back home all dirty with pine gum and ashes and sweat. He has lots of kids. Every fall the barn is as full as an egg and there's a new baby in the house. The years are full. The kids wait for him in the evening. And the man, he finds the day too long because he's anxious to see his kids, especially the smallest ones, but the day is too short too because the sun always sets on unfinished work. When he comes in the house smells of baking bread. There's a smell of milk, too, and fresh laundry. Through the window you can see the wheat growing and you grow taller along with it. The woman is happy and as soon as the children have stopped tossing around under their sheets the man and his wife go happily up to their room where the bed is as good as Heaven.

"Maybe I was Floralie's first man. If I'd had other cirls I would have known if Floralie was like them or different. I must be right: the husband has to break through a wall, a little wall that resists him. And I didn't notice any wall. So there wasn't one. Maybe I was too nervous too. If Floralie is a fallen woman, when she looks at me she doesn't look like one. She looks like a young calf that's never seen the world. I didn't behave like a man: I behaved like a goddamn animal. I love Floralie."

He shouted, "I love you Floralie! I've been crazy! Out of my mind! Like an animal!"

Anthyme deserved to be punished. He would have accepted being sentenced to wander among the black trees for the rest of his days.

"Floralie, I love you! Why didn't you tell me I was the first man you'd given yourself to? You didn't say a thing. You kept your mouth shut — and me, I was practically yelling out loud because I was so happy to be loving you. And then when I got mad you didn't answer. Was I telling the truth? Are you a fallen woman? Are you as open to the public as a street? The street's public, the school's public, even the church is public, but I don't want my wife to be public property. But maybe you aren't. Floralie, I love you, I wanted to spend my whole life with you. I would have held you in my arms every night and then when we were old we would have spent the days rocking side by side in our rocking chairs. But you don't love me Floralie. And I love you!"

*   *   *   *

In the cart, which was creaking and groaning over every hole and every pebble and shaking up the passengers, who were a bit deafened by the blows resounding in their heads, the actors had made Floralie sit down and they had arranged themselves around her.

"I'm hungry," one of them complained.

"Some people only think about their bellies. That's where their brains are."

"Some people don't think about anything except applause. They'd slit their mothers' throats if it meant some applause at the end of the show," retorted the hungry one.

"Shut up! The main thing is for them to throw money on the stage."

"What's the good of money if you always have to work?"

Lust, absent from the argument, was contemplating Floralie's firm, round bosom. On his fingers the breath of memory sang.

"Listen," said Floralie.

"Listen to what?"

"You don't hear anything? It's coming from over there," Floralie pointed to the sky.

"It's the sound of a chain slipping through the sky like on the floor of a barn."

"You're right. I hear it too," said one of the actors.

"Me too."

"You're right. What is it?"

"It sounds like somebody pulling a chain across a wood floor."

"A big chain."

"It's the same sound. It sounds like a man walking in the sky with chains on his feet."

"And his hands."

"It's coming from the sky," Floralie insisted.

Talk became superfluous. They were silent. The horses pricked up their ears and stood still. The rumbling sounded like far-off thunder that didn't let up, but even more it sounded like a man wandering through the sky in chains.

"What is it?"

"Maybe it's a soul condemned to look eternally at the gate of Heaven without being able to enter."

"It's a sign from God," said the driver. "He doesn't talk any more, but he gives people signs."

The actors waited, in a suffocating silence. The sound was neither earthly nor human.

"God wants to remind us that sin is covered with chains," remarked the driver.

"The only chain I've got is on my watch," said Lust jokingly.

"Don't be blasphemous."

"You should be praying instead."

"I'm afraid," said Floralie.

They could feel the cold metal of the chains tightening around their wrists and ankles.

"The chains of sin are invisible."

"Let's pray," said Pride.

"Shut up," said the driver. "My animals are going to get scared. I don't want them to break all our equipment."

"Me, I'm just the way God created me, just the way he wanted me to be. It's impossible that I could be offending him."

"Blessed Virgin, pray for us," pleaded Pride, with the voice of a woman about to give way completely.

The others covered their ears. They wished they were deaf. Floralie got up.

"Our Father who art in Heaven, forgive us our trespasses as we forgive . . ."

As she was praying the sound of the chains became less insistent, as if each of Floralie's words were charming the clamorous serpents. The sky became a silent plain once more.

"It's a miracle!" shouted the driver. "I'm giving up the theatre and opening a place for pilgrimages."

"God obeyed you, Blessed Virgin. But I don't even know your real name. What is it?"

"Floralie."

"Floralie, the good Lord has obeyed you."

Floralie knew who it was who had answered her prayer. Because of her sins God had refused to hear her, but the Prince of Darkness, the King of Hell, where she would be going one day, had made haste to come to her aid. Were these unknown people who had picked her up really men and women? Or were they devils out of Hell come to gather her up in their cart?

The earth opened its monstrous jaw beneath the cart. The actors, laughing diabolically, and Floralie fell into the gulf, whirling around like dead leaves.

"She's fainted, the poor little . . ."

"Let's say the poor little saint."

"Our poor little apparition."

"Me, I'm going to confession as fast as I can. It's a sign from Heaven."

"What do you think, friends, should we make this a place for pilgrimages?"

"Me," bantered Lust, "I'm going to have to ask God to forgive me for trying to seduce his mother."

★   ★   ★   ★

"Except for my little sisters," Anthyme grumbled, "I've never seen a girl naked. I've never tried to play the beast with two backs. I've wanted to often enough — I'm a man, after all. The bulls, the roosters, the stallion — they had the right to jump on the females and do it with them. But I didn't because I'm not an animal. I'm a man, I'm intelligent. Animals have instincts but not intelligence. A man has intelligence but no instincts. Sometimes you'd like to act like the animals, but you don't because you tell yourself you're intelligent. Many times when I've seen a girl I've wanted to rub her belly against mine, but the good Lord would have punished me for behaving like an animal obeying his instinct and not like an intelligent man. Then besides, I didn't get drunk that often. A few times a year, because I'm a man after all and a man likes to lose his head a few times a year, but not often. The good Lord doesn't like to see his creatures vomiting from drinking too much beer. I didn't get drunk as often as lots of other men. There are people who have drowned their minds in alcohol and never found them again. I didn't even get drunk on my wedding day. Anyway, it wasn't an ordinary day. Floralie was the first girl who was all mine. That's saying a lot. At least, that's what I thought till I found out that there's been as many boys on top of her as the LaFleur bridge. Then, before I took Floralie I waited for the priest to tell me officially to go ahead and do it. Not before, because I'm used to being an honest boy, but today, God Almighty how I wanted to be drunk — drunk as a pig, because a drunk pig wouldn't be scared like I am tonight. God in Heaven, blessed be your name, I'm scared. I'm scared the way I used to be at night when I was a kid. I used to have nightmares — wolves running around on the walls in our bedroom. I used to yell. Giants' claws would scratch on the ceiling and you could see the claw-marks in the morning. I cried till my throat was raw. Little red devils, all naked, with skin as red as blood, used to come and dance in front of the window. I'd call for help, but nobody heard. My brothers would never wake up so they wouldn't feel the hunger in their bellies and my father and mother slept like worn-out horses. I'd get up and go and lie down under the bed so I could cry. *Hostie d'hosties,* but I was scared. How can a child stay alive when he's so scared? My fingers and toes should be dead by now. A kid as scared as I was should have stopped growing. *Hostie!* I was scared! My parents' bed used to creak under their weight. That reassured me a little, but you, God, it would take more than a mountain to move *you.* You wouldn't have made your bed creak to reassure me a little. Where were you? Instead of sleeping all night like everybody else you were off chasing a boy who'd had some fun with a girl or you were knocking down some guy who'd had too much to drink. That's more fun than putting a child to sleep. Make a man suffer till he cracks up, then step on him. So where were you that night? *Hostie d'hosties!* I don't understand you any more than I understand Chinese. I just don't get it. I knelt down in front of your image every day of my life. I prayed to you. I honoured my father and mother even though I can't stand the old lady. I didn't blaspheme your name or the names of the priest's holy things except when I had to. Before I had a woman I waited to have her blessed by the priest. And to pay me back for all that you stick me with a dishonest woman, you take away my horse and you make the night come pouring down on me like a flood. I'll never understand. Why, God, why? I don't get it. When a man doesn't understand you shouldn't reproach him for what he says. Listen to me, God. I haven't got anything to drink. But if I did have some booze here I'd drink it right under your nose, I'd get drunk enough to split my guts and then I'd piss and I'd say you were right there in front of me and that I was pissing on your pant leg. I know, I know, God doesn't wear pants. You aren't listening to me, God? Other guys, the ones that used to jump on the neighbours' girls and laughed while they were doing it in the haystacks, the ones that used to go to meet the girls when they were going to milk the cows, the ones that used to go to Québec City every year and try out all the hotel beds with girls in them, one after another like my mother saying her 'Hail Marys,' all those guys have found little women that don't make eyes at men, not even their husbands. Those guys, their little wives give them a baby a year. They've got land and animals and houses that smell of fresh butter and healthy babies' diapers. But me — God — me, you throw a dishonest girl in my arms. Then you take my horse away. Then you throw me in the forest where it's as black as the inside of my mother's belly that I never should have left. How am I supposed to go back to the village without my horse or my wife? I could explain that my wife wanted to stay with her mother for a week and they'd believe me, the people in my village, but I could never make them understand why I'd lost my horse."

With tremendous strength, like the strength that comes out of the earth in spring into the trees and makes them burst out in buds, anger rose up in him. He raised his eyes to Heaven, looked for the spruce tree whose tip was stuck deepest into the sky, chose one and began to climb among its many branches, crawling up between the sharp needles, his arms tight around the gummy trunk. He soon reached the top, his face scratched, his flesh burning under his clothes. He could not hoist himself any higher, because the tip of the tree was as fragile as a feeble branch.

"God," he cried, "listen to me. I'm going to tell you something."

Clutching the tree with one hand he raised the other fist towards the sky.

"God, I'm telling you: you aren't fair! If you think I'm lying, come down and get me. We're going to settle this like men."

The night was stretched tight, ready to tear itself open. God held his breath. From the other side of the silence Anthyme could hear his own heart beating.

"You're hiding as if you weren't real!"

A drop of sweat ran down his forehead and blinded him. The whole universe seemed to sway under the weight of that drop of sweat. He held on tighter.

"I get it. I see what your little game is. You're afraid of a man who isn't afraid of you. Listen to me; I'm going to show you I'm not afraid. Listen to this: if I had a holy wafer and a hammer and a nail I'd nail that wafer right here to this tree and you wouldn't do a thing about it! . . . But I haven't got a hammer, and I haven't got a wafer and I haven't even got a nail."

Relieved, his soul appeased, Anthyme climbed back down the tree, almost happy.

"In other words, God, whether I pray to you or insult you, you're not the one that's going to feed my pigs or find my wife."

★　★　★　★

More than in any other place, potholes and hollows had torn up the road and thrown up pebbles. The cart was pitching violently in the tortuous ruts.

"One day," predicted one of them, "they'll shave this forest like a beard. The wolves will go farther away. They'll find rivers and plant grain and there'll be cows mooing among the women and children under the blessing of the church bell. Right here, under the cart maybe, there'll be a cemetery. People will think it's the gate to Heaven."

"When our cart comes back this way maybe we can put on a show in the village."

"If we aren't too old."

"My father only used to shave on Sundays," Floralie said suddenly.

The actors roared with laughter — she could not have announced the discovery of another America with more conviction.

Her father had a weekday face and a Sunday face. Today, for his daughter's wedding, he had on his Sunday face, but Floralie could only remember the one he wore all week. His hair was beginning to turn grey now; before, his head had been like a big black ball. Black hair, a black beard that hid his cheeks and chin, eyebrows like big black caterpillars, black eyes — and when he opened his mouth his teeth were black too.

For a long time neither Floralie's fingers nor her cheeks had caressed this black ball which, one day, had begun to cringe like a dog that has been beaten; but Floralie could remember how, as a small child, she used to play with this hairy ball that laughed or howled like a man in a rage. Floralie liked to remember how she would hold the black ball on her knees: she would amuse herself by looking for the ears and digging in them with her little fingers; she would comb the hair with an imaginary comb and with an imaginary razor she would cut the beard; it felt rough, like bark.

All of a sudden the black ball would turn the child upside down and crush her, rubbing her face, scratching her cheeks, crushing her nose, grating her ears, becoming hot as fire in her face. Floralie squirmed, complained, twisted to escape the weight of the fierce ball. She was so afraid — her face would be all scratched and bruised until it looked like a skinned knee. She called for her mother, crying, and the big black ball groaned with pleasure as it rolled on her and she sobbed.

"Stop it, Ernest," said her mother. "Can't you see the child's afraid? She's as white as a sheet."

Floralie no longer saw the black ball because her eyes were too full of tears. She only heard it.

"She's ungrateful, the miserable, ill-bred little brat! It gobbles up everything you've sweated to give it, and then you don't even get any thanks for it. You try to play with it and you don't get a word of thanks. You try to play with it for five minutes and it can't stand you. It sneers at you, it's already turning up its nose at its own father."

He was not talking now, he was yelling.

"If it didn't have a soul you could strangle it like a sick calf. But it's been baptised."

And he stamped his boot on the floor. The whole house trembled like the weeping child.

"You should step on it like a bug."

A caressing hand had wiped her eyes with an apron. Now Floralie could see her father, tall as a tree with his black beard and the hair that burst out of the opening in his shirt.

"I wonder why we don't squash them like bugs?"

Then, suddenly gentle, "Come and kiss me, little calf."

Arms were growing under the black ball, hands held out, waiting for the child.

"No, your beard is too prickly."

A scribbler lay on the table between the milk, the molasses and the cold beans.

"Come and give me a kiss or I'll tear up your scribbler and the teacher . . ."

"No, your beard hurts me."

"Come here and let me kiss you!"

"No!"

Without letting go of the scribbler in which she had traced her first words, the big hands moved apart and it seemed to Floralie that it was her flesh that was being torn.

The teacher had punished Floralie, who no longer had the courage to protest when the black beard ravaged her face. Gradually she learned not to suffer when the big black ball rolled on her with groans of delight. She waited with silent hatred for the end of the game.

One day her father completely stopped looking at her while

she was in the house. She had not left home — she was still too young — but she seemed like one of those absent people who are never talked about. At least that was how she felt in front of her father. Had he even noticed her on her wedding day? While her mother . . .

"All forests and all beards should be shaved!" announced Floralie.

"The Blessed Virgin likes them beardless."

"Eunuchs!"

"Saint Joseph had a beard."

"But she was unfaithful to him."

"From now on my cheeks are going to be as smooth as the skin on your behind."

"That young girl will be pretty unhappy if she marries a farmer from her neck of the woods. They've got so much beard they could go without faces!"

"Get married! Go on! Young girls like her don't want a husband, they want a man."

"A husband's a man, isn't he?"

"A man sends his woman to seventh heaven; a husband sends her to look for his pipe."

"Sweet Jesus! Send us a bit of misery so we can cry. I've laughed too much!"

"Blessed Virgin, don't ever get married. You wouldn't have so much to laugh about then."

★   ★   ★   ★

Ahead, the forest was growing light. An island of light animated the branches of the spruce trees but made the trunks more immobile, clutched in their strength.

"We're here, kids," said Néron. "Come on, come on, wake up. Sing! Come on, open your mouths! Sing!"

Like angels miraculously descending above the blessed clearing, the chorus of children intoned the hymn religiously.

Néron, Néron
Is good.
Néron, Néron
Is holy . . .

"More spirit, now. Louder! They'll be more apt to believe you."

From each side of the road, which was lit by flickering lanterns, there sprang up carriages and horses attached to trees, carts, wagons, horses with something to eat in their feedbags, children rolled up in blankets to sleep.

Dozens of buggies were lined up on both sides of the road between the trees, crushing the shrubs. Sometimes two or three horses were tied to the same tree, pushing each other with their muzzles and neighing. Others were sleeping and their open eyes were sparkling. Beams of light could be seen coming from tall pyramids of dry wood that were burning in the midst of the clearing. Some men were stroking their horses' foreheads, others were burrowing in the deepest shadows where only the gleam of the bottles at their mouths could be seen as the men emptied them with guilty gurgles. Women were rummaging in their bags, spreading sweaters and blankets over sleeping children. Older children, laughing, chased each other among the carriages, sneaked in among the horses' legs to surprise the drinkers and, with cries of delight, uncover the lovers. The girls hid their faces in their hands and their lovers pulled up their pants, grumbling, "You come on a pilgrimage and you don't even get a chance to say your prayers in peace."

With great uproar, Néron's retinue swooped down on the clearing, scattering the chattering groups and upsetting old men who were walking with difficulty. A cloud of dust surrounded the buggy, which stopped at a cry from Néron.

"Shut up, children; leave it to me."

He walked towards the back of the buggy. The children did not complain when his nail-studded heels came down on their piled-up toes and ankles. Standing erect, with theatrical gestures, he spoke to the people who were looking at the curious stranger.

"Come here, all of you! Everybody with pains, come to me! All of you with sore bodies, come; all of you with suffering souls, come! Come to Néron, son of Néron, son of the Almouchiquois. Néron knows so much about pain he can kill it just like you kill a fly by pulling off its legs one by one and then its wings and then its eyes and then its head."

Scornful and curious at the same time, the people approached him cautiously. From all directions lanterns were stirring up the night in an eddy of shadows.

"You over there with one leg, come here."

The cripple came up to Néron on his crutches. His face showed the strain of the effort, but his eyes were malicious.

"If you grow me another leg I'll say you're the good Lord and I'll install you in the tabernacle in the church."

Generous laughter exhorted the one-legged man to mock the stranger.

"With one single leg I've made twenty-three children for my wife, and they're all alive except for the five that are dead."

"You don't do that with legs!" teased a man smoking a pipe.

The other groups had broken up. Now there was only one group, gathered around Néron's buggy. The one-legged man went on:

"With two legs I'd have done twice as much: forty-six children, ten of them dead. That's a lot. Too much. The good Lord didn't want it, so he took back the leg he'd loaned me."

"Ladies and gentlemen, admire this man. Twenty-three living children and five dead ones. It's men like him who will save our country," Néron declaimed.

"I've only counted the children I've had with my wife Theodorina. I'm not talking about the others," the one-legged man remarked more precisely.

In their delight the rubber-necks frolicked like calves let loose in the spring grass.

The one-legged man's body was shaken by gasps and hiccups so severe that he began to cough, his face all puffy, his eyes bulging. He lost his balance and fell over, his crutch on top of him.

The laughter dried up in the farmers' throats.

"Move back, everybody," Néron ordered.

They pulled back. Néron jumped to the ground, knelt, and placed a hand on the unfortunate man's head.

"If he hadn't been lucky enough to meet Néron on the way this man would have stayed on his back pinned to the ground."

"That's a lie," shouted the one-legged man, getting up.

"It's a miracle!" shouted the chorus of children.

"I'm getting up because I want to," said the cripple. "That Indian is a liar."

"Néron is telling you: good people, don't pat a lion — you're liable to get clawed."

The country-people came still closer to Néron's buggy. The one-legged man went away, cursing.

"Since my eleventh was born," confessed a woman, "I've had a pain in my belly. It's like a toothache, but a really bad one that goes from my feet right up to my head and then stays in my forehead."

"Woman, give Néron your hand."

He leaned towards her, his head level with the woman's face, her eyes reluctant to tolerate Néron's sharp gaze.

"You're well already. Open your eyes and look into mine. You won't have any more pains tonight or tomorrow if you think of Néron, son of Néron, son of the Almouchiquois. You have been cured. If you want the pain to stay where it belongs and not come back, every Friday the good Lord grants you, at three o'clock, the hour of Christ our brother's death, rub your belly with this water that was drawn at dawn on Easter Sunday. Here's a little bottle. It's free, but don't forget the widow's mite."

"Come, all you who suffer pain!"

Another woman spoke up.

"Me, I'm worn out like a horse that's been beaten too often. It's not my husband, I swear it isn't. He only beats me up when he's had too much to drink or when he's mad or bored. I don't remember a thing any more. I don't remember my sainted mother or my dead father or my happy childhood. I don't remember. It's as if I've never been alive."

"Well, woman, maybe you haven't," suggested Néron.

"I can't remember," said the woman.

"That doesn't matter. In God's Heaven the chosen ones don't remember their life on earth. Woman, you're already in Heaven. God has taken you into paradise before your death. Don't try to remember. That would be setting yourself against the will of God. Look, here's a button from the soutane of Brother Albertus who died in the odour of sanctity. Rub your temples with this button at sunset. It's free, because Néron doesn't work for money. Don't forget the widow's mite. All you who suffer, come!"

A young man held out his hand to Néron.

"Look at my hand, Indian. It's covered with warts. It looks like a rotten potato. Girls are 'as scared of my hand as if it was a skunk. Are you going to let me cut it off or are you going to take off the warts?"

"Give me your hand, young fellow. In three days your warts will be gone if you do as I say. Every day, at dawn, you put your

hand in the first ray of sunlight and spit towards the four points of
the compass. In the evening, when the sun goes down, put your
hand in the last ray of sunlight and put your feet on the places
where you spit in the morning. In three days, if you've really followed my instructions, you'll be able to say, 'Néron, son of Néron,
son of the Almouchiquois, has cured me.' Don't forget to show
your gratitude — a little something for the widow's mite. Néron
relieves your pains."

A peasant with a muscular neck and broad shoulders stood
before Néron.

"Indian, I've got a sickness in my heart. I'm a sad man. My soul
is hidden under sadness, like a field under white November frost.
I'm sad, sad . . ."

He was not going to say any more; sadness was stifling his
voice.

"Speak up, poor man. Néron knows how to listen. So many
words have passed my ears, I can understand everything."

"I'm sad," he repeated. "I don't know how to laugh. I'm a sad
man. When other people laugh, I'm sad. When the sun comes up,
I'm sad. When I've had a good day, I'm sad. I'm always sad. It's as
if I've lost something, I don't know what, and I'm sure I'll never
find it."

"Poor man, give me your hands — put them in mine."

The man obeyed.

"Néron will light the fire in you that will lick away the white
frost that's covering your soul, and it will bring your sad soul back
to life. Feel the fire burning within you, all over. The fire is beginning to dance inside you. Feel the fire in your soul. Your soul is
waking up! It's stirring in you like a flame."

"Watch out! It's the fire of Hell!"

The people looked away from Néron, seeking the woman who
had spoken.

"My good man," Néron went on, "I've restored the fire of life in you. To keep the fire alive, man, think of Néron three times a day. Don't forget the widow's mite."

"That man," Floralie cried accusingly, "is a liar, a charlatan, an exploiter, an adventurer, a highway robber, an abuser of girls and a wild Indian."

What woman dared to insult an Indian endowed with the magical powers of his race? Lanterns circled around her like crows. Who was she to accuse Néron? He pointed a threatening finger at her.

"Young woman, I know your soul and I know you're going under, body and soul, like a leaky boat. But the woman who gives her hand to Néron, who gives him her heart, is saved."

It was only too true that Floralie was shipwrecked, and that she felt as if the forest were the black sea-bottom. An extraordinary sadness caught in her throat, holding back the words. Néron had told the truth, and it was choking her.

"Young woman, Néron sees that your soul is as rotten as a little wildflower in the fall. But Néron can cure you."

He lowered his voice, bent towards her, and whispered in her ear something that the others thought was a magic formula.

"Are you coming to the States with Néron to look for gold?"

"Give up, you charlatan!"

Father Nombrillet untied the cord around his belly and, using it as a whip, jumped into the buggy. With impetuous conviction, he lashed out at the Indian.

"This isn't a carnival; it's the Feast of the Holy Thorn. Get out of here, you devil's sorcerer. I drive you hence, you money-changer! Liar! Thief!"

To get away from the storm of blows and abuse, Néron ran in front of his carriage and gave a command to his horse with a flick of his whip. The horse bolted into the crowd. When he had disappeared into the night you could hear,

Néron, Néron
Is good.
Néron, Néron
Is holy . . .

"My daughter," said Father Nombrillet to Floralie, "if your heart is sad I know the source of all happiness."

"Oh, yes, I'm sad, I'm so sad."

Father Nombrillet placed his hand on Floralie's brow.

"Sin makes you sad, my daughter."

Floralie wished she could come close to him and let her head drop onto his broad shoulder, but she dared not touch a man of God. The big eyes of this big man with the trembling cheeks knew a greater mystery than was hidden by the trees of the forest.

"Sin looks for joy, but it only finds sorrow."

"Yes," said Floralie, whose lips sealed too late to take back the word that escaped.

"Sadness is everywhere. It covers the earth because sin is everywhere. There are more sins than there are men and women; there are more sins than there are cows in the world; there are more sins than blades of grass; more sins than there are insects in all the grass in the world. Sin is vaster than the sea, and there's four times as much water as land. That means there are enough sins to drown the whole human race."

"Is that so?" she asked.

"Come, my child, so I can forgive your soul and your body, which has been a poor servant."

"Blessed Virgin!" someone called.

"Blessed Virgin? Where are you?"

Lust, all out of breath, took her hand, snatching her away from Father Nombrillet.

"Come, Blessed Virgin."

"Blessed Virgin!" repeated Father Nombrillet, incredulous yet respectful.

He genuflected and brought his hands together, dazzled, to thank God for the divine apparition.

"Blessed Virgin," explained the actor, "the Seven Deadly Sins have been looking everywhere for you. Where have you been?"

"The devil reigns over the world," moaned the pious man of God.

*   *   *   *

From all around the clearing, little lantern flames ran up and converged in a low flight near the actors' cart, which had been transformed into a stage by a wall made from a roll of muslin. On the part of the cloth which served as a curtain they had painted quotations from the Bible and religious drawings. On one side, the blonde curly heads of bodiless angels emerged from the clouds; on the other side, smiling out of the fierce red flames, were demons with red eyes and pointed ears, teeth and horns. At the bottom you could read, THE SEVEN DEADLY SINS.

The muslin was held up by upright posts arranged around the cart. Lanterns attached to these uprights by strings swayed as though the cart were in motion. The whole construction seemed very fragile to Floralie, as if the wind could tear it down.

"Blessed Virgin, why are you waiting to put on your white gown? There's one in the green trunk — it's got 'fairies, queens, spirits, angels' marked on it. You'll see it."

"I'm falling asleep," said one of the actors, yawning.

"Come on, hurry up! There's too many of them. I hope they aren't too poor."

"When the Blessed Virgin comes on they'll throw lots of money."

"Sssssh! Quiet! Clear the stage! But be quiet!"

The curtain opened on an actress wrapped in an enormous red tunic and wearing a sparkling crown. The people, with a murmur of wonder, raised their lanterns to see better, but arms blocked their view and there was an uproar of discontent. One by one the arms were lowered and everyone could see the woman, who dominated them all and who was looking at them with cold authority. If she had spread her arms she would have revealed the secret of her body concealed beneath the red tunic. But she was motionless as steel, inaccessible. The night, trembling in her face, made her majesty more fascinating. Soon the night belonged to this woman, waiting till silence had sealed their lips.

"We are the Seven Deadly Sins. We are the kings of the earth — we reign throughout the world. Listen, ladies and gentlemen. We are poor actors condemned to wander through the world without a roof over our heads or a place to stop when it rains or hails. Be generous today, this Feast Day of the Holy Thorn."

The queen disappeared. The stage was empty.

At the back a big brown ball had been drawn on the curtain — the earth; higher up a shining sun, with its golden rays; and higher still, above the sun, a hand burst through a white cloud, blessing, commanding or damning: the hand of God.

The people saw the woman in red return.

"I am Pride. Every man loves me more than he loves his wife."

In the crowd the women hoped that their husbands would press against them, reassuring them, but the men remained cold. The women despised their men.

"Even when they hate me," said the red queen, "they love me. The humble people particularly belong to me."

She drew back into the shadows as a fat man with a cigar approached. Rings gleamed on all his fingers and he laughed in his puffy cheeks.

"I am Avarice. If you are poor, you haven't followed my

advice. If you are rich, you have listened to my advice and you are happy."

His silhouette disappeared, leaving the stage to a woman who came on languorously, her body swathed in a long, tight gown.

"I am Envy. Without me you would be obliged to accept life in all its unfairness, all its inequality. Thanks to me you can hate those whom life has preferred over you."

The actors were telling the truth. No one could have lived without the deadly sins. They secretly loved their deadly sins, but at evening prayers or at confession they had to say they were guilty of acting under their influence. Did they really regret having done so? According to the priests every sin was a gateway to Hell. You had to believe them. So they prayed to God for the gift of believing what the priests told them.

Two men followed Envy. They came on stage dancing, shoving, staggering, their bellies opulent. One was drinking avidly from a bottle, the other was hugging a pillow. They danced first on the left foot, then on the right and capered about as the farmers laughed, their shoulders shaking with delight. The two actors sang:

My name is Gluttony
No thin soup for me!
Sloth is my name
And sloth is my game!
We're both round and soft
As hams that you hang in the loft!

No one had ever seen such good actors. They put down their lanterns and clapped till their hands were sore.

"My name is Wrath," roared a man in a black suit, chasing the two actors who had preceded him. "It's thanks to me that life

hasn't squashed you like common insects, impotent animals paralysed by fear, useless human garbage."

He had shouted his last words like insults. Without another
look at the assembled crowd he went off, breaking his cane.

A pebble intended for him hit the sun on the backdrop instead.

A handsome young man wearing a lace jabot was already on
stage.

"I don't say much, but I say it well. My name is Lust."

He reflected for a moment, then said, with a broad smile, "I
am the father of all your children."

"You're a *baptême* of a liar," shouted an offended spectator.
"When Mélina spreads her legs it's for me and nobody else!"

The laughter of the crowd did not trouble the actor. He carried on.

"I am also the father of all the children you don't have. I am
Lust, the nicest of all the deadly sins. I live in your heads and in
your hearts. You lend me your hands and your wives. I reign in
your beds and your fields. It's through me that you'll be damned
but I'm a very pleasant companion on the road to Hell."

Was he an actor? Was it the devil in flesh and blood there on
the stage in front of all their eyes?

Before he had finished speaking the muslin at the back of the
stage parted to reveal the Virgin in her white gown.

"I am the Virgin Mary," she said, opening her arms.

Sighs of adoration were raised throughout the crowd.

"You'd think it was a real apparition!"

"A real Blessed Virgin couldn't be any more beautiful!"

Women kneeled.

"I am the Blessed Virgin and I shall walk upon the heads of
the deadly sins. I shall stamp them out just as my foot has already
stamped on the head of the serpent."

Hand in hand, the Seven Deadly Sins crossed the stage, singing,

We are the happy
Deadly Sins!
We are the mighty
Deadly Sins!
We're the delightful Deadly Sins!
Happy, mighty, delightful are we!

They went off laughing derisively, like children. The Blessed Virgin advanced towards the crowd.

"I shall stamp out those seven poisonous serpents."

Blessing, beseeching, Father Nombrillet elbowed his way through the crowd, knocking over the kneeling women. Leaping onto the cart he grabbed hold of the Blessed Virgin's hand.

"No, Blessed Virgin, you can't defeat the Seven Deadly Sins. They're stronger than you are."

His face was as sweaty as the face of a man working in the fields under the blazing sun. His breathing was that of a man in an indescribable rage.

"Satan is everywhere. Satan may even be stronger than God himself. Oh God, forgive me! But it seems, my Lord, that you are the weaker one. One could even say that your death on the Cross has not defeated Satan, because he reigns throughout the world. All Catholics should join together against the kingdom of the devil. You alone, my Lord, are our King. My brothers, listen to me. The Seven Deadly Sins are the Devil's army on earth. You can't fight them alone, Blessed Virgin, they'll ruin you. Come on, Blessed Virgin. These actors are the Devil among us. Take away their masks and you'll see the Devil's face. Get out of here, you strangers, get your cart off our land and go get lost. Clear out! Go prowl around somewhere else, you evil-minded wolves. And gorge yourselves on your own flesh!"

Beside himself, Father Nombrillet began to tear up the painted curtain, the earth, the sun, the hand of God.

"Actors, I won't bother damning you because you're damned already. By God himself."

No one in the crowd had the strength to remain standing. All were on their knees, praying, asking God that the Seven Deadly Sins would not try to seek revenge. Their anger was abominable and who could defend himself against the evil spell of the Devil in a rage?

"Go to the everlasting fires of the damned!"

"We're not going to get rich here," one of the actors interjected.

Father Nombrillet extended the protective wing of his arm around Floralie's shoulders.

"And you, little girl; I'm going to snatch you out of Satan's claws."

★　★　★　★

"*Hostie d'hostie!*" Anthyme swore. "At least I didn't get married in the winter. I'd really look smart in the middle of the night, out in the snow. I'd be dead by now."

As a matter of fact the May night was cool, but he was warm from having walked so long. His flesh shivered at the clammy touch of his sweat-soaked shirt. Fatigue had not yet put his muscles to sleep. The joints in his feet moved smoothly and since he had fallen into stride again, his feet moved solidly and without hesitation.

"At least it isn't winter, *hostie!* I wouldn't get out of this alive. And they'd never find my bones."

Around him branches disappeared under the snow and there were white spots floating everywhere in the night. Under his feet the road was somewhere beneath the snow, running east and west, but the snow had obliterated east and west. It hardened under his steps. The white trees walked at the same pace as he. He was as hot as if it were the most torrid part of summer, but a cold wind drifted into his clothing. The cold was biting at his fingers. Soon wolves would come and devour his body. The sweat on his brow froze in his eyebrows and eyes. A misty ice separated him from the world. He hurried but he got no farther ahead. The snow was clinging to his legs, closing its jaws on his ankles. If he freed himself it would catch up with him at the next step. He stamped his feet and a big white cloud swallowed him up. The cold had warm breath and the snow was softer than the white sheets his mother used to pull over him at night. Anthyme fell asleep in the sheets of snow. His mother was leaning over him, telling him to sleep well; she pulled the white sheets, moved her lips towards his forehead — but it was Floralie's face that Anthyme saw.

"Maybe I was her first man, but the truth isn't written down anywhere . . . anyway, I don't know how to read."

It was a blessing from God that this was May and not winter. In December or January, by this time, he wouldn't have been afraid because his body would have been drier than dead wood.

Far away behind the trees Anthyme noticed, veiled at first by the branches, a burning that opened and closed like a red eye.

Soon the trees were long red columns mounting towards the sky. Would the fire spread from tree to tree and cross the forest like a bolt of lightning? He was sorry it wasn't winter, a winter so dead that nothing could set fire to it.

Anthyme ran into a cart without a horse, abandoned, or so he thought. Then he saw another. And horses tied to a spruce tree. And more horses, more carts, with blankets and boxes, sleeping children, buggies. He saw men feeding animals, people strolling about with lanterns in their hands. They were so indifferent to his presence that he did not dare ask what was going on.

"Hostie!" he remembered, from the depths of his tangled memory; "It's the Feast of the Holy Thorn!"

No more black trees sprang up in front of Anthyme; the ground was no longer muddy underfoot. He entered the clearing, where several fires gave off a quavering light. The people carried their lanterns and as they pursued the night it fled, resisting. In the midst of it all a swarm of lights came together. Anthyme headed into the people assembled in front of the cart and the actors. First he searched the crowd for familiar faces.

On the stage, Father Nombrillet was pursuing the actors, swinging his censer, and the Seven Deadly Sins were laughing, cavorting, teasing the priest; they sang.

"We are the happy vices . . ."

Exasperated, Father Nombrillet struck out. The crowd was mute with terror: these actors were devils in disguise, come to disrupt the Feast of the Holy Thorn. The priest, out of breath, sweated and swore; his censer, turning at the end of its chains, struck someone in the back, another in the belly, on the forehead. The priest called on God to help him as the Seven Deadly Sins danced around him, flying like tenacious wasps.

We are the happy vices,

We are the key to joy!

The censer continued to strike without ceasing. Father Nombrillet kept Floralie behind him, protecting her with his body, on which one could have stepped without his giving way. His strength came from Heaven. And his rage. He chastised in the name of a furious God.

Suddenly Anthyme recognized Floralie in her white gown. He pushed, shoved, threw people to the ground, tripped those who were in his way. He leaped into the cart to deliver Floralie from the dangerous madmen. Father Nombrillet saw him charge.

"The Devil has seven vices to serve him. If they aren't strong enough they call for the Devil himself," he explained.

And propelled by all the strength of his Catholic soul, the censer encountered the face of Anthyme.

"*Vade retro Satanas,*" shouted the priest.

Roughly pushed by other demons summoned from Hell, the earth rose up like a wave, turned over and swallowed up, under terrestrial rubbish, all the living who had sinned. When he found the courage to open his eyes, Father Nombrillet understood that only the cart had been overturned by the too brutal exertion of the horses, who had given up under the whip of a maddened actor.

⋆   ⋆   ⋆   ⋆

"Your village is so far," said Floralie.

"If you want to go back to your father's place it's that way," Anthyme indicated the direction, "but if you're coming with me, walk behind."

Father Nombrillet threw himself in front of them, his arms spread out, with the strength of someone who wants to prevent his brother from leaping over a precipice.

"No! God has set me in your path. You shall not pass! A man who meets God in his path should not pass without seeing him. I'll hear your confession because you are great sinners. If you do not purify your souls, they'll decompose like your bodies. Confess!"

Anthyme considered the threat of the censer.

"Save me, Father, but I have not sinned. You can believe me. I hardly smoke at all — only on Sunday afternoons and after supper. I never drink, but when I do I can tell you I don't get drunk very often. I get up early, I go to bed early, and I've never gone with a woman. Except today because it's my wedding day, and she's my wife. I'm poor like the good Lord wants French Canadians to be. I don't see how you can ask me for more than that."

"My son," shouted the priest, as angry as if he had been given a slap in the face, "be quiet! It's wrong to talk like that. Listen: you're a man and every man is a sinner."

"Fine," Anthyme conceded, "I accuse myself of being a man."

"Get on your knees; I'm going to forgive you."

Anthyme knelt, lowered his head and crossed his arms on his chest in the attitude of pious schoolboys. Father Nombrillet's hand, the same one that had torn open his face with a swing of the censer, was placed on his head. As he felt its gentle touch Anthyme realized that it was a protective hand, the hand of God.

"My son, you are forgiven. Get up now. God is within you."

Beneath Anthyme's feet the ground had become hard again because the earth likes the weight of an honest man.

"You, Blessed Virgin, follow me."

"She isn't the Blessed Virgin, she's my wife, Floralie."

"My son," interrupted Father Nombrillet, "the wife of a sinner is a sinner too. Come, so that I can forgive you. What thorn have you stuck in the head of Christ nailed to his cross?"

She objected. "I've never stuck a thorn in anybody's head."

"That's where you're wrong. The worst mistake is to be ignorant of your sins. Come."

Anthyme followed them.

"No, you stay there and pray that God won't send too many misfortunes onto this earth, where we all offend him so greatly."

Father Nombrillet had no lantern but because of the numerous fires crackling in the clearing the night had retreated a little, even if shadows were clouding the ground. Floralie walked behind the priest, who jumped up, stopped, murmured, stretched out his neck, looked for something and speeded up.

"Here, in the midst of so much sin, is the house of God."

Floralie saw, beneath the spruce, a little chapel made of squared-off tree-trunks. The bell-tower was lower than the surrounding trees and the roof was covered with branches. He pushed a silent door on its maple hinges.

"Come in."

The night, suddenly opaque, smelled of rotten earth and urine. There was so much night in the chapel that all the lanterns from the clearing would have been been drowned there. But Floralie could see very clearly the white face of Father Nombrillet. He slipped the bolt in the latch.

"My daughter, how many times have you sinned?"

Floralie reflected. She remembered the Italian.

The priest had come up to her. His breath smelled of potatoes.

"My daughter, is there no remorse squeezing your heart as if Satan's teeth were buried in it?"

She tried, with perfect goodwill, to feel the Devil's fangs in her heart.

"My daughter, if you feel no remorse, your heart is made of stone. Hearts of stone sink in Hell like stones in water."

"..."

"My daughter, all women are sinners."

She declared, "Yes, I have sinned."

Father Nombrillet leaped up. "You too!"

He unbuttoned the collar of his soutane, which was choking him.

"My daughter, let me suffer for your sin too. I share the agony of Christ in the Garden of Olives. Get on your knees."

He prayed. "My God, whose universe is fierce for the souls of your poor children. You put them in the world clothed in the white robes of the angels, but the world where you cast them is a stinking mudhole. My God, spare us, on the day of your most holy wrath."

Father Nombrillet gasped for breath.

"My God, your faithful servant is weary. You have given me

my duty — to empty the sea of the sins that are inundating the earth — but just like Saint Augustine, you've only given me one bucket. I'm tired, Lord. Instead of continuing to empty the sea of sins, in your infinite mercy, which is even vaster than the sea of sins, instead of continuing to do the job you've demanded of me, I would like to let myself sink and drown like a sinner slowly drowning in his sin."

He tore off his soutane.

"But all you demons who cower like wolves, you won't get my soul, because God is with me!"

His ribcage was too narrow to contain his heart, swollen with a torrent of confused emotions.

"Pray, my daughter. The hour of God is at hand. Through my voice and my tongue he is asking you: is it with a man that you have sinned?"

Floralie had to accept the fact that the most precious joy that life had given her was wicked. Her soul could not drink deeply of it, on pain of death. On her knees before Father Nombrillet she was ready to regret every day of her life on which the thought of that joy had created some light.

"Yes," she confessed, "it was through a man that the Devil introduced me to joy."

"Ah! You too! And your soul?"

Father Nombrillet's voice was furious. When he knelt before her, so close to her, Floralie thought he was going to crush her in his arms as punishment for her sins.

"Man," roared the priest, "man corrupts everything he touches."

His hands seized Floralie's wrists, and his fingers were trembling.

"Did the man say, 'Take off your dress'?"

"Yes."

"And you took it off?"

"Yes."

"And God saw you in all the horror of your sin?"

The big lips of Father Nombrillet, like a frog, leaped, sputtering, onto Floralie's face.

"My daughter, admit your sin. You have allowed a man to put his hand here."

A feverish hand pressed Floralie's breast. She dared not push away the hand of God.

"Yes, he put his hand there."

"And you didn't push it away?"

"I didn't push it away."

"And it was good for you?"

Her numb lips could not articulate a single word.

Father Nombrillet panted and sweated. The night weighed on Floralie like a heavy, sweating man. Father Nombrillet trembled, his teeth chattering. A breath, almost a cry, surged from his mouth and resounded under the roof of the chapel. His head fell into Floralie's hair. After a long silence, during which he thought only of breathing, he said, "God and the Devil know that you are a great sinner. What penitence you will have to offer to God!"

And he put his shirt back on because he was afraid of catching cold.

★   ★   ★   ★

An impatient bell rang several times. Slowly, in groups, the crowd headed towards the little chapel dedicated to the cult of the Holy Thorn. Soon they were pushing one another, none of them daring to hope they might have the privilege of entering the tiny chapel. They pushed with elbows and knees and shoved with their shoulders, lanterns colliding. The sick regained their strength for the combat that would bring them into the chapel, now all lit up, the shadows fleeing on the walls as the pilgrims insulted each other and prayed.

"Why don't they let us in in order of preference: first the dying, then the cripples, then the amputees, then the women and men and finally the children?"

"A sinner," retorted someone else, "has as much right to go in there as a sick person. A sinner is twice as important as a sick man."

"But there are sick people who are sinners too."

"They're entitled to go in before the others."

"I know a woman; she's dying, she's sick, she's a widow, she's paralysed, and apparently when she was young there wasn't a girl who knew how to sin like she did. I'd say she's the one that has the right to go in first."

"She's even got the right to sit in the Baby Jesus' cradle!"

"*I'd* say she's entitled to say Mass!"

"Shut up, you apostate; show some respect for holy things and pass the tobacco."

Soon it was impossible to get through the wall of backs. Inside, everyone was wedged into the hot, wet mud. They held their lanterns in their outstretched arms and a glaucous warmth spread through the crowd, where the noises from your neighbour's stomach seemed like your own and you could feel someone else's heart beat in your back. A single body in the chapel was sweating with a single fervour.

"My brothers, *adjuventutem totem nolem:* God is great, the Devil is powerful," cried Father Nombrillet above the mutterings of the crowd.

He had climbed onto a stump that served as a chair.

"Many of you have come here — God will bless you for it — and you know that the souls of the dead are even more numerous and that they are shoving each other too, trying to enter the kingdom of Heaven. But they must wait for the living, through their prayers and incessant mortifications, to force open the gates of Heaven where there reigns a God who is not generous but *just*. My brothers, you have come to observe the night of the Holy Thorn, that is to say the anniversary of the night nearly 2000 years ago — it was a spring night — when a naive, innocent, inoffensive little thorn was growing out of the ground and which, as it grew, became more and more wicked and only grew longer so that it would be sharp enough to sink into the head of Christ, our Saviour. It's a tradition for us to join together on this night of the Holy Thorn to remember that our lives are thorns buried in the head of God, because Christ is God, and to beseech him that, thanks to his forgiveness, Hell will not open beneath our feet like a trap-door in the floor to let you fall into the eternal fire. But nothing will protect you: you do not love God, my brothers, because you love women, alcohol which makes men like beasts, and perverted dances that bring the Devil among you. God wants you to love the spiritual and hate the material. Now, my brothers, you love too much what you can touch, what you can see, what you can taste. We might say that God created the soul while he left it to the Devil to create the body and the senses. I see you, I see the seal the demon's claw has inscribed on your foreheads. Throw yourselves on your knees and pray. The foot of God is upon your heads and only profound regret, confession and penitence will prevent his foot from pressing down and crushing you as in former times the Mother of God crushed the head of the serpent."

Father Nombrillet's sermon was interrupted by a cry. A fire had broken out among the pilgrims. Springing up from the earth, the fire took hold of clothes and held on. The pilgrims wept, pushed, shouted and hit one another. The fire tore off their clothes and scratched their faces. Impressed by Father

Nombrillet's words a pious man had forgotten the lantern in his hand and it had fallen, spattering oil on a woman in front of him. Seized by the flames she had dropped her own lantern. They prayed and cursed and hit and trampled. They tore, but the human wall was impassable.

"God puts to the test those whom he has chosen," shouted Father Nombrillet.

The walls of the chapel opened and the flaming roof gave way and fell onto piles of blazing flesh.

Everywhere in the forest horses were running, trying to make the night extinguish the fire that was crackling in their frightened eyes.

When there was nothing left for its voracious jaws to graze on, the fire slept.

Then they began to look for the missing. The red ashes made a shroud that it was impossible to open, but the souls of the pilgrims who had died on this night of the Holy Thorn were ascending into Heaven. If the people's eyes had not been blinded by sin they would have seen them going towards the Eternal Father.

"The fire has sanctified them!"

"Father Nombrillet is the holiest of all."

Floralie, off to one side in the clearing, was crying. "I didn't confess all my sins to Father Nombrillet. I didn't have the strength. He'll be mad up in Heaven when he finds out I lied to him. His soul won't leave me in peace for a single night."

Pilgrims passing near her stopped to watch her cry.

"What's wrong, little girl?" asked an old man.

"I wish I'd been burned up like the others."

"Believe me, little one, it's better to be a flesh and blood girl than a saint of smoke and ashes. I'm old enough to know."

★   ★   ★   ★

Anthyme had crossed the edge of the forest and he was dragging his heavy feet through a field. The clover was all wet from the night, which had barely ended.

"*Hostie!* I've seen Hell. It wasn't nice."

To forget what he had seen he recited bits of prayers, trying to think only of what he could see in front of his eyes: grass that was clean and neat as a woven blanket and trembling birch trees. But the fire he had seen coming out of the earth and the cries of the demons that had surged up with the fire would leave a horrible scar on his life. He would always remember this night, even when he had forgotten all the others.

His legs could carry him no further. He was too heavy a burden for himself. He stretched out in the clover.

His soul, he thought, left his body, buried itself in the ground, and having got a good grip went drifting up towards Heaven, spreading out in the sky like a beautiful tree. His soul had forgotten the fire of Hell and the memory, changed into leaves, murmured across the sky with a musical sound like water.

In the meadow, a woman's voice was calling, "Anthyme! Anthyme! My husband!"

He opened his eyes. Floralie was bending over him, but she seemed to be on a distant shore.

"Anthyme, your village is so far!"

He went back to sleep.

*   *   *   *

"Here they are!"

"I've found them!"

Cries of triumph made the delicate air of dawn burst out in the sky. The horse and carriage were cropping lightly the new grass.

Villagers, their shirts open and their hair dishevelled from the night's watch, their suits wrinkled, their clothes stained with beer, swooped down on Floralie and Anthyme. They were jubilant. They danced around the couple, swearing to show how happy they really were, to express the beauty of a man and woman entwined in the grass. They flung out obscene cries.

"We've been waiting for them while they were playing in the grass."

"If they spend all their nights counting the stars like that we can count on them, the race won't die out."

"They'll be the ones that wipe out the *maudits Anglais.*"

Laughter turned to hiccups. Floralie had heard everything but she had not yet opened her eyes.

"We spent the whole night waiting for them," a woman complained.

"In the name of God, do you think they were thinking about us? They only had thoughts for themselves!"

Awake, Anthyme smiled to see familiar faces around him, hairy, mussed up as though they had spent the night in the rain. They were holding their bellies, which hurt from so much laughing.

Anthyme and Floralie, sitting in the grass, looked at each other with the expression of people who haven't seen each other for a long time and are trying to bring past and present together in one face.

Revellers held their bottles over Floralie and Anthyme and spilled beer over their heads.

"Is it very far to your village now?" asked Floralie, on the verge of tears.

Hands seized them and lifted them into the carriage, the happy villagers getting in behind.

"Go on! Talk love talk to each other!"

Floralie spread her hand on her husband's arm.

"Anthyme?"

"Floralie?"

"I wonder if I was dreaming?"

"You should never dream."

LA GUERRE, YES SIR!

I dedicate this book, which I have dreamed, to those who have perhaps lived it.

R.C.

The translation is for my teacher, T.J. Casaubon.

S.F.

TRANSLATOR'S NOTE

THE READER MAY be surprised to see words, phrases and even whole sentences left in the original French. The title, to begin with. Although a literal translation would have been simple enough, *The War, Oui Monsieur!* just doesn't have the same force, and Roch Carrier's brilliant title is a succinct comment on the English-French situation in Quebec, particularly as it existed during the second World War.

The swearing has also been left in French. Aside from the war and the conflicts that arose from it, the relationship of the villagers to the Church is perhaps the novel's single most important theme. The people are unquestioning Catholics, faithful church-goers, for whom the parish priest is the most influential person in the community. The relationship is not always a happy one, though, and there is an underlying resentment of it, a desire to escape in some way from its strictures. This rebellion is achieved in a figurative way by the use of a most amazing collection of oaths and curses, which call on virtually every object of religious significance to Roman Catholics, from the wood of the Crucifix to the chrism (Saint Chréme) or sacred oil. These words, uttered in despair or grief or anger — or sometimes in affection — have the same emotional force as some of the Anglo-Saxon expletives. To translate them thus, however, would have been to distort the values of the people who use them; on the other hand, literal translations would have been at best perplexing, more often simply absurd. A "chalice of a host of a tabernacle" just doesn't produce the effect of "calice d'hostie de tabernacle" — pronounced calisse and tabarnaque. "Maudits Anglais" — goddamn Englishmen — is probably only too familiar already.

In a way, the people who used these oaths literally to challenge the Church's authority could be considered the first Quebec revolutionaries; now, of course, the words have lost their strength and revolutionaries have other tactics, other targets.

Then there are the prayers. The villagers' unquestioning attendance at Mass and their observance of the rituals does not preclude an ignorance of what the formulas they faithfully repeat are all about. The result is some marvellously mangled prayers, even the most familiar, that are, unfortunately, completely untranslatable. James Joyce did something similar in his "Hail Mary full of grease, the lard is with you."

A brief glossary may be helpful. "Christ," pronounced "crisse," is one of the strongest expletives; others include "hostie" (host), "ciboire" (ciborium), Crucifix, "Vierge" (the Blessed Virgin), "baptême" (baptism). Nor is the Pope spared.

Anyway, whatever the results of attempts to make Canada officially bilingual, a little personal bilingualism never hurt anybody. Learning to swear in the other language may be an unorthodox way to begin, but it could stir up some interest. And create some understanding that might even help to eliminate one of the most frequently used expressions — "maudits Anglais."

S.F.

JOSEPH WASN'T PANTING.

He approached like a man walking to work. Which hand would he put on the log, his right hand or his left? His right hand was stronger, better for working. His left hand was strong too.

Joseph spread the five fingers of his left hand on the log.

He heard breathing behind him. He turned around. It was his own.

His other fingers, his other hand, seized the axe. It crashed down between the wrist and the hand, which leapt into the snow and was slowly drowned in his blood.

Joseph did not see the red stain or the hand or the snow. When the axe cut through the bone Joseph felt only a warm caress; his suffering began when it was buried in the wood. The cloudy window separating him from life gradually became very clear, transparent. In a moment of dizzy lucidity Joseph was aware of the fear that had tortured him for long months:

"Their Christly shells would have made jam out of me . . ." He drove his stump into the snow. "They've already made jam out of Corriveau with their goddamn war . . . They won't get me . . . me, I'll be making jam next fall: strawberries, blueberries, gooseberries, red apples, raspberries . . ."

Joseph burst into a great laugh, which he could hear going up very high, up above the snow. He hadn't had so much fun since the beginning of the war. The villagers heard his voice. He was calling for help.

★   ★   ★   ★

Amélie rapped on the ceiling with the handle of her broom. It was code. She listened. There was a whispering movement in the attic: a man accustomed to moving around silently. Nothing stirred. Then a mewing sound could be distinguished. That meant: "Is it dangerous?"

Then Amélie called out, "Come on down, gutless!"

Some heavy objects slid, a trap door opened in the ceiling, a boot appeared, then the other, and the legs. Arthur let himself down, a rifle in his hand, a coat folded under his arm.

"No, you don't need all that stuff . . . Come and get into bed," Amélie ordered.

Arthur turned around, looking for a spot to lay down his things.

"Come to bed Arthur," Amélie insisted. "Hurry up. Men! They've got their feet stuck in molasses. I can't figure out why we need them so badly. Arthur, throw your package in the corner and come to bed."

Another head appeared in the opening. Henri.

"It was my turn to sleep with you tonight," he muttered.

"You," she flung the words at him, "shut up! The kids can't get to sleep."

"It's my turn tonight."

"You'll get your turn. Go and hide."

"It's never my turn," Henri protested. "Are you my wife or aren't you?"

Amélie planted herself in the trap-door of the attic, her hands on her hips, and started spitting out insults. Henri heard nothing. He was dazzled by the swelling breasts he could see in the neckline of her dress.

"Yes, I'm your wife," Amélie assured him, "but if I wasn't Arthur's woman too I wouldn't have had kids by him."

"There's no more justice," Henri wept. "Ever since this goddam war started there's been no justice."

Henri had been obliged to dress himself up like a soldier. He had been pushed into a boat, and let out in England.

"What's England?" the gossips used to ask Amélie, who was more than a little proud to have her husband a soldier in England. "England, it's one of the old countries. First there's the sea. The sea is as big as the world. On the other side, there's England. It's at the end of the world, England is. It's a long way away. You can't even go there by train. Oh yes, my Henri is in England. He's fighting the Germans. Then when there aren't any more Germans Henri sweeps the army's floor, in England."

This was how she used to interpret Henri's letters. But with her feminine intuition she knew that Henri was spending his time in England drinking and stroking women's behinds.

"A man on his own," she used to think, "is a tomcat, and besides in those old countries they don't have any morals or religion . . ."

In her prayers Amélie often used to ask the good Lord that if Henri got himself killed by a German his soul wouldn't be dirty like his boots. The good Lord couldn't refuse her that.

Henri had been gone for more than a year. One night someone knocked at her door. Amélie, worried, hesitated to open it. You don't knock at night on the door of the wife of a soldier at the front in England without a very serious motive. Finally Amélie decided to open the latch. It was Arthur, his rifle in his hand.

"Don't kill me," she pleaded, closing the neckline of her dress, which scarcely contained her bosom.

Arthur stared for a moment at the closed hand and the swelling dress. "I want to hide. Hide me."

Amélie stepped aside to let him in.

"Is it on account of the war? If it goes on very long all the women are going to have a man hidden under their skirts."

Arthur laughed. "The military police have got their dogs on my trail. They came to my place, the cops and the dogs. I ducked out the door. I killed one of the dogs. I don't want to go to their goddam war."

"Henri's at the war . . ."

"I don't want to get my face torn up in their goddamn war. Did they ask us if we wanted this goddamn war? No. But when they need men to fight, then they like us well enough. As far as I'm concerned I'm not going to lose a single hair in their goddamn war.

It seemed to Amélie that Arthur was much more right than Henri. Her husband always let himself be taken in by someone or something.

"I don't want to go to their war. The big guys have decided to make their war. Let them do it alone, without us. Let the big guys fight each other if that's what they want; it doesn't hurt them. They always start again. Let them have fun, but let the little guys enjoy themselves the way they want."

Amélie agreed. Arthur was right, Henri was wrong.

"It's the end of the world."

"My God, is it possible?"

"Yes, Madame."

"My God," sighed Amélie, raising her arms in a gesture of supplication. A breast popped out of her open dress. Amélie pushed it inside. "You'll sleep in the attic," she said.

Arthur slept in Amélie's bed. When they woke up at dawn she said to him, "There are cows to milk."

"That's my job."

Arthur got up, got dressed, and on his way out took Henri's jacket which was hanging up near the door. He came back with the milk.

"Those cows were sure glad to see a man."

"How about me; you think I wasn't glad too?"

The children came and sat around the table, and Arthur talked to them about the war that was killing little children, about the Germans who were cutting little children into pieces to feed to their dogs.

The cross-eyed child said, "If a German comes here I'm going to stick my fork in his eye."

"I," said a little girl, "am going to throw a stone at his glasses and the glass will bust his eyes open."

The eldest said, "I'm going to put a snake in a glass of milk and he'll drink the snake."

"I'm going to war like my father," said the youngest.

"Shut up, all of you," Amélie interrupted. "Just be happy you've got something to eat."

"I don't like the war," Arthur explained, "because in a war little children are killed; I don't want little children to be killed." With these words Arthur became the children's father.

Amélie beamed with joy. Henri, their real father, had never known how to talk to the children. Arthur, a bachelor, did. No one thought he should leave. One morning nine months later the children found, in the little bed, two twins, crying and hungry. Amélie laughed happily. "The others are more mine than yours, but the twins are ours."

Arthur kept busy with the chores and the animals; he was never completely free, however, but always afraid that the army dogs would leap on his back. The farm was no longer abandoned. Amélie spoiled Arthur like a favourite child.

One evening Henri appeared in the doorway.

"It's about time you came back," Amélie commented. "We were starting to forget you."

"I've only come for a few days. I've got to go back."

"Why did they send you back here?"

"I was tired. The war wears you out."

"Who's going to fight the Germans while you're here?"

Henri dropped into a chair. "It's tiring, the war."

"You think I'm not tired too, when you've left me here with the kids? Everybody's tired. The twins wear me out, but you don't hear me complain about being tired."

"The twins?"

"Yes, the twins."

Henri didn't understand at all. At the war he had often thought of his children. How could he forget a pair of twins? Perhaps they had been very young when he left. He couldn't have forgotten that he had twins. A man who has twins doesn't forget them.

"Twins," explained Amélie. "Two sets of twins. I have two sets of twin boys. Because the gentleman travels, because the gentleman goes for walks, because the gentleman thinks he's obliged to go off to war, the gentleman thinks the earth stops turning. I've got twins; two sets of twin boys. It's simple. I lugged them around in there," she tapped her belly, "and then they came out."

"What interests me is how they got in."

"I've got twins," she cut in finally, "and they're alive and well."

That evening they bickered, they fought, they swatted the whimpering children, they kicked and punched. When they were worn out they made peace.

After his long absence Henri deserved to be well received. Henri, then, would sleep with his wife. In the future, both Henri and Arthur would have their rights in turn, for as long as the soldier was on leave.

On the last day of his holiday Henri refused to leave Amélie to go back to the war.

"Two men in a house is too much for one woman," Amélie insisted. "There's a war. Somebody's got to do it. There have to be men at the war and men in the house. All the men can't stay at home. Some of them have got to go away. The bravest ones become soldiers and go away to fight."

Arthur added his arguments in a reproachful tone. "The Germans will come along with those boots of theirs that fall on the floor like the blows of an axe and you, you want to stay here and smoke your pipe."

Henri banged his fists on the table; children were crying everywhere in the house. "You," he shouted, "you, are you going to war?"

Arthur lit his pipe and answered calmly, through the smoke. "You're a soldier . . ."

"Germans! I've never seen an *hostie* of a German."

"You're a soldier; you've got the uniform, you've got the boots. Me, I'm a farmer and the father of a family. I've got two sets of twins and Amélie's expecting again. You're a soldier. Soldiers have a duty to protect farmers who are fathers of families, and the children and the cattle and the country."

Henri didn't go back to the front.

"Since this *tabernacle* of a war there's been no more justice," he whined, his head hanging in the opening of the trap-door. "It's never my turn. I should have ended up like Corriveau. Corriveau doesn't see anything any more."

"You're men," said Amélie with a purr in her voice, "and you've got to behave like men and not like children. Listen to each other peacefully. It's not worth it for you two to fight about it — both of you gets his turn in my bed, that's the rule. It's not hard to understand. Each one has his rights. I can't always know whose turn it is. I can't always know if it was Henri who was with me yesterday or Arthur. Shut the trapdoor, Henri, and don't make any more noise. You know they're looking for deserters, and they find the ones that make too much noise."

She grabbed Arthur by the arm.

"Come on. When you get right down to it it's not much fun for my poor Henri. He'd like to spend days in my bed. It's tough, the war."

With his eyes Henri followed his wife and Arthur until they had disappeared into the bedroom.

"*Calice d'hostie de tabernacle!* I'll be glad when this war is over . . ."

He closed the trapdoor and slid some heavy objects over it.

Turning her back to Arthur, Amélie unbuttoned her dress. Arthur watched her. He resisted the desire to leap onto her and crush her breasts in his hands. She let her dress fall; the soft flesh of her back and hips, white and gleaming, blinded Arthur. That back: he could never get used to it. She bent down to take off her pants which she let fall against her legs. Then she turned towards Arthur. He was trembling at the realization that he was about to make his nest in that flesh.

"Corriveau arrives tomorrow," she said.

She fell onto the bed without drawing back the covers. "Hurry up," she said, "I'm cold. Hear the wind? It's sad, a winter wind. Come on, hurry up."

Arthur stretched out on the bed. "I forgot that Corriveau was coming tomorrow. He'll have soldiers with him, so Henri and I can't take a chance and leave the house. Corriveau's going to bust his gut laughing in his coffin."

He felt the generous flesh with rapture. Amélie chuckled. But the fingers loosened. The hand was not ravenous. It fell back on the sheet.

"Corriveau was away for three years," he said. "I remember, it was the beginning of fall. He didn't think he'd be away for long."

"Yeah, and he didn't think he wouldn't be coming back."

"Oh, I don't know if he wanted to come back. The last word he said, I remember as if it was yesterday, he said, 'At last I'm going to have some peace.' He said that. I can still hear it."

"In war, time must pass quickly," she said.

Arthur's sex was too pacific.

"To be away for three years and come back in your coffin, that's no life. Whether you've got a cortège of soldiers or not."

"Dying," murmured Amélie, "that's sad."

"Dying in a war is sad all right."

"Poor Corriveau."

Amélie had rolled onto Arthur; feeling trapped by the heavy breasts and the burning belly, he got out of the bed, picked up his clothes, grabbed the broom, and knocked on the ceiling according to the agreement. The heavy objects slid in the attic, the trapdoor opened, and Henri's head appeared. He yelled, "You can't even sleep around here! They steal your lawful wife who's been blessed by the priest and then they disturb you three or four times a night and just as often in the day. Peace! I want some peace, *hostie!*"

Arthur waited for a moment's silence so that he could talk. It came. "It's sad to come back from the war in your coffin."

"It's sad, but it's no reason to disturb the whole village."

"For me it stirs up my soul, my heart, my liver, my guts, that Corriveau is dead."

"Stir up whatever you want, that won't bring him back."

"It's sad; he was our age."

"He was younger than us," Henri corrected.

"Dying: I couldn't stand that."

"What's wrong with you, stomping around under my trapdoor like a cat pissing in the bran?"

"I'm coming up to the attic. If you want, Henri, you can take my place."

"Okay."

"Take my turn tonight," Arthur went on. "But tomorrow's mine."

★   ★   ★   ★

The scalded pig, all open, the inside of the body a bright red, had its two back legs tied to the ladder on which Arsène had stretched it out. The oldest of his fourteen children, who knew this kind of work well, took hold of one of the animal's front feet and stretched it with all his might, his foot supported on a rung of the ladder. When the beast was sufficiently extended he tied the foot to a rung and seized the fourth foot to begin the same operation over again. Then Arsène and his son lifted the ladder so that it was vertical and leaned it against a wall of the barn. The youth contemplated the skinned pig, the inside of the animal like an immense red wound.

"Every time I see a pig laid out like that I can't help thinking of Christ on Calvary."

"Philibert! " his father yelled. "Atheist! You'll be damned! Ask the good Lord's pardon right now and come here so I can give you a boot in the ass!"

Philibert, his eyes fixed on the opened pig, didn't move a hair. His father came up to him, grumbling that he was a damn blasphemer, that he would bring down misfortunes on the house, such as foot-and-mouth disease, thunder, cancer, debts, and hunch-backed children.

"Every time somebody insults Christ, the pope and holy things, he pays for it," explained Arsène.

He would have liked his son to understand, but he knew that gentleness is never effective. So he buried his boot in Philibert's behind and repeated the action until his leg was tired.

Tears flowed from Philibert's eyes. Was this what life was all about? Was this why a child was supposed to honour his father all the days of his life? Philibert had no desire to honour his father. He wouldn't honour him to the end of his days. He'd go away soon like all the boys in the village. The young boys left the village because they had no intention of honouring their fathers to the end of their days. Philibert knew what he wanted to be when the day came for him to leave . . . And he wouldn't come back before he'd forgotten the kicks he had received. These kicks, he thought, should never be forgotten, so maybe he'd never come back.

"You're a kid with one hell of a mouth; you're possessed by the devil, my boy, the living devil. May God protect me, his father, from eternal damnation."

Arsène gave Philibert his most powerful kick.

"It's not worth killing me," said Philibert craftily. "I didn't mean anything bad. I just meant that Christ must have suffered a lot, stretched out on his cross like that pig."

Arsène replied with another kick. Philibert pursued his idea. "Getting stuck on a cross and having knives stuck in your belly, that can't be very much fun."

"You're still blaspheming! Are you dead set on making hell come down on us like a rain of fire?"

Arsène hit his resigned son several times. Then he calmed down. A long silence paralysed them. Father and son were back to back; they remained motionless for some time, not daring to let out the insults they exchanged internally, silently. Arsène resolved to speak. He couldn't be silent till the end of the world.

"You know, my boy, that punishment on the cross is still practised today. And it must be more painful today than in the olden days because nowadays our flesh isn't so tough."

Philibert had nothing to say.

"The Germans are still putting prisoners on the cross," Arsène went on.

"I'd sure like to see a German. I'd see how it's done and then I'd kill him."

"The Germans put women on the cross."

"Why not men?"

"The Germans prefer women on the cross. With men they couldn't do the same thing."

"Because the men would bust their teeth."

"I think I can tell you now, you're big enough to understand. I was telling you that the Germans stretch the women out on crosses . . ."

"Yes, you told me that."

"Women are women, but the crosses aren't crosses . . ."

"Ah!"

"The crosses are beds."

Philibert looked at his father wide-eyed with astonishment.

"The Germans get on top of the woman attached to the bed one after another, and then they take advantage of her till she's dead."

"What do the Germans do to the woman?"

"Nitwit!" cried Arsène, booting him in the rear.

The child suddenly caught on. "Did Corriveau do that too?"

Arsène looked at his son indulgently. "What am I going to do with you? I'm trying to educate you and then, *Sainte Vierge*, you refuse to understand a thing. Are you a birdbrain? Corriveau didn't do that. Corriveau isn't a German. Our soldiers don't behave like Germans. Our soldiers fight clean," explained Arsène; "they defend our rights, our religion, our animals, everything that belongs to us."

When would Philibert be able to go to war with the Germans, kill a German?

"Did Corriveau knock down any Germans?"

"Today they kill without seeing each other, and without seeing each other they die. Anyway, even if he did see any, Corriveau won't be able to tell us now."

*   *   *   *

Joseph appeared, his arm wrapped up in rags soaked in alcohol and red with blood that was beginning to harden because of the cold.

"It's the Anglais, that's for sure, that are coming with Corriveau," he announced. "The army told Anthyme Corriveau. There'll be seven. Seven Anglais."

"Anthyme was right to buy a whole pig from me," Arsène noted.

"There'll be seven of them."

"That'll make a lot of people trying to find a hair on my pig."

"There'll be seven Anglais, seven soldiers. That means that six are going to carry Corriveau, three on each side. The seventh is the most important. He gives the orders. A soldier doesn't do a thing, he doesn't even fart without an order."

Philibert was amazed.

"I can't wait to see these Anglais; I've never seen one."

Arsène looked at him in the manner of a man who knows everything. "The Anglais, my boy, are like everybody else. The men pee standing up and the women do it sitting down."

He held out a bucket to the boy. "Go ask your mother if she has some boiling water. There can't be a single *hostie* of a bristle on this pig. Hurry up!"

Philibert ran towards the house, the bucket in his hand, thinking of the insulting things he could say to the real Anglais. Arsène noticed some blood on Joseph's bandages.

"What's the matter, Joseph my friend, did you scratch yourself?"

⋆   ⋆   ⋆   ⋆

Bralington Station.

The train could be seen in the distance, the engine ploughing through the snow covering the forest. At the station you couldn't see it approaching, there was so much frost on the windows. You could only tell it was coming by the noise. The stationmaster withdrew into the shed, sliding the door on its rusted pulleys so that the employees could unload the merchandise there. In his little station, smelling of charcoal and the loafers' tobacco, the station agent had forgotten about all the snow.

He swore, "May God change my mother into a horse with the head of a cow if I've ever seen so much snow in my life. And I've seen some."

"Snow," said the storekeeper. "There's more snow than there are *hosties* in all the *tabernacles*. This morning I want to go out the door, like a gentleman. So I can't even open it! It was blocked by the snow. Hard snow, like ice. Okay, so I climb up the stairs, I open a window, and I go out the window like a *ciboire* of a savage."

"I used to be in the Royal Navy," said the stationmaster. "The first time I found myself in front of the ocean I said to myself, I said: 'Open your eyes. By Christ, you've never seen so much water all at once.'"

"Me, I don't like water. A glass of water makes me seasick. Goddamn water. There's only one way not to make me seasick: put alcohol in my water."

"Okay," continued the stationmaster, who had not lost his train of thought, "today when I saw all that snow I said to myself, 'Open your eyes, grandpa, you've never seen so much snow.'"

"You can't please everybody, but the polar bears must be pretty happy."

The conductor loomed into sight in a cloud of snow, as though blown by a gust of wind. In his hand he held a watch that was attached to his stomach by a little chain, and he watched it beat as if it were his heart. "With all this snow," he said, "you don't move very fast. We're behind two hours, seventeen minutes and forty-four seconds."

"With all this snow," repeated the stationmaster, "there's a danger that polar bears will come down from the North. It's been known to happen: polar bears have come down into the villages. Because of the snow they thought they were on home ground. In cases like that they devour everybody in the village. Polar bears never have indigestion. When I was sailing in the navy . . ."

The conductor didn't have time to listen to another fragment of the stationmaster's autobiography. "We're late," he interrupted. "At every station everybody has to work faster: the time lost by the train has to be made up by men."

Storekeepers were bringing down cases and packages. The stationmaster checked to see that they were in good condition, to make sure that the fastening had not been broken or the wrapping undone during the trip. As each object was inspected he made a little mark on a list that he brought up close to his nose so he could read it.

"Eaton's? OK. Mont-Rouge? OK. Brunswick? OK. Montreal Shipping? OK. Clark Beans? OK. Marini Spaghetti? OK. Black and White? OK. Black Horse? OK. William Scotch? OK. l, 2, 3, 4, 5, 6, 7, . . . Corriveau? Corriveau?" he shouted. "Corriveau? Where have you put Corriveau?"

"Corriveau?" somebody asked from the inside of the car, "What's that, Corriveau?"

"Corriveau's a coffin."

The voice in the car gave an order. "The dead guy gets off here. Where did you put the dead guy?"

"Are you going to let him off?" asked the stationmaster impatiently.

"He isn't here now," said the voice in the car. "He must have got off to stretch his legs."

"He should have better come and help me shovel," said an employee who was trying to clear the platform.

"That *baptême* of a corpse, he isn't there," complained the voice in the car. "There's always trouble with these dead guys. I'd rather ship ten living men than one dead one."

The stationmaster's voice took on the dry tone of someone in authority. "Friends, I don't want you to make a mistake with that package. Corriveau is one of us. He's going to get off here. I want Corriveau to get off with his Anglais."

"Ah!" sighed the man inside, relieved. "I get it. If you're talking about the Anglais, all their baggage is off."

The man appeared in the door of the car, triumphant. The stationmaster marked his sheet in the necessary place and went back into his office.

Through his wicket he noticed the képis of some soldiers who were sitting in the waiting room. "Hey! boys," he asked, "did you get a nice trip?"

"Not too lovely, monsieur," one of the soldiers replied in French.

"I understand English, boys. You may speak English. I learned when I was in the navy — Royal Navy."

"All the peoples speaks English," said the same soldier, still speaking French.

"Where is Corriveau?"

"What means Corllivouuw?"

"Corriveau is the name of our poor boy, boys."

"The man is in there," said one of the soldiers, indicating the coffin on which they were sitting and smoking cigarettes.

The one who was the leader got up; with a single military movement the other six soldiers took up their positions. Then they gave the stationmaster a military salute and carried away the coffin, leaving the waiting room door open to the cold.

The stationmaster grumbled: "You can see these *maudits* Anglais are used to having niggers or French Canadians to shut their doors. That's what Corriveau must have done: open and shut doors for the Anglais."

A thin man, an employee who had finished his work, was going from one window to another as though he were looking for something important. He wasn't discouraged although he kept running into opaque frost. He walked as though he knew where he was going. The man pulled his finger out of his nostril. "Life," he declared, "is nothing but this: there's the big guys and the little guys. There's the good Lord and there's me. There's the Germans and there was Corriveau. There's the Anglais and us; you, Corriveau, me, everybody in the village . . ."

The man plunged his finger back into the nostril, where it had lots to do.

"Corriveau," said the stationmaster "is the first child the war has taken from us."

The man removed his finger from his nose and pointed it accusingly towards the stationmaster. "You mean Corriveau is the first child the big guys have grabbed away from us. Shit on the big guys. They're all the same: Germans, Anglais, French, Russians, Chinese, Japs; they're all so much alike they have to wear different costumes to tell each other apart before they throw their grenades. I shit on all the big guys, but not on the good Lord, because he's even bigger than the big guys. But he's a big guy too. They're all big guys. That's why I think this war, it's a war of the big guys against the little ones. Corriveau's dead. The little guys are dying. The big guys last forever."

The man stuck his finger back in his nose and began again his promenade from one window to another, all of them covered with frost.

The stationmaster lit his pipe. "If Corriveau had died here, in the village, in his bed, that would have been very sad for a young man. But he died in his soldier suit and far away from the village; that must mean something."

"That means that the big guys get bigger and the little ones go bust."

★   ★   ★   ★

Madame Joseph wished she were a dog. With sharp claws and furious barks she would have chased, dispersed and bitten the legs of the gang of urchins blocking her way.

Madame Joseph was going back to her house. She could not endure, on her own, the pain of becoming the wife of a man who had chopped off his own hand with an axe. She had gone to tell her neighbours about her troubles. "Life is hard," she had said, tears in her eyes. "You marry a man and you find out you're sleeping with an invalid. What's Joseph going to do with his stump in my bed?"

It was a sad story indeed. The neighbours, helpless before her misfortune, all promised to pray for her and Joseph. In any case it was not certain whether Joseph had done wrong, because it said in the Gospel, "Tear out thy hand or throw it on the fire." Because that was truly said in the Gospel, Madame Joseph was almost consoled.

She returned, then, along the snowy path dug in the piled-up snow by the horses and villagers. She walked with as much dignity as possible because, behind the curtains, they were watching her; in the houses they were talking about her and Joseph.

The children in the street were too busy with their game to see her coming. Divided into two teams, everyone was armed with a curved stick as in a hockey game; they were fighting over an object, probably a frozen horse turd, trying to push it into the other side's goal. Sticks were raised and came crashing down; the players held on, knocked each other around, waved their sticks, banged them together with a dry sound. Suddenly the object shot outside the milling group; the players ran after it, tripped each other, exchanged blows with their sticks, their elbows, got hold of it again, all the time shouting and swearing as the sticks came crashing down, clattering on one another. The object was rolling farther along on the snow again, among the shouts of joy and swearing of those who had scored a point.

Madame Joseph didn't dare go on. She couldn't attempt a detour off the road. She'd sink in the snow.

How would she manage to get by this horde? Would she shout, "Let me past?" They would leap on her; they would roll her in the snow and amuse themselves by looking at her thighs and seeing her pants. The thighs and pants of Madame Joseph were spots of great interest for the boys of the village. Other women could go along the road with no trouble, without being bothered, but as soon as Madame Joseph went out the boys invented a new way to get a look at her thighs.

"We hatch them and they turn out to be vicious little morons who will always prefer the bordellos to the Church," she thought, a little sadly. "There isn't one of those kids who isn't the spitting image of his father. We don't beat them enough."

With an instinctive movement she tightened her thighs and advanced cautiously.

Suddenly furious, she raised her arms and brought her fists down on the little boy closest to her. She grabbed hold of a stick, struck out at random, fiercely, shouting threats. "Little morons! vicious little monsters! damn brats! pigs! *I'll* show you how to play hockey!"

Madame Joseph grabbed a second stick, waved it around in front of her head, and struck out to the left, to the right, everywhere at once, in front, behind. Her sticks hit noses, ears, eyes, heads. The boys were soon dispersed. From a distance they shouted their insults: "Fat ass! Big tits! You've got the face of a cow walking backwards! You look like a holy Virgin turned upside down!"

"Vicious little monsters! Damned brats! You're all set to visit the bordellos in town!"

They replied, "If we go to the bordellos we go to see your daughters!"

She stopped speaking their language. She could not insult them. They knew all the insults. "We don't beat them enough," she complained.

She got down on her knees and picked up the object they had been fighting over with their sticks — her husband's chopped-off hand. The fingers were closed and hard as a rock. There were black marks where. their sticks had struck it. Madame Joseph put it in the pocket of her fur coat and went back to her house, announcing to the boys, who were choking with laughter, that the devil would punish them in hell.

★   ★   ★   ★

Joseph was sitting in his chair, pale, with a tortured face.

"I've found your hand, Joseph."

He looked at her indifferently.

"It's a good thing I went that way; the kids were playing hockey with your hand."

Joseph said nothing.

"If I hadn't got there in time the brats would have broken it. You should thank me."

Bored by his wife's insistence he finally answered. "What do you want to do with my hand? Make soup?"

"You're a lazy good-for-nothing."

Joseph looked at his wife sadly. "Apparently Corriveau's arrived at the station."

Waving his battered arm, all covered with bloody rags, he exclaimed, "Now let them come and take me off to fight their Christly war! I'll cut off their dinks, if they've got any. I'll cut them off like I cut off my hand. I'm not going to fight their god-damn war."

Madame Joseph whistled between her teeth at the dog, who woke up and obeyed her call. She threw the hand out the door into the snow. The dog ran after it, growling with pleasure.

"You think it makes me happy to sleep with a man who's only got one hand . . ."

"I always thought you'd have liked to see me go off to the war and you wouldn't have minded too much if I'd come back like Corriveau. At a certain age all women want to be widows."

Madame Joseph stood in front of her husband, her hands on her hips, and spoke to him as though she were spitting in his face. "A man who doesn't have the courage to go and fight a war to pro-tect his country is no man. You'd let the Germans walk all over you. You're not a man. I wonder what I'm sleeping with."

Joseph murmured gently between his teeth. "Corriveau? Is Corriveau a man?"

★   ★   ★   ★

The road between the village and the station had disappeared in the snow like a stream in a white, blinding flood. No one lived here. No house. The forest was weighted down by the snow, which spread out as far as the eye could see, sparkling in all its dunes, its rises, its very shadows; because of the snow it seemed no longer alive, but a mute white plaster.

On the other side of the endless forest the snow continued to the horizon.

How could they have got away, these men who were bent
under a coffin and sinking into the snow up to their· belts? They
were six soldiers carrying the burden, three on each side, and
in front of them a sergeant shouted to make them go on. Each
step required an effort. First they had to lift a leg out of the snow,
which gripped the foot with a strong suction, then raise the foot
as high as possible without losing balance, stretch the leg then,
and push the foot energetically, press it into the snow until it was
hard, still without losing balance, and without moving the coffin too much, because all the weight carried by one man would
be transferred to the shoulders of another; they had to hurry. It
was already later than they had expected. The sergeant was in a
bad mood. He nagged his men, who were sweating in this plain
of snow, under the coffin they were carrying on their shoulders
from the station to the village. It was not the first coffin they had
carried, but they had never gone as far as they had that day, and
at each step the village on the mountain seemed farther away, as
though they had changed directions in the snow.

The soldiers were sweating. Their clothes were soaked. The
sweat rolled down their backs in cold globules. Sweat poured
onto their faces too, and froze after sitting motionless on their
chins; they could feel the skin growing stiff. Their swollen lips
had slowly become paralyzed. They didn't dare to say a word, to
swear or laugh or complain, they were so close to the breaking
point. Their wet hair was steaming. The cold stung their hands
like spiny bushes.

The soldiers didn't even suspect that there was a road hidden under the snow. They simply walked on like animals. They
went on towards the mountains where they saw chimneys above
the snow, their smoke like a comforting balm to the men. In the
silence, where nothing vibrated but the effort of their breathing, they remembered, bent down under their fatigue, their own

houses which they hadn't seen for months.

With no order from the sergeant, with a spontaneous gesture, they lowered the coffin from their shoulders and put it down.

"I'm dead hungry," said one.

They took up their burden again and continued on in the snow.

*   *   *   *

Busy surveying the unloading of merchandise, the station master had not seen the soldier Bérubé get off the train, accompanied by his wife, Molly, whom he was bringing home from Newfoundland. What a surprise this arrival would be. He had not warned his family, either that he was coming home or that he had recently been married. His letters didn't say a thing.

Basically, Bérubé had only one topic to write about: that he could tell nothing about his life as a soldier, or about the war, and that he didn't know what would happen to him tomorrow. He kept himself ready for everything, he wrote. His mother couldn't read a line without bursting into sobs: how painful this war was, when a son couldn't tell his mother about his life.

Bérubé was responsible for looking after the toilets in G wing of B building at the airforce base in Gander, Newfoundland. Bérubé had learned to speak English. He spoke it as well as all the other toilet-cleaners, whether they were Poles, Italians, Hungarians or Greeks.

Waiting for the plane that would take him to Montreal, where he would catch a train, Bérubé decided to stay at the Aviator Hotel. Before he had even ordered a drink at the bar a soft hand stroked him, and an insinuating English voice said, "Come with me, darling."

"Darling?"

"Come . . ."

"Where are you going, by the way?"

"To my bedroom."

"OK, let's go!"

Bérubé followed the girl. As he watched her walking ahead of him, her hips swaying in her narrow skirt, and as he speculated about the well-formed behind, Bérubé's legs felt numb; the rug in the corridor became rough and lumpy for him. He had the feeling that each of the girl's steps and each movement of her body tightened invisible ties around him. He hurried, because she was walking quickly. When he put a hand on her behind and she did not take it away his disagreeable paralysis dissolved and he was suddenly sure of himself and even a little cold.

"*Tu es un bien beau bébé, chérie.*"

"What did you say?"

"Be a good girl."

The girl turned towards him and, laughing, stuck out her tongue and pushed away his hand. She opened the door of her room. "Shut the door behind you!" she ordered. Then, making her voice more caressing, she said, "Give me five dollars. Take off your clothes."

Bérubé feverishly tore off his tunic and sat on the bed to undo his shirt. He was trembling; he had the feeling that the bed was charged with electricity. He undid his fly and took off his trousers, which he threw onto a chair. He turned his head towards Molly. What kind of modesty was making her turn her back as she undressed? Bérubé wanted to see a naked girl.

"Hey! look at me," he said.

Bérubé felt it was ridiculous to be sitting on a bed when a girl was getting undressed on the other side, but he didn't dare stand up: the girl would make fun of what had happened to him. He remained seated and blushed.

"Come, darling."

The girl was before him, naked. She had kept on her brassiere, which was full to bursting. She held out her arms to Bérubé who was incapable of getting up, of leaping towards the naked girl, of seizing her in his arms, of clutching her violently and throwing her on the bed. Bérubé felt completely weak, as if he had had too much to drink. In his head he heard a tick-tack like a drumbeat. "Always, never," repeated the monstrous clock which had marked the hours of his childhood, the clock of hell which throughout eternity would say "always, never"; the damned are in hell for ever, they never leave. "Always, never." Under the clock Bérubé saw the viscous caverns of hell where serpents climbed, mingled with the eternal flames. And he saw the damned — naked, strangling in the flames — and the serpents. "Always, never": the clock of his childhood beat out the measure, the clock of eternal damnation for those who go naked and those who touch naked women; "always, never," sounded the clock and Bérubé had to beg, "Do you want to marry me?"

"Yes," replied the girl, who had never been asked this question.

"What's your name?"

"Molly."

"Oh! Molly, I want you to be mine," said Bérubé, getting up and going towards her. They embraced. Molly let herself fall onto the bed, and the marriage was celebrated.

Then they got dressed again. Bérubé took her in a taxi to the Padre, to confess and receive the sacrament. The Padre did not hesitate to give his blessing.

Before they took the plane to Montreal Bérubé and Molly went to buy a wedding dress, which she insisted on putting on right away.

★   ★   ★   ★

Molly was shivering in her long bouffant white gown, which the wind was trying to snatch away from her. Neither the horse-drawn carriages nor the snowmobiles had been able to get to the station to pick up the travellers. Bérubé said simply, "Molly, climb up on my shoulders. Get on my back, we'll take our bags another day."

They started to go up towards the village. Bérubé powerfully dug a passage through the snow, which came up to his chest. Because of the white lace tickling his face and because of Molly's warm thighs which were pressed tightly against his cheeks, Bérubé felt a desire to toss her into the snow and leap onto her, but that would have rumpled her dress and made Molly all snowy; when they arrived at the village people would soon guess what had gone on and they would be amused at Bérubé's impatience.

This way, in the snow, Bérubé tried to think of nothing in order not to think of Molly's thighs, of her breasts, bigger than fine apples, of her buttocks beneath the white dress. But it was impossible to think of nothing; one always has a picture inside one's head, or a sensation, or the memory of a picture of a sensation, or even a desire. A feeling of warmth, the good warmth of Molly's thighs, of her belly, of the warmth between her breasts, clouded Bérubé's thoughts, threw into his head and before his eyes a fog that dazed him. He did not know if he was still going in the right direction; he could no longer see the village on the mountain, and the snow was as deep as the sea. Bérubé could think of nothing but the warmth of Molly, and this warmth moved over his body like a caressing hand, so that even the snow pressing against his legs, his stomach, his chest, had the warmth of Molly's body, seated on his shoulders and silent as though she didn't want to distract him from his sweet obsession.

Bérubé forced himself to think of a cow, an airplane, the wreck of a big ship, the *Satanic*, that he had heard stories about, of Hitler's moustache, of the toilets he had cleaned and washed for months and months. In his head one image was supreme, one image that hid the rest of the universe behind it: Bérubé saw, as though for the first time, Molly standing up near the bed, naked, her breasts spilling out of her brassiere; then he thought of the pleasure he had had. Ah! his pleasure had been so intense he had wept like a child.

Bérubé, completely swallowed up, could not pull himself out of the snow or even move his foot. It was making him dizzy. He let Molly down, jumped on her, and caught her mouth between his lips, trying to bite it. Roughly, he caressed her breasts.

"Oh!" complained Molly, who was floundering about. After a fierce struggle she succeeded in freeing an arm, and gave him a slap in the face. "Nothing but animals, these French Canadians. I don't want my dress to get creased," she said, to excuse herself.

He did not reply. He had decided simply to abandon her there, in the snow. He got up. Free of the load on his shoulders he was less troubled by the snow. He went away. Molly did not call him. Anyway, he would not have answered if she had called. Something warm tickled him in the corner of his mouth. He put his finger to it. It was blood.

"*La bon Dieu de Vierge!*"

He picked up a handful of snow and stopped up his wound.

"Let her freeze there standing in the snow, *la Vierge*. I won't let any woman break my jaw; not a whore, not an Anglaise. Not an Anglaise. Let her freeze there, *la Vierge*."

Bérubé turned around to see his wish come true. Almost disappearing in the snow because of her white dress, Molly was waving her arms about to call her husband, but she was quiet. Bérubé after savouring his triumph for a moment, cried: "Go ahead and freeze to death."

Lower down, at the foot of the mountain, Molly noticed a group of men carrying a long box on their shoulders. "That French Canadian has got blood on my dress."

Bérubé arrived in the village alone; that was when he learned about Corriveau's death.

★   ★   ★   ★

The gossips were saying, "Now that Amélie's got two men in the house she must be satisfied."

Amélie had started to prepare a meal. She was alone in the house. Saucepans sang on the wood fire, perfuming the kitchen. She wanted a man. Arthur had gone out; Henri was in the attic. She smiled. In a long caress she slid her hands over her bosom and slowly onto her belly and thighs. She stood up again, went to the stove, lifted the covers off the pots, the aroma of the roasting meat drifting out.

She tested it with her fork, checking to see how much longer the meat had to cook, replaced the cover and climbed upstairs. Amélie needed a man.

Was it Henri's turn, or Arthur's? Who had slept with her the last time. Her two men made her keep a strict accounting; that was very difficult.

Amélie wanted a man, and in a few minutes the meat would be burning on the roaring fire. She took the broom and, according to the code, rapped on the ceiling. Someone moved in the attic. The heavy trunks were pulled aside and the trap door opened.

"What is it?" asked Henri in a voice choked with sleep.

"Get down here, I need you."

"What for?"

"Hurry up, I can't wait till Arthur gets back."

"What for?" Henri repeated, hardly convinced.

"Get undressed and come here!"

"It's not my turn," he yawned. "I don't want to cut in when Arthur's away."

Amélie had already undone the buttons on her dress. Henri leapt from the attic. He started to undo his trousers.

"Hurry up," Amélie ordered, hurrying towards the bed. "I've got some meat on the stove."

"Hurry up," repeated Henri, "that's easy for you to say; a man isn't always ready."

He finished undressing, getting out of his clothes as though they were a thornbush.

"What's the weather like today?" he asked Amélie, who was already stretched out on the bed.

"Winter, same as yesterday."

"I know that. I know perfectly well that it's winter. I'm dying of cold up there in the attic."

"It's your own fault. If you'd been willing to go to war you wouldn't have to hide in an attic and be cold. Hurry up; thaw out."

"There isn't even a goddamn window in my attic. And the cracks in the ceiling are blocked up with ice. That's how I know it's winter."

"Hurry up. You can keep your wool socks on . . . Don't complain about nothing. If you weren't so well off in your attic you'd go to war. Come on."

Then Amélie became gentle. "And besides," she said with a smile, "you're not always in the attic . . ." Her voice was caressing. "Isn't that right, Henri?"

Henri was undressed now. Rather bored by this tenderness and curious to see the village, he went to the window and pulled aside the curtain. The glass was covered with frost. He brought his mouth close to it and breathed out a long breath. Under the warmth of his breath the frost melted a little. Then Henri scratched with his fingernail.

"Henri!" begged Amélie, impatient.

He continued to scratch the frost until he could see. He stuck his eye into the little hole. Who was coming up the road?

"Amélie, there's something in the road."

"If you don't come here Henri, I'll get mad." Amélie, in her bed, was worked up. Henri continued to scratch at the frost. "Come see what I see, Amélie." "Henri, if you don't come and get on top of me right now it'll be a long time before you put your behind in my sheets."

"Come here, I tell you."

Persuaded by his insistence, Amélie got up and went to the window. Henri gave her his observation post. She looked for a long time, then drew back. Henri looked again.

A soldier was holding a bugle at the end of his arm, which was stretched out horizontally. A coffin followed behind him, carried by six other soldiers and enveloped in a flag. A woman in a white wedding gown was escorting the coffin. The cortège ended with the boys of the village who were marching solemnly along with it, their hockey sticks on their shoulders.

They passed in front of Amélie's house and disappeared towards the other end of the village.

"It's Corriveau," said Henri.

"Yes, it's Corriveau coming home." Amélie returned to lie down on her bed. Her husband accompanied her.

Their embrace became more and more violent, and, for a moment, without their daring to admit it, they loved one another.

*   *   *   *

The door was narrow. It wasn't easy to bring the coffin into the house. The soldiers were very embarrassed not to be able to keep the symmetry of their movements. The door of the Corriveaus' little house had not been built to accommodate a coffin. The bearers put it down in the snow, calculated at what angle it could pass, studied how they should arrange themselves around it, argued. Finally the sergeant gave an order; they picked up the heavy coffin again, inclined it, placed it almost on edge, made themselves as narrow as possible, and finally succeeded in entering, out of breath and exhausted.

"Leave it now," grumbled old man Corriveau. "It's enough that he's dead, you don't have to swing him around like that."

The door opened into the kitchen. In the middle was a big wooden table.

"Put him there," said Mother Corriveau, "on the table. And put his head here, at this end. It's his place. Like that he'll feel more at home."

The English soldiers didn't understand the language the old people were speaking. They knew it was French, but they had rarely heard it.

"On the table!" repeated Mr. Corriveau.

The carriers put the coffin back on their shoulders and looked around for a place to put it.

"On the table!" ordered Mother Corriveau.

The Anglais shrugged their shoulders to show that they did not understand. Mr. Corriveau was getting angry. He said, very loud, "On the table! We want him on the table!"

The sergeant smiled. He had understood. He gave a command. The obedient soliders turned towards the door: they were going to take the coffin outside.

Mr. Corriveau ran to the door and spread his arms to block their passage. *Vieux pape de Christ*! They come and take him by force, they get him killed without asking our permission, and now we're going to have to use our fists to get him back from them." The old man, red with anger, threatened the sergeant with his fist; the latter wondered why everyone didn't speak English like he did.

"*Vieux pape de Christ!*"

"Put it on the table," said Molly in English. She had come in after carefully shaking the snow from her dress.

"What's she come here for, that one?" asked Mother Corriveau. "He's our dead."

When she saw the soldiers obey Molly, Mother Corriveau accepted her presence, and asked her, with an air of recognition on her face, "Tell them to take away the cover; our little boy is going to be too hot in there."

Molly translated. The soldiers gave Mother Corriveau a withering look. How dare she refer to the British flag as a "cover"! The old lady had no idea she had offended England; she would have been astounded if someone had told her that this "cover" was the flag her son had died for. If she had been told that, she would have kissed the flag as she kissed the relics of the tunic of the twenty-three-year-old Jesus Christ every night.

The sergeant decided to ignore the insult. The soldiers folded the flag, the sergeant blew on his bugle a plaint that made the windowpanes shudder and the villagers, already assembled around Corriveau, weep. The sound of the bugle stunned Anthyme Corriveau, who nervously dropped his pipe. He cursed his rotten teeth that couldn't hold a pipe any more. At twenty, Anthyme had had hard teeth that could crumble a glass, chew it. Now his rotten teeth were a sign that all his bones were going rotten too. He was so old, Anthyme, his sons were beginning to die. "When your sons begin to leave you, it won't be long before you go to join them."

"Anthyme," said his wife, "go find your screwdriver. I want to see if our boy's face has been all mashed up or if he knew enough to protect it like I told him. In all my letters I used to tell him, 'My child, think first of all of your face. A one-legged man, or even a man with no legs at all, is less frightening for a woman than a man with only one eye or no nose.' When he wrote back the dear child always said, 'I'm taking good care to protect my face.' Anthyme! I asked you for your screwdriver. I want that coffin opened."

Molly, in practising her trade, had learned several words of French. The French Canadians in Newfoundland liked Molly a lot. She explained, according to what she had understood, the Corriveaus' wish. The sergeant said, "No! No! No! No!"

His men shook their heads to say "No" too. Mother Corriveau took the sergeant's hand and squeezed it with all her might: she would have liked to squash it like an egg. The sergeant, with a courteous strength, freed himself. His face was pale, but he smiled.

The sergeant felt sorry for these ignorant French Canadians who did not even recognize their country's flag.

"Anthyme Corriveau, you're going to take your shotgun and get these *maudits* Anglais out of my house. They take my son from me, they let him get killed for me, and now they won't let me see him. Anthyme Corriveau, take out your shotgun and shoot them right between the buttocks, if they've got any."

Crushed by the heaviest despair, old man Corriveau relit his pipe. At this moment there was nothing more important than managing to light his pipe.

"Anthyme!" shouted his wife. "If you don't want to use your shotgun, give them a kick. And get busy! After that you're going to look for your screwdriver."

"*Vieille pipe de Christ*! You can ask me for my screwdriver as often as you want. I can't remember where I put it last time I . . ."

"Anthyme! Get these *maudits* Anglais out of this house!"

The old man put out his match; the flame was burning his fingers. He spoke after several puffs. "Mother, we can't do a thing. Whether you see him or not, our boy is gone."

Mother Corriveau said simply, "We're going to pray."

Her husband had reminded her of the most obvious fact: "We can't do anything," Anthyme had said. An entire life-time had taught them that they could do nothing. Mother Corriveau was no longer angry. It was with a gentle voice that she had said, "We're going to pray."

She knelt, her husband did the same, then the villagers who had come, then Molly, taking care not to crease her wedding dress. The old woman started the prayer, the prayer she had learned from the lips of her mother, who had learned it from hers: "Our Lady of the faithful dead: may he rest in peace among the saints of the Lord."

The seven soldiers knelt: the old lady was so astonished that she could not remember the rest of the formula.

"Anthyme," she muttered, "instead of getting all distracted while your son is burning in the fires of purgatory it might be a good thing if you'd pray for him. Your prayers will shorten his suffering. But then when I think of how you brought him up, I don't know if he's in purgatory or already in hell. Maybe he's in hell. In hell . . ."

She was choked by sobs. Anthyme started again, with the words of a man who has had to pray every time his wife threatens him with hell: "*Que le Seigneur des fidèles défont les lunes en paix dans la lumière du paradis.*"

Everyone replied, "Amen."

"*Je vous salue Marie, pleine et grasse, le Seigneur avez-vous et Bénedict et toutes les femmes et le fruit de vos entailles, Albanie.*"

"Amen."

The incantation was taken up several times. Then, Anthyme Corriveau was praying alone. No one was re.plying to his invocations any more. What was going on? He continued to pray, but he opened his eyes. Everyone was looking at his wife, who was lost in a happy dream. She was smiling.

The Blessed Virgin had given her mother's heart to understand that her son was in heaven. All of his sins, his oaths, his blasphemies, the caresses he had given the girls of the village, and especially the girls in the old country where had had gone to war, his drunken evenings when he used to go walking in the village throwing his clothes in the snow, the evenings when bare-chested and drunk her son would raise his fist to Heaven and shout, "God, the proof that you don't exist is that you aren't striking me down right now," all these sins of Corriveau had been pardoned; the Blessed Virgin had breathed it to his mother.

If the hand of God had not struck down Corriveau on those nights it had weighed on the roofs of the houses. People in the village would not forget those alcoholic evenings, even if God had forgiven Corriveau for them. His mother felt in her soul the peace that must now be her child's. Her son had been pardoned because he had died in the war. The old lady felt in her heart that God was obliged to pardon soldiers who had died in the war.

Her son had been reclothed in the immaculate gown of the elect. He was beautiful. He had changed a little since he had gone off to war. A mother gets used to seeing her children look more and more like strangers. Dying transforms a face too. Mother Corriveau saw her son among the angels. She would have liked him to lower his eyes towards her, but he was completely absorbed in the prayer that he was murmuring, smiling. The old lady wept, but she wept for joy. She rose.

"Take my son out of the kitchen and put him in the living room. We're going to eat. I've made twenty-one tourtières. Anthyme, go dig up five or six bottles of cider."

*   *   *   *

Furniture was shifted to free a wall against which the coffin was placed. In front of it rows of chairs were arranged, like in church. Anthyme had gone to the shed to look for some big cherry-wood stumps that would make solid legs for the coffin. Mother Corriveau had taken all her candles from the drawers, the tallow ones and those made of beeswax, the ones that had been blessed and the others. The blessed ones had protected her family during thunder and lightning; the others served very well for giving light when the electricity was cut off by storms or by ice on the wires. The soldiers stood at attention. Anthyme, with some other villagers, installed himself in front of them and fell asleep immediately, as he always did when he sat down. Mother Corriveau stuffed her stove with wood, because twenty-one *tourtières* would not be enough. "When there's a dead person in the house the living have to eat for those who have passed away."

"Everyone" as An thyme said — even the villagers who had not spoken to the Corriveaus for ten years — had arrived or were on their way, all dressed in black.

"We're going to say a little prayer so that his soul will requiescat in pace."

On her knees, hands joined on the coffin, Molly prayed. What prayer could she say, she who could speak only English? "She must pray to her God, the English God," thought Anthyme. "The God of the English and the God of the French Canadians couldn't be the same one; that isn't possible. The English protestants are damned, so there couldn't be a God for the damned in hell. She isn't praying at all; she's only pretending."

Mother Corriveau interrupted her work for a minute to look at Molly. "I didn't think of asking her, but she could be the wife of our son . . . Maybe our little boy got married during a break when there wasn't any war. Maybe he told us about his marriage in a letter that was bombed by the Germans. There's no way of knowing. This war is turning life inside out. Anyway, if she is our son's wife we'll keep her with us just like our own daugher . . . I'll talk to her about that later. It's not a question you can easily ask a young girl who has just been married when there's a dead man in the house and the dead man has married her just a couple of days before."

To keep awake Anthyme got up and was leaning against the doorframe. He was contemplating Molly's lush body: her breasts — it would have taken both Anthyme's hands to hold just one — where they swelled out her bodice, and her waist, which heralded buttocks that could make a man lose his head. Looking at Molly made him young, gave him a rest from Mother Corriveau all swallowed up in her own fat.

Suddenly the door was opened, almost torn off its hinges, by a kick that shook the whole house. Everyone found themselves, prayers on their lips, in the kitchen. A soldier was standing on the doorstep, paralysed before all those people whom he recognized, pale and frightened. It was Bérubé.

"I've come to get my wife," he explained. "They said Molly was here with the *maudits* Anglais." He spoke almost politely.

"She's in there," indicated Mother Corriveau, relieved now that Molly was not the wife of her son. "Don't put your dirty feet on the rug. And before you enter a house, you ask permission."

"I'm sorry."

"Don't say that, you cheeky little hoodlum. When you were little you used to say 'excuse me.' It always meant you were going to come back and do something worse."

Molly understood, but she didn't turn around. She stayed alone on her knees with Corriveau. Bérubé ran into the living room, grabbed Molly by the arm, shook her, and with his other hand he slapped her.

"Whore!"

Molly didn't try to protect herself.

"When you're married you don't turn on the charm, either to dead men or living ones."

Molly's nose was bleeding. Her dress would be stained.

"I'm going to make you understand you're my wife and not a whore."

He struck her with both hands. Molly collapsed, wedged between the foot of the coffin and the wall. Bérubé brought back his big leather boot and prepared to kick.

"Atten — shun!!!" thundered the guttural voice of the sergeant.

Bérubé stood at attention. He clicked his heels. Bérubé was nothing but a ball of obedient muscles. The sergeant who had barked out the order walked towards Bérubé and gave him a steely look. Bérubé waited to be hit. The sergeant, two steps away from him, breathed in his face. Bérubé felt as if his eyes were melting and trickling down his cheeks; in fact, he was crying. He was crying because there was nothing he could do. Bérubé felt like attacking the sergeant, dislocating his jaw, blackening his eyes, making him bleed.

After a long, silent confrontation the sergeant said, "Dismiss."

Bérubé turned on his heel and Molly followed him, holding his arm. Mother Corriveau detained them just as they were going out. "As far as I'm concerned I don't want you not to stay. I don't want you to have to go out in the snow. Even dogs don't go out at this hour. I offer you my boy's room; he doesn't need to sleep now."

In the bedroom Molly took off her dress.

"Whore of a woman," said Bérubé as he took down his pants. He was laughing. Undressed, he lay down against her; they embraced, the world spun around them. For a moment they were happy.

Bérubé opened his eyes abruptly and said, "Corriveau isn't going to like this, us having fun, making love in his bed."

*   *   *   *

Night darkened the snow. The candle flames were dancing on the flag-covered coffin. The living-room was filled with men and

women from the village packed tightly against one another. The
soldiers were lined up against the wall, motionless, erect, looking towards Corriveau, silent. Everyone was praying, mumbling
"Mother of God," "Save us sinners," "At the hour of our death":
tirelessly they repeated the phrases, "Forgive us our mortal faults,"
"Welcome them into the kingdom of the Father," "Requiescat-
in-pace"; they purred "God," "Amen," "Holy Ghost," "Deliver
him from the claws of the devil." Pronouncing these prayers
they began to miss Corriveau; they were sorry that they had not
liked him when he was among them, before the war; they prayed
loudly as though Corriveau could hear them and recognize their
voices, as if their prayers could make Corriveau happy under his
British flag. The villagers were alive, they were praying to remind
themselves, to remember that they were not with Corriveau, that
their life was not over; and all the time thinking they were praying for Corriveau's salvation, it was their own joy in being alive
that they proclaimed in their sad prayers. The happier they were
the more they prayed, and the little flames on Corriveau's coffin
wavered, danced, as though they were trying to free themselves
from their wicks. Shadow and light played on the wall, making
strange designs that perhaps meant something. The air disturbed
the flag a little. It seemed as if Corriveau was going to get up.
They prayed, they murmured, they whispered; they finished their
prayers, began again; they swallowed their words to pray more
quickly, while in the kitchen Mother Corriveau beat at her pie
dough with her fists, and the sweat ran down her back, onto her
forehead, into her eyes; she wiped it with her floury hands. Her
face was white with flour and the sweat ran into the flour. She
stopped a drop that was tickling between her breasts, and started
again to prepare her pastry, stirring, rolling, twisting, while on
the stove the pork was crackling in its boiling fat.

   "Don't go to too much trouble, Mother Corriveau."

"When there's a dead man in the house the house shouldn't smell of death."

She opened the oven. The golden crust whispered at its contact with the air and a perfume that reawakened appetites spread through the kitchen. One by one the villagers got up, abandoned their prayers and Corriveau, and went into the kitchen. Mother Corriveau welcomed them with a plate on which she had put a quarter of a *tourtière* under a sauce made of a mixture of apples, strawberries, bilberries and currants. As for Anthyme, he was holding out a glass filled with foaming cider. For years he had been making his cider in the fall when, as he said, "The wind is ready to scratch the apples." Then he buried his bottles in the cellar where they remained hidden in the ground for a very long time. His children became men and the bottles were still in the ground. At times, on great occasions, Anthyme would parsimoniously draw out a bottle and quickly fill in the hole so that, as he said, "The light of the cider won't get out." Over the years Anthyme's cider became charged with marvellous forces in the earth.

A bottle in each hand, Anthyme was now looking for empty glasses. When a glass was filled the old man wore a smile like God the creator.

Meanwhile, in the living room, the tide of prayers subsided; people were talking, laughing, arguing; in the kitchen they ate and drank and were happy, while Mother Corriveau looked on with brimming eyes. From time to time she wiped a tear that came as she thought of her son, loved by so many people: not only the people from the village, but also the army, which had sent a delegation of seven soldiers because her son had given his life in the war. So many people joined together for her son; Mother Corriveau could have no finer consolation. She wouldn't have believed that her son was so well-liked.

They ate and prayed; they were thirsty and hungry; they

prayed again, they smoked and drank. They had the whole night before them.

"You're not trying to tell me there are really men like that in town!"

"You mean if our boys leave home to work in town they'll turn into homosexuals?"

The third blew his nose too energetically; his eyes were filled with tears. "Hey, have you forgotten there's a war on? Our boys don't have to go off to town any more."

The first kept to his story. "I'm telling you, I'm not lying."

Father Anthyrne arrived with his bottle of cider and filled their glasses.

"I mean it," the first one went on, "I've seen two . . ."

"Two what?"

"Two homosexuals. When I went to town. Two homosexuals pushing a baby carriage."

The three men laughed until they couldn't stand up. They choked and chortled, they wept, they laughed till they seemed about to burst. Their faces were red. When they stopped laughing, the first man took up his story again.

"Two homosexuals. When I noticed their baby carriage I went up to them. I couldn't believe they were taking a baby for a walk. I looked in the carriage and there inside it was a little homosexual!"

The other two were genuinely astonished. "Things are happening nowadays you wouldn't have thought possible thirty years ago."

"You don't even know any more if there's a God. There are people who say if there was a God he wouldn't be allowing this war."

"But there have always been wars, or it seems like it."

"Then that means maybe there's no God."

"You could talk about something else," suggested Louisiana, who had heard them even though she had been gossiping in another group. "That takes some nerve, saying there's no God when a little boy from the village is roasting in purgatory."

The wife of the man who had told the anecdote had heard too. "If you go on blaspheming I'm taking you home to bed, and your hands will stay on top of the covers."

At least twelve men had a good laugh at her threat.

The man who had been caught out indicated the living room with his nose, and pointed his finger towards Corriveau. "Fatso, if it was your son in there, would you still believe there was a God?"

"I'd believe it because He is everywhere, even in the heads of idiots like you."

"According to you, God would be in your big tits." Anthyme came to serve him some cider. The man drank his glassful in one gulp.

"I didn't say there isn't a God, and I didn't say there is one. Me, I don't know. If Corriveau has seen him, let him raise his hand. Me, I don't know."

Father Corriveau, who was listening, stupefied, with his two bottles of cider, had nothing to say. He refilled the glass.

"It's not my child who's in the coffin," the man said; "it's yours, Anthyme."

"So it is; you shouldn't have that trouble," said Anthyme to the weeping man; "It's my boy, not yours."

"It's not my boy in the coffin, but I wonder: if there is a God, why does he spend so much time sending children into these holes? Why, Anthyme?"

"An old man in a coffin, I find that just as hard to look at as a young one." Anthyme was weeping too.

The villagers were very gay. "Ha! Ha!" laughed one of them. "I've seen some nice behinds, some real nice ones. (Not my wife's, of course.) So I say to myself, if there are nice behinds like that on earth, what is there going to be in Heaven?"

"What a lot of hell Corriveau'll raise! When he was alive he was quite a rooster."

"Father Anthyme, we haven't got any cider!"

Mother Corriveau took more *tourtières* from the oven. The whole house was an oven that smelled of fat golden pork. Through this perfume floated phrases from prayers: *"Salut pleine et grasse"*; *"Entrailles ébenies"*; *"Pour nous pauvres pêcheurs"*; *"Repas éternel"*; these mingled with pungent clouds of tobacco smoke. They had to stay all night. The soldiers remained at attention, against their wall. There were distractions for the young girls as they prayed: they forgot the words of their Ave's as they admired how handsome the soldiers were, these Anglais who didn't have coarse, dark hairs on their cheeks but beautiful fair skin; it would be good to put their lips there.

It wasn't human for them to stay fixed there all night, stiff and motionless. It's not a position for the living. The Corriveaus went to offer them cider or *tourtière*, but the soldiers refused anything.

"Why don't you drink a little glass of cider?" asked Anthyme. "Have a little piece of my *tourtière* then," coaxed his wife.

The Anglais didn't budge, didn't even answer "No" at the ends of their lips.

"They turn up their noses at our food," thought Anthyme.

Mother Corriveau found the laughter too generous. "You're going to wake up my son."

"Would you like a little glass of cider?" offered Anthyme, filling the glass before he had an answer.

In the living room, they were praying: "Jesus Christ," "So be it," "Save us," "The eternal flames"; they were juggling syllables, words, as they prayed, rushing through their prayers. The faster they prayed the sooner Corriveau would leave the flames of purgatory. And if he was condemned to the eternal fires of hell perhaps their prayers would ease the burning.

In the kitchen the people were talking:

"I'd bet my dog that if you climb on a woman three times a day, not counting the nights, that's hard on the heart."

"It's better to kill yourself by climbing on your wife than by working."

"Pig!"

The one who had made the accusation was a bachelor. The other reproached him. "I like people who climb on their wives better than the ones who enjoy themselves all alone like bachelors."

The bachelor was used to this. "I prefer climbing on other men's wives."

The villagers roared with laughter, they belched, they swallowed mouthfuls of cider, and without retying their ties they went, by common consent, into the living room to pray. Those who were in the living room got up and went into the kitchen, where Mother Corriveau never stopped caressing her *tourtières*, and Anthyme worked just as hard filling glasses with cider.

"Listen, here's a good one."

"I'm not in the habit of listening in on dirty stories," insisted Anthyme, who wanted to hear the story. "But tonight, laughing a little might help me forget my sad sorrow. Losing my boy has made me suffer as much as if both my arms had been torn off. Worse, even. I can still see myself, one morning in spring. He had come home well after sunrise. His shirt was undone. It was stained with blood. A white shirt. His lip was as thick as my fist. His left eye, or maybe it was the right, was closed it was so swollen. I stood in the doorway of his bedroom and I said, 'We won't argue. Just go back where you came from and don't set foot in this house again, drunkard.' He left, and he's come back to us today."

Anthyme could not talk any more. He was sobbing. His wife was looking at him hard, like someone who will not allow herself to be tender.

"He's drunk too much, the dirty old man. He throws his sons out the door, but he doesn't notice that it's him they take after. He gives everybody cider but he doesn't forget himself. He takes advantage of the death of his son to let himself get drunk like an animal. You old bum, you're drunk."

"I'm sad, wife, I've never been so sad."

"Come on Anthyme, give me a little cider and don't cry. What the good Lord has taken away he'll give you back a hundredfold."

"At my age, you know I can't make another boy. Not with my wife, anyway . . ."

"Drink a little faster, Father Anthyme, and listen to my story."

"My wife doesn't want me to drink."

"You're too sad. It's bad luck to be as sad as you are. You need a little distraction. Listen to this; it's a good one . . . Once there was . . ."

The raconteur put his arm around Anthyme's shoulders and told him, in a tone confidential enough to attract the curious: "Once a young girl from town came to my place, a cousin of mine. She asked if she could milk a cow. Sit on my little stool, I told her; you know what to do? .Yes. I went on to something else. I came back five minutes later. She was still sitting beside the cow, tickling the tits with the ends of her fingers, caressing them tenderly. Would you mind telling me what you're doing there? I asked her. — I'm making them hard, Uncle."

They laughed heartily till they choked; they struck their thighs and punched one another. They had never heard such a funny story. Anthyme had tears in his eyes, and laugh! right now he was laughing so hard, shaking so much, that he was spilling cider on the floor.

"You're going to kill me," he said.

And he went on to another group where the thirst was great. In the living room, on Corriveau's coffin, the candleflame was clinging stubbornly.

Anthyme Corriveau found himself again, after he had served the drinks, in front of the storyteller, who was proud of his success and still enjoying it.

"Father Anthyme, that story was told to me by your son. He should be laughing at it with us."

"Oh!" said Anthyme, "he shouldn't want to laugh."

★   ★   ★   ★

Mother Corriveau was still cooking her *tourtières*. She was soaked in sweat as though she had been caught in a storm. She was tearing around the stove. Feeling something sticking into her breast she stuck her hand into her bodice. She had forgotten, in her grief, the letter the sergeant had presented to her when he arrived.

"Anthyme," she ordered, drawing the letter out from between her breasts, "come here. I forgot."

She waved the letter.

"Come here. I've got a letter from my boy."

"From our boy," Anthyme corrected. "Open it. Hurry up."

Because of this letter Corriveau was alive. They forgot that their child was lying in his coffin. The old lady feverishly tore open the envelope. It wasn't true that he was dead; he had written. The letter would correct the facts. The villagers spread the word from one group to the next that the Corriveaus had received a letter from their son. They continued to laugh, to eat, to drink, to pray. Mother Corriveau started slowly to puzzle out the letter that had been found in her son's pocket.

"My dearest parents,

I won't write you very much because I have to keep my steel helmet on my head and if I think too hard the heat could melt my helmet and then it wouldn't protect me very well. The socks mother sent me are really warm. Give me news about my brothers. Have any of them got themselves killed? As for my sisters, they're probably still washing their dishes and diapers. I'd rather get a shell in the rear than think about all that. I've won a decoration; it's nice. The more decorations you have, the farther you stay from the Germans." (Everyone insisted, so Mother Corriveau started reading this part again.) "I've won a decoration . . ."

Father Corriveau, amazed, snatched the letter from his wife and proclaimed, pushing people around in his excitement, "My boy got a decoration! My boy won a decoration!"

From all their hearts, from the bottoms of the hearts of those who were praying and those who were drinking, a hymn was raised up that made the ceiling shake:

Il a gagné ses épaulettes
Maluron malurette
Il a gagné ses épaulettes
Maluron malure.

*   *   *   *

Eventually the feast spread to the living room too. The flag covering Corriveau's coffin became a tablecloth where plates and glasses were left and cider was spilled. People sitting at the kitchen table leaned against a wall because it was hard to keep your balance with a plate in one hand, a glass of cider in the other, fat from the *tourtière* streaming down cheeks and chin; or they kept their heads high and dry on a pile of greasy dishes, or else standing in the doorway which was open to the snow and cold, they tried to vomit to get rid of their dizziness; or they put both hands on Antoinette's generous backside or tried to see through the wool covering Philomene's breasts; and they ate juicy *tourtière* in the living room, in the odour of the candles which were going out, and they prayed in the heavy odour of the kitchen where the smell of grease mingled with that of the sweat of the men and women.

They prayed: "*Sainte-Marie pleine et grasse, le seigneur, avez-vous? Entrez toutes les femmes . . .*"

These people did not doubt that their prayer would be understood. They prayed with all their strength as men, all their strength as women who had borne children. They did not ask God for Corriveau to come back on earth; they begged God quite simply not to abandon him for too long in the flames of purgatory. Corriveau couldn't be in hell. He was a boy from the village, and it would have seemed unfair to these villagers for one of their children to be condemned to the eternal flames. Perhaps some people deserved a very long time in purgatory, but no one really deserved hell.

Amélie had come with Arthur while Henri, her deserter husband, remained cowering in his attic, well protected by the heavy trunks slid across the trapdoor.

"In purgatory the fire doesn't hurt as much as in hell. You know that you can get out of purgatory; you think of that while you're burning. Then the fire doesn't bite so bad. So let us pray for the flre of purgatory to purify Corriveau. Hail Mary . . ."

Amélie strung all her prayers end to end, formulas learned at school, responses from her little catechism, and she felt that she was right.

"Let us pray again," she said.

How could a woman leading a dishonest life with two men in her house be so pious? How could she explain supernatural things about religion and hell with so much wisdom? Despite her impure life Amélie was a good woman. Occasions like this evening were fortunate, people would say: you have to have deaths and burials from time to time to remember the goodness of people. The villagers felt a great warmth in their hearts: it wasn't possible that there was a hell. To imaginations steeped in pork fat and cider, the flames of hell were scarcely bigger than the candleflames on

Corriveau's coffin. The flames could not burn through all eternity; all the fires they were familiar with were extinguished after a certain time: fires made to clear the land, or wood fires, or the fires of love. An eternal flame seemed impossible. Only God is eternal, and as Corriveau was a boy from the village where people are good despite their weaknesses, he would not stay long in purgatory. They would bring him out through the strength of their prayers: perhaps he was out even now.

"Memento domine domini domino . . ."

"Requiescat in pace!"

Mother Corriveau was still filling the plates held out to her like starving mouths; in the cellar Anthyme was unearthing new bottles of cider.

The Anglais were at attention, impassive, like statues. Even their eyes did not move. Nobody noticed them. They were part of the decor, like the windows, the lamps, the crucifix, the coffin, the furniture. If someone had observed them up close he would have noticed a gesture of disdain at the edges of their nostrils and the creases of their lips.

"What a bunch of savages, these French Canadians!"

They neither moved nor looked at one another. They were made of wood. They didn't even sweat.

Hands in their pockets, Jos and Pit, the latter leaning against the coffin, were chatting. "That damn Corriveau, I'd like to know what he's thinking about in his coffin with all these women prowling around him."

"There are lots of women going to cry when he's buried."

"Some of them are going to be dreaming about a ghost with soft hands."

"Me, I'll stick my hand in shit if he hasn't undressed at least twenty-two of the women here: Amélie, Rosalia, Alma, Théodelia, Josephine, Arthurise, Zelia . . ."

"So where does that get him?" Jos cut in: "Now Corriveau's lying between his four boards all by himself. He won't get up again."

"Albina," Pit continued, "Léopoldine, Patricia, then your wife . . ."

"What are you talking about, *Calvaire*?"

"I'm telling the truth."

Before he had pronounced the last syllable Pit received a fist in his teeth. He fell over backwards among the plates and glasses, onto Corriveau's coffin. The soldiers moved forward in unison, took hold of the two men, threw them out the open door into the snow, and returned to take up their post again.

The two enemies could be heard shouting and swearing in the cold air. While they tore at each other, the rest were praying for Corriveau's salvation.

"Grant him eternal salvation. Forgive him his trespasses."

They stopped eating. They did not dare to raise another glass to their lips. Everyone was praying. The winter became silent once more.

"They've killed each other," moaned one of the women.

Then the two men appeared in the doorway, faces bloody and blue, snowy, their clothes torn, arms around each other.

"It's not worth going to the bother of fighting if Corriveau isn't in it," Pit explained.

They moved towards the coffin. "You missed a Vierge of a good fight," Jos said.

Pit put two fingers into his mouth. He was missing some teeth.

"Peace deserves a glass of cider! " proclaimed Anthyme.

★   ★   ★   ★

Molly was watching Bérubé sleep, his head on his folded tunic which served as a pillow. She had awakened because she was cold.

She pressed against his chest. The warmth of this sleeping man felt good. Bérubé was snoring. Each time he exhaled he enveloped Molly in a cloud that smelled of Scotch and rotten sausage.

"What a stink — a sleeping man!"

She turned her head to avoid the disagreeable odour, but she remained fastened to him, flesh against flesh. She slid her arm under Bérubé's shoulder and pressed her chest a little more closely against his, as though she wanted to merge her breasts with his hard torso. Bérubé's sex slowly rose. Near him, overcome by a burning dizziness, Molly would have liked to throw herself into him, as into a bottomless pit. Downstairs people were laughing, praying too, and under his flag Corriveau was dead. He would never laugh again, never pray again, never eat or see the snow or a woman or make love. With her whole mouth Molly kissed the sleeper; she would have liked to take his breath away. Bérubé stirred a little, and Molly felt his flesh come alive, rouse itself from sleep.

She sighed, "Darling, let's make love. I'm afraid you'll die too."

Bérubé moved, grunted, farted.

"Let's make love, please."

Bérubé rolled onto Molly. It was death that they stabbed at, violently.

★   ★   ★   ★

Three sudden little knocks at the living-room window above Corriveau's coffin made everyone shudder. The villagers were quiet, listening. Every time someone dies, inexplicable things happen. The soul of the dead person does not want to leave the earth. Now nothing disturbed the silence. The villagers pricked up their ears: all they could hear was their own breathing, hoarse from fear. The cold twisted the beams in the whining walls. The silence was sharp enough to cut a throat.

Three little blows shook the window again. The villagers looked at each other questioningly. They were not mistaken; they had certainly heard it. The men stuck their hands in their pockets, stiffening their chests in a challenging way. The women pressed against the men. Less terrified than the others, Anthyme said, "Something's going on at the window."

He pulled the curtain, which was never opened. Night had fallen long ago. It was very black outside the window. The eyes of the villagers were fixed on the blackness.

"If there was a noise at the window it's because somebody's out there," reasoned Mother Corriveau. "Have a better look, Anthyme, and not with your eyes shut."

"Maybe it isn't something you can see," suggested one of the women.

Then a shadow moved in the shadows. Anthyme took a candle from the coffin and approached the window. The light shone first of all on the sparkling frost. In the centre of the frame the glass was bare, but Anthyme could see nothing but his reflection.

The knocking began again.

"*Vieille pipe de Christ*," he swore. "If you want to come in, come in the door."

A little voice from the other side of the window tried to make itself stronger than the wind. "Don't you recognize me?" she asked.

"*Vieille pipe de Christ*, if you'd let us see you maybe I'd recognize you. Are you ashamed of your face?"

"Open up! " the little voice implored. "It's me."

"*Vieux pape de Christ*, don't you know the difference between a door and a window?"

Anthyme climbed up with both feet on his son's coffin.

"Open . . ."

"Open!" repeated Anthyme. "*Baptême*! It isn't summer!"

"It's me, Esmalda!"

"Esmalda! *Vieille pipe du petit Jésus*! Esmalda! It's my daughter Esmalda, the nun," Anthyme explained. "It's our little nun. Come in, little Memalda!"

"The blessed rule of our community forbids me to enter my father's house."

"Little Esmalda!" Mother Corriveau cried with delight. "My little Esmalda! I haven't seen her since the morning when she left with her little suitcase that had nothing in it but her rosary; she left me a lock of her hair, beautiful blonde hair and I hung it at the feet of Christ on the crucifix." She was weeping with joy; she rubbed her eyes to wipe the tears. "My little Esmalda! Our little saint!"

The villagers got on their knees and bowed their heads.

"I'm not allowed to come into my father's house."

"*Vieille pipe de Christ*! I'd like to see anybody try and stop you from coming into your father's house."

". . . and your mother's. Come and get warm. And I've made some good *tourtières*. Don't stay outside."

"But I must obey."

"I'm your father. If you didn't have me the good sisters in your community wouldn't be able to forbid you to enter my house."

"I must obey."

"*Vieux pape . . .*"

His wife cut him off. "Anthyme, you don't understand a thing about holy matters!"

Esmalda's face near the window pane, her breath and her voice, her warmth, had enlarged a circle in the frost. You could make out her face more clearly, though it was still flooded in darkness.

"I would like to pray for my brother. Open the window."

"Come in by the door," shouted Anthyme. "We're glad to see you. The window will *not* be opened. It isn't summer. If you don't want to take the trouble to come in to see your little brother who was killed in the war you can stay outside and go back with the women who ask you to turn your nose up at the people who brought you into the world."

Mother Corriveau interrupted. "Anthyme, go and get the screwdriver and the hammer. Are you going to refuse hospitality to a little sister of Jesus?"

Using the screwdriver like a wedge, which he struck with the hammer into the space between the window and the frame, Anthyme tried to pull the window out of the ice. Although he hit it with the hammer and his shoulder, the window remained fixed in its place.

Arsène and Jos joined Anthyme on the coffin. The three of them pulled away the window the way you tear cloth.

A cold wind blew into the living room. The nun's face appeared, under her coif, rumpled in the lamplight. "It's good to come back to the house of one's parents, dead or alive," she declared.

Soaked in sweat, the villagers were shivering now. The sweat turned to ice on their backs.

The nun's head was motionless. A thin smile uncovered her sharp teeth.

"Who is dead? Who is alive? Perhaps the dead man is alive. Perhaps the living are dead."

The villagers crossed themselves.

"Sin may have killed the person who is alive. Who is without sin? Grace, the gift of God, may have revived someone who is dead. Who has the grace of God?" Then Esmalda was quiet. She looked at the villagers assembled before Corriveau's coffin. She looked a long time at each one, trying to recognize them. She had not seen them for many years, since her adolescence. She noted how voracious time had been, how it had ravaged the people of the village. When she recognized someone she smiled less parsimoniously. They would not forget that smile.

"All together, men can damn a soul. All together, they cannot save a soul that has been damned. All together, men can lead one of their own behind the door that opens only once, and behind which eternity is a fire. But all together men cannot have one of their own admitted into the kingdom of the Father."

"Hail Mary," implored a voice which sounded like the last cry before the shipwreck.

The villagers replied in chorus. "The Lord is with you; have mercy on us poor sinners."

The nun waited for the end of the prayer; then she said, "I won't ask you to open the coffin to see my brother. If he has been damned I will not recognize his face; the face of one who has been damned is like a tortured demon. And if he has been saved I am not worthy of setting my eyes upon the face of an angel chosen by God."

"Hail Mary . . ." began another voice, as if it wanted to chase away what it had heard.

"Forgive us sinners!"

The nun lowered her head over her brother, gathered herself together for a moment, prayed in silence, and then raised her eyes to the villagers. "All men live together, but they follow different paths. But there is only one path, the one that leads to God."

The nun's decayed teeth could be seen in her rather sad smile. "How sweet it is to come back among one's own people!"

She turned around and disappeared into the night and the snow.

"She's a saint!" exclaimed Mother Corriveau.

"Let's shut that window fast," said Anthyme.

★   ★   ★   ★

Stretching out his arms to show how long the pig was that he had killed for Anthyme, that was now being eaten chopped up in Mother Corriveau's *tourtières*, Arsène awkwardly bumped into the man next to him. The glass he was holding broke and slashed Arthur's cheek. Blood spurted out. Arthur stopped up the wound with the sleeve of his jacket. Amélie held him by the arm.

"Arthur, don't go and dirty my Sunday clothes. Blood stains don't come out."

Arthur refused to sit down. He remained standing in the middle of the kitchen. The villagers formed a circle around him to watch the blood flow. Arthur was amazed to see so much blood gushing out of such a little cut. He felt as if he was being drained of his contents like a bottle. When he started to bring his hand up to the wound, to put pressure on it and ease the flow of blood, Amélie lowered his arm. He was surprised that the blood was so red. Dazed, he put his hand on the wound again, and the blood burned his fingers, flowing onto his hand, his fist, his suit.

"What a baby!" said Amélie. "I tell him not to put his hands in his blood, but he can't resist it."

Anthyme arrived with a towel. He soaked it in cider.

"Cider's good for the blood."

"Arthur's bleeding like the pig I killed."

"Instead of laughing," suggested Amélie, "how about bringing me some snow?"

Several men went out and came back with their hands full of snow. Amélie got busy and applied some to Arthur's wound. He grimaced because of the cold. The snow, all red from the blood, dropped onto the floor where it melted. Arsène, who was responsible for the wound, could only apologize awkwardly.

"If I'd hit you a litte harder they'd be burying you with Corriveau."

Arsène laughed derisively. Everyone laughed. The clothing of Arthur and Amélie was red with blood. Grouped around them, everyone contemplated all the blood.

"Arthur didn't want to go to the war, but he looks as good as a lovely war wounded."

"Keep quiet," a woman begged.

"A handsome wounded man isn't as sad as a handsome man dead in the war," insisted Mother Corriveau who, after the accident, had returned to her pastry, in which a tear fell, and to her *tourtières* crackling in the oven.

Arsène insisted. "Seeing that much blood and a face chopped up so nice makes me sorry I didn't go to the war. Arthur makes me want to go to war. I think that having a German at your feet, losing all his goddamn German blood, that must satisfy a man. But it seems as if our soldiers don't see the Germans when they lose their blood. Our soldiers shoot their little rifles, then they go right away and hide, pissing in their pants for fear they've caught a German, because the Germans know how to defend themselves."

"Shut your big yaps!" shouted a demented voice that terrified the villagers. "Shut your yaps," the same voice repeated more calmly.

★   ★   ★   ★

Bérubé appeared on the staircase, barechested, his face flat as though he had no eyes, barefoot, his khaki trousers too wide and his fly open.

"Shut up!"

No one opened his mouth. His cries had stifled their laughter and their prayers. The men, anticipating a good fight, didn't dare put down their glasses and plates. Rosaries were still in the hands of the women. Bérubé came down the last step buttoning himself up. They cleared a path for him, stepping back as he approached. He punched several stomachs, several breasts, and found himself in front of Arsène, who was convulsed. But his laughter was stopped in his throat when Bérubé grabbed him by the jacket. Buttons flew, cloth tore. The villagers were still as mice.

"*Calice de ciboire d'hostie! Christ en bicyclette sur son Calvaire!* So you think we enjoy ourselves in the war? You pile of shit! War is funny? I'll show you what the war's all about. You'll laugh."

While he was spitting his blasphemies Bérubé was hitting Arsène in the face ("*maudit ciboire de Christ!*"), not with his fist but with his open hand, and Arsène's big face was twisted with pain. Bérubé's eyes were red, and Arsène's big face was swinging with the blows ("*cochon de tabernacle!*"); his jacket was in shreds, his shirt was torn. Bérubé was in full cry.

"Oh!" cried Zeldina, "I've peed on the floor!"

"Shut up or I'll make you lick it up!"

He pushed Arsène against a wall, and tossed him about until the house shook.

"Ah! " he said, "soldiers have lots of fun in the war! War is fun! You don't know anything but the asses on your cows that look like your wives. It's funny, the war. You like having Corriveau there in his coffin; he can't laugh any more, he'll never be able to laugh any more, *crucifix!*"

Bérubé could no longer shout or swear or speak. He was choked by his bitter anger; his eyes burned, and like a child he burst into sobs.

Was he the devil in flesh and blood? Terrified, the villagers stopped their prayers.

Arsène, waiting to take advantage of Bérubé's softening up to get away, took a chance and moved his foot. There was no reaction to his movement; Bérubé hadn't noticed it. Then Arsène threw himself forward. But Bérubé had caught up with him again. He held his head tight in the vise of his hands. "War is funny, eh, you big shit? I'll make a man out of you! Forward march!"

Bérubé pushed him, shoved him towards the mirror hanging

on the kitchen wall. The villagers dispersed, closed their ears, broke glasses and plates, spilled cider on their coats and jackets. Bérubé flattened Arsène's face against the mirror.

"We have fun in the war, do we? It's a funny man who has a bloody face like a crushed strawberry. Laugh! There's nothing funnier than the war."

Arsène didn't dare move a pore of his skin.

"I told you to laugh," Bérubé repeated, punching his ears.

Arsène looked in the mirror and saw his rotten, tobacco-stained teeth; they were revealed as his lips unstuck and were clenched into a kind of smile.

"Laugh!"

Bérubé struck Arsène. The blows resounded and echoed in his head, which felt immense. His head felt as if it was going to burst, and his brains come out through his eyes.

"War's funny. Laugh."

Finally, Arsène succeeded in releasing a loud, phony laugh.

"So you laugh when men get themselves massacred by the goddamn Germans. I'll make you understand, by the sweet shit of holy Jesus."

Once more he struck, crushing his head between his two hands. After several blows Bérubé stopped the torture.

"Tell us what you see in the mirror."

"I see myself," Arsène replied fearfully.

"You see a big pile of shit. Have a good look. What do you see in the mirror?"

Bérubé grabbed Arsène by the neck and shook him until he begged for mercy. Then Bérubé calmed down. "In the war you have to look carefully; you have to see everything. Looking is learning. You learn everything through the seat of your pants. Watch out."

He let fly a few kicks.

"Okay," asked Bérubé, "what do you see if you look in the mirror?"

"I see Arsène."

"He doesn't understand a thing."

Bérubé began to hit him around the ears again. Arsène was so stunned that he wanted to vomit, as though everything in his head had fallen down into his throat. Bérubé threatened him now, waving his closed fist in front of his eyes.

"Arsène, I'm going to make a good soldier out of you. Tell me exactly what you see when you look in the mirror."

"I see myself."

Bérubé brought back his fist to make him understand that the threat was stronger. "One last time. What do you see in the mirror?"

"I see a pile of shit."

Bérubé had won. He smiled; he hugged Arsène. He patted his cheek. "Now you're a real good soldier."

★　★　★　★

The shouting had awakened Molly. She stretched out her hand to caress Bérubé, but finding that he was not in the bed she started as though she had just awakened from a nightmare. At that moment Bérubé was shouting some blasphemy. Recognizing his voice, she jumped out of bed onto the cold floor, slipped on her dress, which she had let fall on the floor and, worried ran downstairs.

She appeared like another incarnation of the devil, in this house where they were holding a wake for a dead man. In her haste Molly had put on the dress without taking the trouble to put her petticoat on first. She was completely naked because the dress was made of very sheer tulle. No one dared raise his voice to tell her to go and get dressed.

Molly stopped on the stairs for a moment, trying to understand what was going on. She held herself regally under the long transparent gown. The women closed their eyes and imagined that they too were beginning to look like this girl — before the children, the sleepless nights, their husbands' rough words, before those winters, each one more interminable than the last. They would never look like that again; they despised her. The men were devoured by that flame so sweetly sculptured beneath the tulle. A fire was trembling in their bodies. That belly, rounded for caresses, wasn't a swollen sack of guts; those breasts, firm as hot rolls, didn't wobble down onto the belly. The young men put a hand in their pockets and drew their legs close together.

Molly had learned not to get mixed up in men's quarrels. She crossed the kitchen, head held high as though nothing had happened, and went to the living room. There was no reaction, no movement from the soldiers at attention. Molly knelt down before Corriveau's coffin and prayed to God not to condemn to his terrible hell the soul of Corriveau, whom she had never known, but who had such respectable parents. He had been born a French Canadian so he couldn't have been very happy.

Corriveau must have looked like all those young soldiers who used to come to her bed to forget that no one loved them; Molly used to feel very pleased when, after they had got dressed again, they would give her a last kiss, with a certain happiness in their eyes. She liked these young soldiers very much. Their desires were never complicated like those of the old officers or the travelling salesmen who always asked her for all sorts of fancy stuff which she didn't like but which she agreed to because they paid well. Only the young soldiers made her happy. Corriveau would have been like those young soldiers; when he had closed the bedroom door perhaps she would have been sorry to see him leave. Some returned to her bed, and she sometimes recognized them, but there were also some who didn't come back.

Now the young soldiers, the old officers, the travelling salesmen and all the others would never come to her bed again to
knead her flesh with avid hands, as though they wanted to model
in that flesh another woman's body: the body of the woman they
were thinking about. Bérubé alone would love her now.

Molly became very sad at the thought of those young soldiers
who would never come again to her bedroom with their affected
coarseness, who would never again let an "I love you" escape into
her ear at the moment when they were swollen with all their useless love. Molly wiped a tear. All her love would be destined for
Bérubé. They would forget her quickly enough: Molly wasn't the
only one in the hotel, and there were other hotels. Some of them,
of course, could not forget her — the little soldiers who had not
come back from the war, who would never come back. If Molly
were ever unhappy they would be the ones whose help she would
ask. Those little soldiers who had given their lives in the war
could not refuse to help Molly. She prayed that God would open
the doors of his Heaven to all the young soldiers who looked like
Corriveau. She recited several prayers, but is was very difficult.
She did not manage to recite them all the way to the end because
the desire to sleep was stronger than her desire to save the souls of
young war-heroes, stronger than her distress at seeing young men
like Corriveau know death before they had known life. It would
be better to go to sleep right away. Molly would get up very early,
at dawn, well rested. Then she would ask God for the salvation of
Corriveau and all those like him.

"Here little girl, little lady, eat this bit of *tourtière*." Mother Corriveau put a plate on Corriveau's coffin in front of Molly, who took
a mouthful to be polite.

"You," said Mother Corriveau to the soldiers, "you're not having much fun. Goodness but you look sad. You're soldiers, you
shouldn't be sad. You'd think you were in mourning. What if you

are Anglais? We don't wish you any harm. We won't send you back home to England. We like you alright. Would you each like a little plate with a piece of *tourtière* like I've given our little Molly?"

The soldiers didn't move. Only the sergeant's eyes turned in their sockets. His lips barely unfastened as he said, "Sorry, we're on duty."

And, to harden his men's positions, he shouted, "Attention!"

Molly nibbled another mouthful and got up to go to bed. When she went into the kitchen Bérubé seized her arm and said to her, "Come here you, all naked, we need your help."

Would Bérubé beat her? She noticed that she was, as her husband had said, really naked under the tulle dress.

Arsène, ludicrously, was standing in front of Bérubé, who kept hitting him with his open hand. Would Bérubé mistreat her like that too? The big man's face was so red that the flesh seemed to want to burst.

"What do you want?" she asked submissively.

Arsène was wearing a buttoned coat; a wool scarf was tied around his neck. Seeing him bundled up like that Molly could not know that under his top coat he was wearing two others.

Arsène did not try to dodge the blows. He was pale, sweaty, suffering.

"Get on his shoulders, get on his back. I don't know how to say it to you. *Baptême*, that language of yours wasn't invented by Christians. Get on his shoulders. That *baptême* is going to learn what a soldier's life is like."

Bérubé seized Molly by the waist, lifted her, and installed her on Arsène's shoulders.

"That's enough," said someone who had come up to them. He couldn't go on: he was silenced by a fist. The man recoiled, surprised at the blood that was running down his chin.

The villagers laughed derisively. "By Christ, you're going to learn what war's all about. Dance! It isn't finished. Dance!"

Arsène's eyes were burning with sweat. Under his coats his suit was soaked as if a bucket of water, boiling water, had been poured over him. During his lifetime he had carried few things as heavy as little Molly; he'd be crushed by her weight. But he danced so that he wouldn't be hit any more. He would even have kissed Bérubé's feet. He danced with all his strength; his feet were scarcely moving, they were so heavy that when he moved he felt as if he were buried in snow up to his thighs, snow that burned like fire and clung like mud. He would have liked to dance still more so that Bérubé would stop being angry.

"Dance!"

Arsène gathered up all his strength and thought he had speeded up his rhythm. "Dance, by Christ! Dance!"

Bérubé struck. Molly told herself that she wasn't dreaming.

"Dance faster!"

On Arsène's shoulders Molly looked like a queen. The old men marvelled at the pink tips of her breasts under the tulle, two fascinating little stars. Basically they were no better off than Corriveau. They would never again have the privilege of gently kissing such little pink tips on such tender breasts. They would never again caress such beautiful breasts, all warm in their hands. They were sad. Their lives were over already. And they cursed from the bottoms of their hearts the young men who were devouring Molly with their eyes.

"*Allez! Hop! Allez! Hop! Vivent the soldiers!* Go on! Dance, *hostie!* Dance! Faster! Run! *Vive* the army! *Vive la guerre!* Left! Right! Left! Right! Left . . . Left . . . Left . . ."

Bérubé didn't stop Arsène, who was completely under his command.

"Left . . . Left . . . Right! Dance, you stinking vermin! Dance! *Vive la guerre et les soldats!* Dance! Left! Right! Here's a shell!"

Bérubé kicked him in the rear.

"Here's a grenade!"

Bérubé slapped him.

"Here's a bomb!"

Bérubé spat in his face.

"Run! You're rottener than Corriveau will be after the spring thaw. Faster! Left, turn!" Arsène obeyed as well he could. He ran in place, more and more slowly; his face was drowned in sweat. He couldn't breathe. There was a cold stone in place of his lungs. He was stifling. The air was not coming to either his mouth or his nose. He was as thirsty as if he had eaten sand.

"Go on, soldier! Left! Right! Left! Right! Left! Right! Soldier, left turn!"

If Bérubé judged that he was not being obeyed promptly enough, he crushed Arsène's head between his two hands, cracking them over Arsène's ears. Bérubé was as sweaty as Arsène. Molly felt drunk.

"It's lovely, a soldier's life. You would have liked to be a soldier. Look out! It's a mine!"

Bérubé gave him a few kicks on the shin. Hadn't Arsène felt some pain? He showed no reaction, no contortions, no grimaces. He was shaking.

"Ah! the lovely war. Left! Right! *Hostie* of a mule, forward march. Look out! a torpedo!"

Bérubé sank his fist into Arsène's stomach. He was doubled over by the blow. His face was purple. His coats and his wool scarf were strangling him. Would he be strong enough to get up? He was staggering.

No one came to interfere. No one was brave enough. In order not to feel like cowards they tried to be amused, and laughed as they had never laughed before.

"March!"

Arsène felt as if there was a bar of red hot iron in his skull, from one ear to the other. He could no longer see anything; he would have sworn that his eyes were running down his cheeks. What was that flowing, thick and hot, down his temples? Was it sweat or blood? Arsène sank into a deeper and deeper torpor.

"Left! Right!"

Arsène's legs were melting like the pats of butter in Mother Corriveau's saucepans. She was as quiet as she used to be when her son, the one lying there in his coffin, used to come in drunk and insult Anthyme.

Arsène's legs had melted. He was resting now against his fat belly. He could no longer run or dance. He was an exhausted, legless cripple in his soaked coats. Arsène was thinking "I'm plastered, I'm asleep, I've had too much to drink. I'm letting myself fall on the ground."

Bérubé was hitting him. "Left! Right! Left . . . Left! Here's the beautiful life of a little soldier. Look out! Here's a shell!"

Bérubé flattened his hand in Arsène's face.

"When are those Christly Germans going to leave us in peace?" asked Bérubé.

Arsène no longer had any arms. He had become a sack of potatoes, but he still obeyed.

"You're a good soldier. Left! Right!"

On Arsène's shoulders Molly felt humiliated.

Suddenly, Arsène stumbled. Molly fell onto one of the men, who received her in his arms like a flaming log.

"Narcisse!" cried his wife. "Don't touch that!"

Bérubé came up to Arsène, who had passed out on the floor. He stuck his foot in his face and shook his head. "That's a real good little soldier; not as good as Corriveau, but better than me. Arsène is a *Christ* of a good soldier. He deserves medals, stacks of medals as high as churches. Arsène lets himself be pulled apart. He doesn't try to save a single tiny bit of his skin. He's no miser. A *hostie* of a good little soldier."

With his left toe he turned over Arsène's face.

"He'd let them make mincemeat out of him if they told him they needed his skin to plug up the walls of the shithouses. A real good little soldier. But he hasn't got a uniform."

Bérubé pulled off the coats that he had made Arsène pile into, one on top of the other. He took off his jacket, tore off his shirt, which he threw into the woodstove, and pulled off his trousers; the women no longer dared to look. The men were snorting with laughter. Arsène, motionless, submitted to all the outrages. He was nothing but a mass of obedient flesh.

"You're a real good little soldier," said Bérubé, who was no longer pale, whose eyes were no longer haggard. He looked more gentle. "You're a real good little soldier and you've done a goddamn good job for your country, but you've got to have a uniform. It's your duty to fight the war: it's the most glorious job, to fight a war. It's fun to fight a war; it's nice. You're a good soldier, but you haven't got a uniform."

Arsène, dazed, dressed in his long wool underwear that covered him from his ankles to his neck, listened to Bérubé. He repeated, "You need a uniform." The women had an equivocal smile on their lips; the men, their mouths wide open, were amused. Bérubé grabbed hold of the neck of Arsène's underwear, one hand on either side of the long row of buttons that started at the neck and went down to the crotch. Without loosening his grip he pulled, vigorously. Buttons flew, the underwear fell down, Arsène's white chest appeared, then his fat shiny belly. When Arsène, unresisting, was completely naked, the women laughed as hard as their husbands.

Arsène himself burst out laughing.

"Soldier, never forget that your uniform represents your native land, your *patrie* our country, and Liberty."

Bérubé kicked Arsène towards the door and pushed him out into the snow.

"Go on, soldier, go and stomp out three or four goddamn Germans for me."

The villagers gurgled as they emptied themselves of their laughter, and all their insides seemed to escape with their laughter. They held their stomachs, they wept, they stamped their feet, they pranced about, they choked.

Bérubé seized the arm of the astonished Molly.

"Darling," she asked, "why did you do that?"

"What?"

"It was a bad joke."

"Let's go to bed; let's have a little nap."

"Darling . . ."

"Sometimes I feel a little crazy."

★   ★   ★   ★

The candles on Corriveau's coffin had burned out. Now the living room was lit only by the light coming from the kitchen. The light was yellow, greasy looking. The soldiers had been present, imperturbable, at Arsène's massacre. They had looked impassively at the savage rites, drowned in heavy laughter, cider and greasy tourtières, but their lips were sealed by disgust.

What kind of animals *were* these French Canadians? They had the manners of pigs in a pigpen. Besides, if you looked at them carefully, objectively, French Canadians really looked like pigs too. The long thin Anglais looked at the French Canadians' double chins, their swollen bellies, the big flaccid breasts of their women; they scrutinized the French Canadians' eyes, floating inertly in the white fat of their faces — they were real pigs, these French Canadians, whose civilization consisted of drinking, eating, farting, belching. The soldiers had known for a long time that

French Canadians were pigs. "Give them something to eat and a place to shit and we'll have peace in the country," they used to say. That night the soldiers had proof before their eyes that the French Canadians were pigs.

Corriveau, the French Canadian they had transported on their shoulders through snow so deep it made them want to stretch out and freeze they were so tired, Corriveau, this French Canadian sleeping under their flag, in a uniform like the one they were so proud of, this Corriveau was a pig too.

French Canadians were pigs. Where would it end? The sergeant decided that it was time to take the situation in hand. French Canadians were unmanageable, undisciplined, crazy pigs. The sergeant prepared a plan of attack in his head.

His subalterns remembered what they had learned in school: French Canadians were solitary, fearful, barely intelligent; they didn't have a talent for government or business or agriculture, but they made lots of babies.

When the English arrived in the colony the French Canadians were less civilized than the Indians. The French Canadians lived grouped in little villages along the shores of the St. Lawrence, in wooden cabins filled with dirty, sick, starving children, and lousy, dying old men. Every year English ships used to go up the St. Lawrence because England had decided to get involved in New France, which had been neglected and abandoned by the Frenchmen. The English ships were anchored in front of the villages, and the Englishmen got off to offer their protection to the French Canadians, to become friends with them. But as soon as they had seen the British flag waving on the St. Lawrence the French Canadians had gone and hidden in the woods. Real animals. They hadn't a vestige of politeness, these pigs. They didn't even think of defending themselves. What they left behind — their cabins, animals, furniture, clothes — were so dirty, so crawling with vermin, so smelly, that the English had had to burn it all in order to disinfect the area. If they hadn't destroyed it the vermin would have invaded the whole country.

Then the boats went away, but the French Canadians stayed in the woods until autumn. Then they got busy building new cabins.

Why did they not accept the help offered by the English? Because France had abandoned them, why would they not accept the privilege of becoming English? England would have civilized them. They wouldn't be French Canadian pigs then. They would know how to understand a civilized language. They would speak a civilized language, not a *patois*.

Accustomed to obeying, the soldiers felt that they were being given an order. They turned their eyes towards the sergeant, who motioned with his head. The soldiers understood. They carried out the order fervently.

They went through the house picking up boots, coats, scarves and hats, and threw them outside. The villagers were invited to leave.

More preoccupied with finding their clothes than protesting the insult, they left, pushing each other as they went.

*   *   *   *

When they were outside, their feet buried in snow crusted from the same coid that froze the saliva on their lips, the villagers realized that they had been kicked out of Corriveau's house by the Anglais. The Anglais had prevented them from praying for the repose of the soul of Corriveau, a boy from the village, dead in the war, the Anglais' war. Their humiliation was as painful as a physical wound. The Anglais were preventing them from gathering together to mourn at the coffin of one of their people. Because life in the village was lived in common, each villager was Corriveau's father to some extent, each woman his mother. The women wept bitterly; the men held in their anger. Gradually they all found their clothes. They were not cold now: their anger protected them from the wind.

Mother Corriveau had not liked the soldiers' behaviour, but she couldn't communicate with them in their language. She put some wood in the stove. "You have to hit these Anglais over the head to make them understand."

Anthyme didn't say whether he agreed or not. Mother Corriveau, without saying another word, indicated to the Anglais that they should sit down at the table, where she served them generous portions of *tourtière* swimming in fragrant sauce.

Father Anthyme didn't want his cider drunk by these Anglais who had kicked out the people who had come to pray for his son. But he went down to his cellar and dug up some more bottles. "We know how to live," he said to the soldiers, who smiled because they didn't understand a word.

★   ★   ★   ★

Henri, the deserter, in order not to risk being caught and taken back to the army by the Anglais soldiers, remained under cover in his attic, motionless in his bed, while Amélie and Arthur went out to pray for Corriveau's salvation. Henri breathed carefully, avoiding any movement, any creaking of his old mattress that could reveal, in this too perfect silence, the presence of a man who refused to go to war.

Henri even had to force his children and those of his wife — that is, the ones she had had with Arthur — to forget about him.

The presence in the village of those seven soldiers who had accompanied Corriveau gave him palpitations; the soldiers could very well go back with their hands not empty: there were a number of deserters in the village. Because Amélie wanted to live with two men in the house Henri would be one of the first to be captured.

The people in the village didn't like two men living with the same woman. Henri knew he was superfluous. It wouldn't take the soldiers long to find him if they looked.

He despised his fear as he despised himself for having lost Amélie. Even if he had his turn in bed with her, even if she called him when Arthur went out, Henri was well aware that she preferred Arthur.

Under his skin, in his flesh, the smarting of his anguish tormented him; he wanted to scratch himself, to claw until the blood came. He would not forgive himself for hiding away in a glacial attic, a man whose wife had been taken away from him and who was afraid that they would come to this black hole where he was scared, where he despised himself; and force him to go back to the war.

The sun had set very early as it always does in winter, when even the light does not resist the cold. But despite the invading night Henri did not sleep.

In all fairness, it was his turn to sleep with Amélie tonight, but because of Corriveau he would lose it. He didn't dare let himself be seen on the outside. Amélie had had Arthur go along with her to see Corriveau. Suddenly it occurred to Henri that it was just as dangerous for Arthur to go out and be seen by the seven soldiers as it was for him, because Arthur was as much a deserter as he was. In fact, Arthur was even more of a criminal because he had never even worn a uniform. Because he was going to pray with Amélie, Arthur had insisted on spending the night in her bed. Henri had had the wool pulled over his eyes once too often. He despised himself. Perhaps Amélie and Arthur would give themselves up to the soldiers? Henri flattened himself into his bed and pulled the covers over his head. Arthur would spend two consecutive nights with Amélie while Henri, in his attic, was bored to death.

Every night he was tortured by the same thought: his wife

no longer belonged to him, his house no longer belonged to him, nor his animals, not even his children, who all called Arthur "papa." He cursed the war; he gathered up all the curses he knew, inventing some that came from the bottom of his heart, and loosed them against the war. He hated the war with all his heart. But he thought sometimes that he would be less unhappy in the mud of the war. It even seemed to him more desirable to be unhappy with his family, in his own house, than to be happy in the war. Then he would tell himself that it was better to be unhappy in a cold attic than happy in the mud of the war. But he knew above all that man is unhappy wherever he is, that in the village the only man who was not unhappy was Corriveau, on condition that there was no hell and no purgatory. Drowned in the untidy remorse of his thoughts, Henri fell asleep.

Shortly after, he awoke, thinking of the sun. The thought of the sun had awakened him just like a real ray of sunlight caressing your face on a summer morning.

Henri's sun was only a mirage, a poor thought that would not revive the dead earth beneath the ice and snow, an idea that would not light up the attic where Henri feared the night and the mysterious shadows. He pulled the covers over his head again to give himself the illusion of warmth and security. Henri's sun would not even light up the sad recesses of his mind.

Henri had dreamed of a big sun, round as an orange; he could still see it in his mind, precise, high, immense, dizzily motionless. He imagined it was suspended by a wire; if the wire were cut the sun would fall and, opening its mouth, it would swallow the whole world. Henri contemplated this sun. There was nothing above it or beside it. It was indeed a solitary sun.

Henri noticed that, beneath this sun, something was arranging itself on the ground. It looked like a house, but as he observed more carefully he saw that it was not a house but a big box, and as he thought better he realized that it was Corriveau's coffin, which he had seen going by in the street covered with the Anglais' flag. Henri saw the sun, then, very high, and on the earth he could see nothing but Corriveau's coffin.

To tell the truth, this coffin beneath the sun was bigger than Corriveau's, because the people from the village were entering it, one by one, one after the other, just as they entered church, bent over, submissive, and the last villagers brought their animals with them — cows, horses, and the others following. It was a silent cortège. The coffin was much more vast than the village church for, as well as the villagers and their animals, squirrels, snakes, dogs and foxes were entering the coffin; even the river suddenly climbed up like a snake to enter the coffin. Birds came down from the sky to go into it, and people from neighbouring villages. The cortège was interrupted; people were arriving with their baggage and their children and their animals. Henri was among these strangers, and he went into the coffin too. Houses were moving like awkward turtles; covered with ice and snow they slid along heavily and disappeared into Corriveau's coffin. Now people were arriving in crowds, whole villages at a time, huge numbers of people patiently waiting their turn. They came in trains, hundreds of trains, then giant steamboats drew up and spilled their crowds into Corriveau's coffin. From the four corners of the earth people came running up, rushing into Corriveau's coffin which was swelling up like a stomach. The sea too, even the sea had become gentle as a river and was emptying itself into Corriveau's coffin: he saw fish with eight hands, with three heads, crabs with terrifying teeth, insects too, creatures in shells that seemed like pebbles, then nothing more. The entire ocean had been drunk up and in the whole world nothing remained but Corriveau's coffin.

"Now it's all over," thought Henri.

The earth was deserted. Now the coffin seemed very small,

hardly as big as the one Henri had seen going by on the shoulders of the Anglais soldiers. The earth was silent, motionless. Henri was relieved not to be thinking of anything.

Then groups of men, mechanically disciplined, began spilling out from the torn horizon. They were soldiers, armed, marching in step. Countless armies were marching towards one another; their march was fierce, implacable. Henri understood that they would converge at Corriveau's coffin. They did not raise their weapons but, soldierlike, entered Corriveau's coffin. Henri waited a long time. Nothing more happened. On the whole earth, only Corriveau's coffin under the Anglais flag still existed.

He cried to himself, "I'm going crazy! " He moaned again, "I'm losing my mind!"

He sat up in his bed. Night was over and day had begun in his attic. Henri noticed Corriveau's coffin. It was in his attic. Henri saw it, at the back of the attic. A hand was pushing Henri's back, pushing him towards Corriveau's coffin which now was just big enough to contain one man: Corriveau or himself.

"Help!"

He leapt from his bed, pushed aside the trunks, lifted the trapdoor, let himself down and ran downstairs. The children were asleep; the walls were cracking as though the devil was nibbling at them.

Henri slipped into Arthur's boots, put on his wool jacket and his fur cap. Despite the danger of being caught by the soldiers and taken back to the war, Henri decided to join the others at Corriveau's house. The door was open: he hesitated on the step.

The night was so black, the village so flooded by the night, it seemed so deep that Henri felt dizzy.

He stuck the shotgun in his hand.

$\star$ $\star$ $\star$ $\star$

When the villagers found themselves in front of Anthyme Corriveau's house, their feet in the snow which was as sharp as
splinters of glass, when they understood that they had been
expelled from Anthyme Corriveau's house, that they had been
thrown out into this icy sea where they were trembling in their
soaking clothes, when they thought again that it was outsiders,
Anglais, who had chased them out of Corriveau's house, a house
that had come down through five generations of Corriveaus, all
living in the village and in the same house on the same bit of land
for more than a hundred years; when they reminded themselves
that Corriveau, a little French Canadian boy, a son of the village,
had been killed in a war that the Anglais from England, the United
States and Canada had declared on the Germans (Corriveau had
been killed in the mud of the old country while the Anglais were
sitting on cushions in their offices; the Anglais left their shelters
sometimes, but only to go and bring a young French Canadian,
dead in the war, back to his family); when the villagers realized
that they had been sent out like dogs that had peed on the rug
by the Anglais who weren't from their village or their county or
their province, or even their country, Anglais who weren't even
Canadians but only *maudits* Anglais then the villagers knew the
depth of their humiliation.

Gesticulating, swearing, bickering, arguing, pushing and
shoving, spitting, drunk, they swore inflammatory oaths agains
the Anglais who had settled themselves into Corriveau's house.

Joseph waved his stump, wrapped up in its bandages, and
shouted louder than the others. "The *maudits* Anglais have taken
everything away from us, but they haven't got our Corriveau.
They won't get Corriveau's last night!"

★   ★   ★   ★

Sweat was streaming over the body of little Mireille, over her face, and wetting the sheets.

She didn't move.

She couldn't stir; her limbs refused. The night weighed on her like the stories of the loaded wagon that had capsized on her the summer before. Only her eyelids were moving. She opened her eyes, then closed them. Though her eyes were shut she could still see.

Mireille wished that she could see nothing.

She raised her foot and looked at it as though it wasn't hers, as though there was only her foot in the bedroom.

In the light Mireille could see her toes at the end of her foot. She curled them, uncurled them, and watched them move. Then she stopped. She saw her foot as it really was: it was wax. She could no longer shake her wax toes, she could no longer pivot her foot around her ankle. She didn't dare touch her wax foot, even with her fingertips.

She wanted to yell, but she had lost her voice. She couldn't call for help.

Mireille especially did not think of her fear. She was busy instead watching the smile of Corriveau who was lying in her little brother's place.

Mireille had seen Corriveau sometimes when he was still in the village, and today she had seen his cortège go by.

Corriveau was smiling.

Mireille knew that Corriveau would get up. She waited, stiff, paralysed, mute. She waited dutifully. Then Mireille heard the sound of the straw in the mattress. She saw Corriveau get up, look in the pockets of his trousers and take out a match. He lit it with his thumbnail. He looked around him. Then he walked towards Mireille's feet, lighting his way with the match.

Corriveau brought the match near Mireille's foot. She saw little flames start up at the erid of her wax foot.

Satisfied, Corriveau went back to lie down in the coffin, which was in the place of her brother's bed.

Corriveau lay down, stretched out with satisfaction, and fell asleep smiling.

Mireille was suffocating. But she could do nothing with her toes, those ten little burning candles that were watching over Corriveau.

★   ★   ★   ★

Anthyme Corriveau and his wife had fed the Anglais as though they were boys from the village. They watched them. The Anglais ate little. They spoke little. They drank little. If one of the Anglais spoke, the others were quiet and listened. If a question were asked one at a time would answer. They didn't laugh: instead, they compressed their lips in a miserly smile. Anthyme and his wife could not understand what the Anglais were saying, but they didn't like to hear the sounds of their language because of their eyes. "Their eyes aren't frank," thought Anthyme. They had the impression that the Anglais were making fun of them when they spoke.

"We're all French Canadians here," thought Father Corriveau; "my little boy who is dead is a French Canadian, everyone is a French Canadian. The whole province is French Canadian, there are French all across Canada, even in the United States. So why did they send these Anglais to bring back my son?"

Anthyme Corriveau could not overcome a certain sadness; it was not because he had lost his child, but another sorrow that he couldn't explain.

Listening to her rattling saucepans in the sink the old man knew that his wife was not pleased with the way things had worked out.

"We were among our own people, all from the village," she was thinking. "We all knew each other, because we all live the same life; we raise our children together. My son is the son of the whole village. All the people who were here are a little bit his parents and I could even say that the young people were his brothers or sisters. Even when trouble comes to the village we like to be together; we all share the trouble, and then it's not so hard to bear. When we're all together we're stronger, and the trouble doesn't bother us as much. Why did the Anglais break up our get-together? My son would have been happy to see us all around him. But the Anglais have broken up our evening. I'll remember it for the rest of my life."

Mother Corriveau didn't want to serve the Anglais at the table any more. She offered them three or four *tourtières* and went into the living room. Anthyme put a bottle of cider on the table and found his wife kneeling in front of their son's coffin.

In the kitchen the Anglais were speaking in low voices, saying words that Mother Corriveau and her husband could no longer take the trouble to understand. Hands joined on the coffin, Anthyme Corriveau and his wife forgot about the Anglais whose voices came to them discreet, distant. The old couple were alone. It was the first time they had been alone with their son. They were close to each other as they had been on their wedding day. Mother Corriveau was wiping away tears as she had on that day. Anthyme's eyes would not permit tears but, as on his wedding day, he had a violent desire to cry, to swear, to hit himself, to break something. Had they lived their lives to come to this dismay, this sorrow?

The paths of everyone's lives, they were thinking, lead to the coffin. They could only accept that this law was a fair one. She wept. He raged. Mother Corriveau did not want life to be like this. Anthyme could not remake it, but he was convinced that if it was necessary for coffins to go by, and for life to stop at a coffin, it was not fair for people to have such an obvious love of life.

The old people wept.

What was the use of having been a child with blue eyes, of having learned about life, its names, its colours, its laws, painfully as though it were against nature? What was the use of having been a child so unlucky in life? What was the use of the prayers of that pious child, who had been as pale as the pictures of the Saints? What was the use of the blasphemies of the child become a man?

Everything was as useless as tears.

What was the use then of the sleepless nights that Mother Corriveau had spent consoling the child who cried from the pain of living? What was the use of the old people's grief?

Anthyme could not stay on his knees. He wanted to destroy something. He went to the stove, took some logs, and threw them on the fire. Mother Corriveau wiped her tears with her apron.

"God isn't reasonable."

She wanted to say that he was exaggerating, that he was not being fair. Anthyme came back to her. "It's not worth the trouble to have children if God does that," he said, indicating his son.

His wife thought of the others: Albéric, Ferdinand, Toussaint, Gaston, Alonzo, and Anatole who were in countries where they were fighting the war against the Germans. There was even Ernest and Nazaire in countries where they were fighting the Japanese. They were shooting bullets at this moment, without knowing that their brother had been killed. Mother Corriveau realized that it was night; no, right now her children were not fighting: they were asleep, because it was night. The thought reassured her. When would they learn that their brother was dead? Would they know before the war was over? Letters arrived at their destinations so seldom.

Suddenly, Mother Corriveau got up. An image had come to her, terrifying, an image to make her die of grief. She had seen in her mind the coffins of all her boys piled up one on top of another.

"Anthyme! Anthyme!" she begged.

He started. "What is it?"

She ran to him in tears, pressed herself against him. Anthyme's arms dosed around her.

"We have to say a lot of prayers."

"I'm going to the barn. I want to swear."

★   ★   ★   ★

Joseph-with-the-hand-cut-off was the first to dash towards the house. The others followed. He smashed into the door. The house shook as if a bull had fallen on the roof. The windows trembled. The door sprang open as if someone had pulled it. Joseph brandished his stump in its bloody rags. "We want our Corriveau! We want our Corriveau! You're not taking our Corriveau!"

Anthyme went to Joseph calmly. "Cut off your hands, cut off your feet too if you want, cut off your neck if that's what you want, but don't tear out my doors!"

Mother Corriveau stayed beside her husband, an iron pot in her hand, ready to strike. "I've just taken it off the fire, and it's red hot. I'll fry your face, you with the hand cut off."

The Anglais had got up politely as the villagers came in. Plates were broken on the floor, glasses too. Threats were shouted: "You won't get our Corriveau! Go back to England, *maudits Anglais de calice!* There's a train at noon tomorrow; take it and don't come back!"

A woman remarked, "He's cute, the little one there. Too bad he's an Anglais."

"A *Christ* of an Anglais," her husband specified, kicking her in the ankle as punishment.

"They aren't even real Anglais. They came to Canada because the real Anglais in England wanted to get rid of them."

"You're not taking our Corriveau!"

"Our Corriveau belongs to us!"

The villagers fought over the Anglais. Each of them wanted to catch one. When an Anglais was taken over by two or three villagers they shook him, pulled his moustache, flicked their fingers against his ears. The soldiers grimaced with disgust as they received right in their faces the alcoholic breath coming out of these French Canadians. They barely defended themselves. The villagers spun the soldiers around like tops. They staggered. The villagers pulled their neckties; shirt buttons went flying. The women amused themselves by groping at the Anglais' trousers; each time they found what they were looking for they chortled, "He's got one!"

Then the sergeant cried, "Let's go boys! Let's kill 'em"

The soldiers obeyed, attacking men and women. The villagers redoubled their violence and their anger. The Anglais defended themselves with their fists or their boots, their big leather boots; they struck out at faces, at stomachs, at teeth; faces were bloody; they trampled over bodies stretched out on the floor, crushed fingers, and fought with plates and chairs.

"You're not getting our Corriveau!"

"Let's kill 'em! Let's kill 'em!"

Mouths were spitting blood.

"Christ de calice de tabernacle!"

"Maudit wagon de Christ à deux rangées de bancs, deux Christs par banc!"

"Saint-Chrême d'Anglais!"

"We're going to get our Corriveau!" Bérubé appeared in the stairway again, barefoot, bare-chested, in his trousers. The uproar and the shouting had wakened him. He looked over the situation. He understood that the soldiers were fighting against the villagers. He jumped over the stairs. He wanted to smash some Anglais jaws. He'd show these Anglais what a French Canadian had in his fist.

"Attention!" shouted an English voice. Bérubé was paralysed by these words. The sergeant had given an order: Bérubé, simple soldier, was hypnotised.

"Let's kill 'em!"

These words brought Bérubé back to life. The soldier without rank obeyed as he knew how. He struck out at the villagers as though his life were in danger. He had to hit harder than the people from the village and harder than the Anglais if he wanted anyone to respect him.

Little by little the villagers lost the battle. Bloody, burning with fever, humiliated, disgusted, swearing, they went after each other, and one after the other they came to, defeated, their heads in the snow.

Outside, the villagers continued to threaten. "You're not getting our Corriveau!"

The sergeant ordered the Anglais and Bérubé to go out and end the brawl.

Under the gray light of the moon, in the cold air that seemed to be bursting into pieces like a thin skin of ice, the little war refused to be extinguished. It calmed down, then all at once burst out again, on all sides. People were twisted with pain, groaning, swearing, weeping with impotence.

Suddenly, a shot — dry, like the crack of a whip.

★   ★   ★   ★

Henri had run towards Anthyme's house, pursued by Corriveau's coffin which was following him through the night like a starving dog.

A soldier appeared before him. He thought the soldier wanted to arrest him and take him back to the war.

He fired.

The scuffle was over. The Anglais picked up the wounded

man, carried him into the house and laid him out on the kitchen table. The soldier was dead.

The Anglais carried the table and the soldier into the living room, across from Corriveau's coffin.

"It's very sad," said Mother Corriveau; "I have no more candles."

★   ★   ★   ★

Everyone got down on their knees. The Anglais prayed in their language for their compatriot. The villagers prayed in French Canadian for their Corriveau. Bérubé didn't know whether he should pray in English for the Anglais or in French Canadian for Corriveau. He started to recite the words of a prayer he had learned in school. *"Au fond tu m'abimes, Seigneur, Seigneur . . ."*

He didn't go on. The villagers were looking at him with hatred, the hatred they felt for a traitor. Because he had fought with the Anglais against the people of his village, Bérubé had become an Anglais to them. He didn't have the right to pray for Corriveau: their hard looks told him that. So Bérubé decided to pray in English. "My Lord! Thou . . ."

The Anglais turned towards him. In their eyes Bérubé read that they would not tolerate a French Canadian praying for an Anglais. Bérubé left.

Several bottles of cider were abandoned on the floor, open. He grabbed one and drank it. The cider gurgled, poured down his cheeks onto his chest. Then he went up to the bedroom where Molly was sleeping, threw his clothes across the room, tore off the covers, and threw himself onto Molly, without even bothering to wake her up.

"Ma ciboire d'Anglaise. I'll show you what a French Canadian is."

She dreamed that a knife was tearing her stomach open. She started. Then, reassured, she pretended to be asleep.

Bérubé grew agitated, frantic; he sweated, whimpered, kissed, embraced. He hated.

"Those *crucifix d'Anglais* sleep all the time. No wonder they have such small families. And when the Anglais make a war they come and look for the French Canadians."

Bérubé had spoken out loud. Molly understood. She smiled. Slowly, she caressed his back. He shivered.

"That *ciboire* will be the death of me . . ."

Molly mocked him. "Are you asleep, darling?"

★　★　★　★

Some of the villagers felt an urgent need for sleep. They lay down three or four to a bed, or on the braided rugs, or on the bare floor, or a fur coat. Several were sitting in chairs, another was on his knees before Corriveau and the Anglais. But most got through the night as though it had been daylight. The night passed quite peacefully. They chatted, exchanged memories, repeated the adventures that are always told on such occasions, counted the people who had disappeared, recalled Corriveau's deeds and gestures, ate *tourtières*, drank cider, prayed, pinched a passing bottom, made up stories, choked with laughter, and went back to their prayers, the tears coming to their eyes: such injustice to die at Corriveau's age while suffering old people were begging the Lord to call them to him. They blew their noses, wiped their foreheads, cursed the war, prayed God that the Germans would not come to destroy their village, asked Mother Corriveau for another piece of *tourtière*, reassured Henri who was desperate at having killed a soldier. "It was a case of legitimate self-defence. Have a drink! War's war." The women were sad to see their dresses in such a pitiful state.

The soldiers kneeling by their colleague dead at his duty were so attentive to their prayers that God himself seemed to be at their side.

"*Vieille pipe de Christ!*" said Anthyme. "Those damn protestants know how to pray as well as the French Canadians!"

Mother Corriveau announced that the time had come to form the cortège and go to mass and the burial of her son.

★   ★   ★   ★

Henri watched over the soldier he had struck down. The others followed Corriveau's coffin, carried on the shoulders of the Anglais and of Bérubé, whose services had been requisitioned.

Henri was afraid. He had deserted because he didn't like the idea of death, and now he was obliged to keep company with a dead man, a dead man killed by Henri himself. He was not afraid of punishment. That was war. During a war you are not punished for killing. Henri was quite happy that the Anglais had not attacked him in peacetime: then, Henri would have been punished.

He saw his body swinging at the end of a rope, suspended from a scaffold planted in the snow that went on as far as the eye could see, and his body had become an icicle; if someone had touched it his body would have tinkled and broken into splinters. Henri was cold; the wind whistled as it moved a dry dust that came to brush against his body, oscillating at the end of its rope. Henri was cold; he buttoned the sweater he had borrowed from Arthur.

It was the idea of being hung from a rope over the snow in the cold that made him tremble: it was a cold fear. He was afraid of this house where he had a dead man for company. He laid his shotgun across his knees. He did not want to pray for the Anglais. He kept quiet, waiting.

The wind was trying to take off the roof. Nails were crackling, beams were twisting and whining. Like a child, Henri was afraid to be alone with this wintry music. He wished that there was someone with him. Then he would not have been afraid. In fact, he did have someone with him, but it was a dead man and that made Henri ten times more alone. With a live companion Henri could have talked, shared some tobacco. But a dead man doesn't talk or smoke.

Henri listened. "What does a dead man think about under his white sheets? Does he hate the person that killed him? A dead man, if he's damned like this vierge of a protestant, does he burn inside before he's buried? Dead men get mad at the living. It's the dead who put the fires of hell into barns; you often see it: a house that bursts into flames all of a sudden, without reason, that's hell-fire. There are dead men who walk in the walls of houses too. We cheer ourselves up and say it's winter that's making the houses whine, but it's dead men . . . As long as we haven't prayed enough to rescue their souls from purgatory, the dead come back to earth begging for prayers, and if we don't understand they spread trouble to make us think about them."

Was it Corriveau climbing around in the walls?

Henri tightened his grip on the rifle. He wouldn't fire at the soul of a French Canadian. He wasn't afraid of Corriveau's soul.

But the Anglais . . . perhaps the Anglais would take advantage of his death to revenge himself for not succeeding in wiping out the French Canadians. Henri tightened his grip again: he was ready to shoot.

"If he comes I'll let him have a bullet right through the heart."

All the beams in the house were whining. Henri remembered an evening when he had been lost in the forest. Everything was so damp that it was impossible to light a fire. A soft, heavy wind had come up. Trees, big hundred-year-old spruce, waved their arms and sang like so many souls in distress. Afterwards, Henri did not know if it was trees he had heard or souls.

Perhaps it would calm his imagination if he stared fixedly at the Anglais. When you see someone motionless in front of you you know he isn't moving. A dead man doesn't move.

He was reassured. He was no longer afraid. The Anglais under his sheet was as well-behaved as a stick of wood. Even if all of a sudden the sheet moved, Henri was not afraid. He was not afraid because it was winter, and the wind could come in through a crack in the window, strong enough to make the sheet Mother Corriveau had thrown over the Anglais tremble.

The sheet lifted, and some hair emerged. Henri fired.

He was out of the house already, running in the snow.

Henri had killed the Corriveau's cat.

*   *   *   *

The priest was talking. When he opened his mouth his tongue looked like a toad that did not dare to jump.

"Veni, vidi, vici, Caesar wrote; Caesar, who like Corriveau, this boy of our parish, practised the most noble profession of arms — that most noble profession after the profession of holiness that is practised by your priests. It was of a military truth that he was speaking. If he had spoken of a human truth Caesar would have written veni, vidi, mortuus sum: I came, I saw, I died.

"My brothers, never forget that we live to die and we die to live.

"The short time of life on earth, this short time is far too long because we have enough time to damn ourselves several times over. Let us be careful that one day Christ does not get tired of wiping out, of washing our consciences; let us be careful that, seeing the deluge of our sins, he does not spill on your heads, my brothers, the fires of hell, just as he spilled on them, through the hand of his priest, the holy waters of baptism. Perhaps the war, at this moment, is a little like the fires of hell that God is pouring over the old countries which are known for their disbelief in the teachings of the Church.

"Life on earth is far too long for many of the faithful who

damn themselves for all eternity. Even some of my dear parish-
ioners have been damned, are damning themselves and will walk
for all eternity on the poisonous snakes of hell, on the scorpions
of hell (they look like little lobsters, but there are big ones too,
and they bite); their bodies will be filled with leprosy, the leprosy
of sin as it can be seen in pagan countries; they will wander, these
damned souls, through all eternity in flames that burn without
consuming.

"That is why we must bless God for having come among us to
seek the soul of our young Corriveau who, since he is dead, will
no longer offend God and the saints. Our son Corriveau, after a
life that only God can judge — but God is a fair judge and pitiless,
punishing the wicked and rewarding the good — our son Corriveau, dead in a holy way, fighting the war against the Germans.

"My brothers, this black catafalque you see before you and
under which our son Corriveau has been placed, you will all enter
it one day as Corriveau has entered it today. For you as for him the
six torches of the angels of the catafalque will be lit, symbolising the
flames that purify the sinner, these flames to which you will submit
because of your sinful voluptuous nature. You will submit to the
flames of hell if you do not live like the angels who carry them. Do
not lose sight, my brothers, of this holy symbol of the church.

"Because you are men and women, because the flesh is weak,
you are condemned to perish in the flames of hell, to perish without perishing unless God in his infinite goodness forgives your
offences.

"My brothers, every day of your lives, think, think several
times a day, that this catafalque that you will all come to will be
the gate of hell if you do not have a perfect contrition for your
faults, even for your venial faults, for God, all-powerful and
immensely perfect, could not tolerate even a venial imperfection.

"If you were in Corriveau's place this morning, Corriveau who died like a saint defending his religion against the devil disguised as Germans, would you be saved?

"I, your priest, to whom God has given the privilege of knowing, through holy confession, the most intimate secrets of your consciences, I know, God permits me to know that there are several among you, blasphemers, immodest, fornicators, violators of God's sixth commandment which forbids sins of the flesh, drunkards, and you, women, who refuse the children that God would give you, women who are not happy with the ten children God has entrusted to you, and who refuse to have others, women who threaten by your weakness the future of our Catholic faith on this continent; I know that without Christ, who dies every day on the altar when I celebrate the holy mass, I know that you would be damned.

"Let us pray together for the conversion of our sheep who have strayed . . ." Mother Corriveau was weeping; it was true, then that her son was saved!

*   *   *   *

Arsène was also the gravedigger. For him a death in the village was a gift from God, because he sold a pig to the stricken family and also dug a grave. For a long time now his son, Philibert, had been helping him with his work.

As a child, Philibert used to follow his father with his little shovel on his shoulder as he went to the cemetery. Arsène was proud of the child. "I'll make a good worker out of him." At this time Philibert was so small he could not get out of the grave by himself. Arsène would hoist him up in his arms, laughing. At times he would amuse himself by leaving the boy alone in the grave, pretending to abandon him there. In the pit the child would cry, calling to his father until he seemed about to burst. Arsène would not answer: he was seeing to other tasks. When he came back

Philibert would often be asleep. Arsène picked up a handful of wet earth and threw it in his face. The child woke up, bewildered.

"So, lazybones, asleep on the job?"

Arsène would bend over the grave, hold out his arms, lift up the child. He leaped to his father's neck and kissed him, furiously. Arsène replied, "A real female, this little *baptême*; affectionate."

It was of such good times past that Arsène was thinking as Philibert declared, from the bottom of the grave, "This ground is frozen like Christ's shit."

Hearing him, Arsène brandished his shovel and threatened him. "You little foulmouth, I'll teach you to have some respect for holy things."

He stuck his shovel in the ground, came up to his son, and sunk his boot in the boy's behind. The blow was painless because Philibert was used to it. He turned to his father calmly, "I'm not defending myself because you're my father, but every time you kick me I think how I'm itching to dig *your* grave."

These words shook Arsène more than a blow from a fist. For a moment, he was stunned. Arsène was no longer the father of a child, but of a man. Philibert had become a man. Time had certainly passed quickly.

"You're right, son. The ground is as hard as frozen *Saint-Chrême*."

"The ground is as hard as a knot in the wood of the crucifix."

"It's as hard as the Pope's mattress."

At each oath father and son bent over with laughter in the grave they had almost finished digging. If they had not had the walls of the grave for support they would have collapsed, they were laughing so hard.

"Son, listen to me. Now you're a man. You know how to talk like a man. Listen to me. Because you're a man I promise never to boot you up the ass again, except in special circumstances."

"Am I really a man?"

"Don't be so innocent — you think I haven't noticed you're like a little stallion in the spring?"

"It's true that I'm a man? *Hostie de tabernacle*, that's good news!"

"Yes, my boy, it's good news!"

Shivering with joy, Philibert jumped out of the grave. Standing on the earth that had been dug up he turned to Arsène. "*Mon vieux Christ* if I'm a man I'm getting the hell out. You can bury yourself all alone!"

"Little *Calvaire!*" roared his father.

They had to finish digging the grave. The earth was hard, chalky.

"Independent little bugger! At noon when you come to ask for your piece of meat I'll give you a boot in the ass. You're going to learn what life's all about!"

Philibert walked through the snow toward the station. He had decided that he would never come back to the house.

"If I'm a man I'm going to be a soldier like Corriveau."

Arsène went on digging. It was hard to loosen the earth. The pick scarcely bit into it. Arsène hurried.

The first few times he had done this work he had made a notch in the handle of his shovel for every villager who was buried. Now he no longer counted them. There was only a little bit of dirt left to remove, and all he thought of was that little bit of dirt. "This ground is so hard that Corriveau will stay fresh till late spring."

★   ★   ★   ★

Elsewhere in the world there was night, war. Harami, come to study commercial law in Europe, had been sent out to the backwash of the war.

His duty was to sleep for several hours in his wet, muddy sleeping bag so that he would be rested for the call that would sound in a few hours. He did not sleep. He was desperate.

Distant gunshots.

So many men had died beside him and everywhere in Europe and elsewhere, Harami had so often seen guts bursting out of an open belly, he had seen so many men drowned in the mud, he had seen so many limbs torn off, strewn over the ground like demented plants.

Harami thought of a man he had seen die, a new man, arrived that very day. Harami had found himself beside the new man at supper. He had asked a question that Harami had not understood. Then the new one had spoken English with a very heavy accent. "Are you a real nigger from Africa?"

Harami had been offended by the insolence of the question. "No," he had replied, with the unctuous politeness he had picked up in London.

"Is there snow where you come from?"

"In the mountains, yes, there is snow."

"*Bon Dieu de Christ*," exclaimed the new one, "there's so much snow in my village maybe that means I was living on a mountain too."

Harami had smiled.

"They probably haven't got any real toilets here," sneered Corriveau.

"The w.c.'s over there," Harami indicated.

"You've got to line up, wait your turn. I can't."

"Go over there, then, behind the hedge."

"Thanks."

The new one ran, undoing his belt. He disappeared behind the hedge. Harami heard a loud detonation: a mine. A cloud of earth was raised. Harami ran.

Once again there were several shreds of flesh, several bloody bits of clothing, a billfold. By reading the papers Harami had learned Corriveau's name.

★   ★   ★   ★

As they were leaving the church they saw the sky, very high, distant, deep as the sea where icebergs would be adrift, because the
clouds were white and hard under the sky; when they lowered
their eyes the snow was spread out like a sea too, as vast as the sky
and the water.

The soldiers who were carrying Corriveau's coffin dosed their
eyes because the snow reflected the light so brightly that it hurt
their eyes, tired from the night's watch. Mother Corriveau, in
tears, was leaning with all her weight on the arm of her husband,
who was not weeping but who kept repeating that it was he who
was being carried to the grave. Behind the old parents of the dead
boy they had left a space for the members of the family who had
not been able to come to the funeral. Then the villagers followed,
silently, this one of their own whom they were about to render
unto heaven and to earth.

The clock struck, marking the steps of the cortège. The slow-
ness was infinitely sad.

Little by little Corriveau was forgotten, they were so taken up
with hating the snow in which they were hobbling around, and
which was melting in their boots and shoes.

Finally they arrived, covered with snow, out of breath, wet
and shivering.

The soldiers placed the coffin on the two planks thrown
across the grave. They held themselves rigid at the sergeant's
order.

"Atten . . . shun! ! !"

The villagers were arranged in a circle around the grave.

The sergeant brought his bugle to his mouth, puffed out his
cheeks, and blew. The very earth wept under the snow. From the
depths of their memories of Corriveau alive, the tears came. Those
who did not want to cry choked. In her wedding dress Molly wept

beside Anthyme Corriveau and his wife. Only the eyes of the soldiers were dry.

*   *   *   *

Then, holding the coffin by cables they let slip between their hands, the soldiers lowered Corriveau into his grave.

Arsène prepared to throw the first pellet of earth.

"Wait!" the sergeant ordered.

He jumped into the grave, took the flag off Corriveau's coffin, and climbed out. "Now you can go . . ." The gravedigger hastily filled in the hole with snow and earth.

The priest in his long black cope threw holy water, which didn't take long to freeze.

*   *   *   *

For Bérubé it was not over yet. The sergeant ordered him to find a carpenter in the village who knew how to make a coffin.

Bérubé returned in the afternoon with a roughly made coffin. The Anglais Henri had killed was laid in it. The coffin was covered with Corriveau's flag.

Bérubé realized that his punishment was finally going to begin.

The sergeant ordered him to carry the Anglais' coffin with the other soldiers.

Without speaking, they carried away the body of the hero killed while he was doing his duty.

Molly walked behind them. Because of her white gown, she was the first to disappear.

*   *   *   *

The war had dirtied the snow.

IS IT THE SUN, PHILIBERT?

This story is dedicated to those who never told it because they wanted to forget.

TRANSLATOR'S FOREWORD

IS IT THE SUN, PHILIBERT? completes the trilogy that began with *La Guerre, Yes Sir!*, then skipped back a generation or so to *Floralie, Where Are You?* While the first two novels took place over long, drawn-out nights, here most of a lifetime is telescoped into a few pages. And while the first two novels had a rural setting, where the snow was so white it took a war to leave a stain on it, here the setting is Montreal, where in the first few pages Philibert, son of the grave-digger in *La Guerre, Yes Sir!*, finds the snow an unfamiliar element that tastes of mud.

It's not just the snow that makes Montreal a hostile environment for Philibert. His first encounters with the legendary English-speaking minority are devastating and in another personality might have marked the beginings of political awareness. But, although there are some resemblances to the real life of Pierre Vallières, Philibert would never think of himself as a "white nigger," or even as a Québécois. He considers himself, rather, "un petit Canadien-français" and a born loser, destined always to suffer at the hands of "les gros" — who might comprise anyone from "le boss" (who might speak any one of a number of languages, including French) to God himself. Philibert does take some steps towards rejecting his traditional role. By openly declaring his loss of faith and by changing newspapers, forsaking *Montréal-Matin,* house-organ of the then-ruling Union-Nationale party, for *La Presse,* he rejects two powerful institutions of the Québec of the forties and fifties.

He does not question the need to learn English to help advance himself, and in one of the novel's more poignant moments, when Philibert at last has a job that promises him a measure of self-respect, his first impulse is to change his name, to call himself "Mister Phil." Duddy Kravitz became Dudley Kane too, but Philibert is no Duddy Kravitz. His life is a series of put-downs and failures and his dreams of success seem sadly misdirected. "Philibert did not understand" is a recurring complaint. Duddy Kravitz understood only too well.

Readers of *La Guerre, Yes Sir!* should have no trouble understanding the curses and swearing here. The litany is much the same, with some emphasis on "ciboire" (ciborium) as a term of insult. Just as Anglo-Saxon four-letter words are rarely decorated with asterisks, many Québec oaths are written out as pronounced, as "crisse" or "tabernaque," for example. Roch Carrier prefers to emphasize the original intent of these blasphemies and to write them in their proper form.

Roch Carrier sees this account of one not untypical life as representative of what he calls the last third of Québec's dark ages. And, as in the earlier novels, he has used his incomparable humour to make it palatable, to himself as well as to his readers. Its ambiguous conclusion and title are suggestive of many more questions, not just for Philibert but for all the "petits Canadien-français — and for the Québécois as well as for the *Anglais, maudits* or otherwise. Philibert's story, like those that preceded it, may be at least as helpful as many official reports in understanding various public events and personalities. And certainly more entertaining.

S.F.

PHILIBERT WOULD NEVER forget the sound the crumpled paper made, green paper with gaily-coloured designs, pictures of snow, little red men, deer and spruce trees with lights on them. His mother saved it from year to year, smoothing it out with her iron and storing it away for the next Christmas. He had found a box wrapped in Christmas paper in the dust under his parents' bed. Wait until Christmas Eve to open it . . . but Philibert could not wait. He ripped open the package. In his impatient fingers the paper made a noise he would remember for the rest of his life. In the box there was a toy car. Philibert picked it up and ran happily to the kitchen to give his mother a kiss. His father grabbed him by the arm ("That toy's for Christmas. Not before."), snatched the toy away from him, threw it on the floor and stomped on it with that big leather boot of his that made the stairs tremble, and the ceiling on its axe-hewn beams; that big foot that could dig a hole in the snow big enough to hold Philibert like a grave.

"No! No!" cried the child.

The man opened the door and threw the flattened toy into the snow.

"In this life you got to learn to wait for things," the big voice told him.

The child looked for the remains of his toy in the falling snow. The car was lost. It was useless to crawl around and look for it, digging through the snow with his swollen hand.

Christmas drew near, like the muzzle of a wolf. There would be no present for Philibert. But under the tree, among the brightly-coloured boxes, there was a tag with his name on it. He tore frantically at the paper. The rustling sound delighted him.

The box was empty.

It was the box that had contained the toy car.

Every day he dug in the snow, looking for the lost toy. When spring came he examined the melting snow, waiting, hoping. But when the yellow grass appeared he was forced to admit that even though it was impossible, the toy had melted with the snow.

★　★　★　★

Every year, when the stubble in the fields was white with the first frosts and the trees' crooked fingers came through the windows to scratch at the walls and grapple with Philibert's blankets, a man with long boots and a red runny nose came to tell him a story, always the same one.

"This morning I was walking along the river, in there where the little trees are, you know, like little balls of needles. Nothing but branches; no more leaves. They whip at your face, those little branches. They're all stiff like porcupine quills. All of a sudden, what do I see but thirty-nine ducks. I could count them because they weren't moving. They were stuck in the river because the river was all frozen over. Just their necks were sticking out: thirty-nine heads squirming around and thirty-nine quacking beaks. Arsène, can you see yourself stuck in the river like that with nothing but your beard showing over the top? Philibert, can you see yourself, little fellow?"

The ice squeezes the ducks and pulls out their feathers. Their heads are drooping flowers.

The old hunter goes to look for a weapon and comes back to the river with a scythe as though he were going to cut grass. At this time of year! With one great swath he slices off several heads and they go skittering along the ice. The old man strikes out again and cuts more heads, which slide across the ice as they fall until finally they stop in their own frozen blood.

When his crimson harvest is complete the man takes an axe to cut, around the birds, the ice which is already softening in the autumn sun.

That night the sliced-off heads appeared like sorrowful stars. Red stars that cried out in the silence and bled onto Philibert. They slithered across the floor of his bedroom like snails, climbed into his bed and got tangled in his sheets.

*   *   *   *

His parents' bed creaked and groaned like a buggy on a bumpy road, behind the imperfectly joined green boards of the dividing wall. Every night Philibert was awakened by the noisy clamour in which his father and mother fell silent and even their breathing seemed to stop. Only the bed complained, creaking and crying, a tortured beast in the night.

*   *   *   *

The child was peacefully digging a little hole next to his father, who was preparing a grave for the coffin of one of the villagers. When the big hole had been dug his father went off through the muddy earth towards a little white cabin at the back of the grave-yard. Three or four coffins had been piled up there since winter, waiting for spring to soften the ground so they could be buried. Winter keeps dead men stiff and odourless.

His father pulled out a coffin, loaded it onto his wheelbarrow and tossed it into the hole which he hastily filled in with shovelfuls of dirt, as though he wanted to have it forgotten under the ground. What was there for Philibert to bury? The coffins in the white cabin were too big. Only his father could move them, and it was hard even for him. His face turned all red, the big muscles swelling in his neck, and he puffed like a horse. Philibert had noticed a white coffin, smaller than the others: the coffin of a child. He would make the grave he was digging a little bigger and put the white coffin in it. He was able to lift one end of the coffin and he could feel the small corpse sliding around inside it — was it the head or the feet that had struck against the inner wall? — but he could not lift the coffin all the way off the ground.

He went back to his little grave rather sadly and knelt down. He put his hand at the bottom and threw some dirt over it, saying that his hand was dead, the worms were eating it up, that his hand was rotting, it was damned, the fire of hell with all its shiny teeth was devouring his hand and it would suffer eternally. The child raised his other hand to his mouth, curled his fingers to make a trumpet, puffed out his cheeks and blew.

"Toot, toot, toot, ta-ta toot, toota, toota . . ."

It was the trumpet of the Last Judgment. The dead began to stir beneath the ground like dreamers clutching at the last remnants of sleep before it fled. Philibert pulled his hand out of the ground. It had not rotted. It was not pitted with worm-holes, nor had it been marked by fiery fangs. His hand was as new as the other one.

Next to him, his father pushed aside some dirt. It fell onto the coffin with a heavy thump. He was humming, unaware that the dead were stirring under their blanket of earth. He sang as he filled in the grave.

Philibert ran to the house, took a doll out of the box that served as its bed and went back to the graveyard. He ran among the white crosses and black epitaphs. Then he laid the doll on the floor of the grave, used his little shovel to cover it with dirt, and was finished at the same time as his father, who had filled in a man-sized grave. Philibert made a cross out of two bits of branch. His sister, in tears, was looking for her baby.

Philibert was happy. It was just like a real funeral.

★   ★   ★   ★

"Mama! Mama! I'm dreaming!"

The silence and the night had big hairy hands that pressed on his neck. Philibert was trembling, afraid. He got up, staggering with sleep. The earth beneath his feet was eternally still. He moved his hand towards some tall plants, but the stems and flowers and bushes and thorns slipped away as though they had turned to night. He looked for his village. He broke into a run. Tripped. Ran. His breathing was in the mouth of someone behind him. He climbed up the night as though he were going against a current. He walked. Ran. His village was no longer there. Nor the mountain. Nor the smell of fresh bread. The child was searching in the tall grasses of night as though he had lost a ball.

In the place where all the houses in the village came together there was only his father, tall and strong throwing the last shovelfuls of dirt onto a coffin. The stirred-up earth formed a lump that he flattened with his big feet. In the cool black night his father too was all black: face, hands and clothes. The sweat on his forehead was black as well. His father had buried the whole village.

"Mama! I'm having a bad dream!"

"Shut up!"

★   ★   ★   ★

Philibert and his father were running through the snow trying to catch a pig. They laughed at the ridiculous mass of lard trying to make itself agile, running away from them as it wept like a baby. The creature got stuck in the snow. Philibert and his father, taking their time, climbed on the pig's back to immobilize it. Seated there they were like two mad kings on a throne. Taking hold of an ear, the father planted his big knife in the neck of screaming flesh and the blood sprayed his face. The entire field turned red and the snow remained the colour of blood until the next storm. The pig squealed loud enough to burst God's eardrums, but the laughter of Philibert and his father was louder still. The pig seemed to grow silent only when it had been stretched out on a vertical ladder, its belly split open and its insides all cleaned out.

"It's got to be as clean as a nun's bum," said the father.

The boiling water was steaming away, sizzling on the animal's belly. And sometimes at night, when the wind was blowing, Philibert heard it cry.

On slaughter days his father talked in the morning at breakfast time, between spoonfuls of porridge which he gulped down with a grunt. On those days Arsène never beat the children. When he came back in the evening, his hands all red, if he did run after the squealing children it was not to slap them. His favourite would receive as a gift the animal's frozen tail, slipped into his shirt by a big cold red hand.

Arsène would have liked to find a job where he just had to kill pigs or cows, or any other animal for that matter. One day he asked his wife to write to an abattoir in Chicago to ask the head slaughterer if he might need the help of the best pig-sticker in the Appalachian Townships.

"There's no future in this country. You can't kill ten pigs a day. You got to have more people getting married or more people dying. Either that or we need a war. There's one going on but it's in the Old Countries so we've got peace here; but if I was ten years younger and I didn't have so many kids I think I'd have got on the train and gone away to fight that war in the Old Countries."

*   *   *   *

Philibert loved to watch the cut-off tongue on the floor. It was still. It had bristles. Then all of a sudden it would contract. It was the movement Philibert had been waiting for, but he was still startled to see the evidence of life in the dead tongue. It curled up, uncurled, seemed to want to have a life of its own, to go off and leap like a toad, perhaps turn around in the pig's mouth or run away as far as the horizon or fly off into the sky. Philibert stepped back; that tongue could very well leap up into his face and go right into his mouth. But it stayed on the big worn-out floorboards. It quivered and trembled and shook. Philibert was fascinated, but even though he was used to it he could not help being afraid. Every time the tongue was shaken by a contraction it was a sign of life that was not life, because the pig had had its throat cut.

In the big voice that whistled through his yellow teeth and spread out over his three-day beard, his father said, "Listen, son. The tongue's talking. Can you hear it?"

"What's it saying?"

"What do you thing it's saying? Prayers? It's talking dirty: pig-talk."

A burst of laughter split his father's face. It started at his feet and shook and inundated his whole body. Words appeared on his lips and flowed back into his laughter. Later, the child would understand.

Philibert sat down in front of the pig's tongue and tried to understand its language. Each tremor contained a word. He listened. The tongue spoke, dirty words. The pig's tongue cursed like a man. Seated in front of the tongue, his chin in his hands,

Philibert listened for hours to the pig's tongue uttering tremendous oaths, oaths that would make the ground tremble, they resounded so deeply into hell. The tongue uttered everything it knew about what men and women do together in their beds at night, or in the hay or straw.

"*Christ!*" said the pig's tongue.

Philibert repeated the word from the depths of his soul. When he was a man he would be entitled to swear out loud, to curse as loud as he wanted, like his father and all the other men. He wouldn't have to go and hide in the bushes at the end of the field when he wanted to insult the saints in Heaven.

"Tits," said the tongue.

Philibert thought of the dark dizzying pit he had seen in the opening of Madame Joseph's dress in church on Sunday when she bent over to genuflect.

Philibert listened for hours to the tongue uttering forbidden words, hoping that one day he would be a man. Then the words became gradually more widely spaced, the tongue was frozen in silence and it stopped moving. He was sad. Silence stopped his own tongue.

*   *   *   *

It was an old wooden house, always repainted white to erase the years. Philibert loved it, because in order to reach it he had to go along a dirt path that was almost a secret path. It disappeared beneath the willow leaves like an egg under a hen. When the light of day had left a bitter taste in his mouth Philibert would set off towards the house, walking under the canopy of fragrant leaves that sang softly for him. making the day fresh again.

With rough, resin-scented words his grandfather would reconstruct the past and the child Philibert shivered with the delight of being alive so that when he was old enough he too would be able to tell stories that would make children long for old age.

Today the hand of sadness weighed heavily on his back. He went towards the old wooden house. He recognized the road, the pebbles. The tracks of passing cars in the mud were a writing that he knew. But the willows had disappeared. It was as though they had gone back into the earth from which they had sprung long before Grandfather was a child.

The willows had been cut down.

The grass was pale, deprived of their green shade, and at the end of the denuded lane his grandparents' house seemed ashamed of its poor peeling wood. Rats had gnawed around the base of the house. One day it would tumble down. There would be no more willows to give the wood of the house the desire not to die.

Troubled and uncomprehending, Philibert pushed at the door as cautiously as though he were entering an unknown house. His fingers were clenched with anguish on the handle, which creaked because of the rust. Inside, his grandparents were sitting in their usual places, in their chairs that danced like ships on the seas of the past. Grandmother was embroidering a cushion; she said she was making a sky. Grandfather spat. There were pigs nosing about in the room. Philibert was amazed. He wanted to leave. One pig was dozing silently, leaning against a door. Another was tumbling down the stairs and its weight made the house shake.

"We were young once," said Grandfather.

"We were young like you," said Grandmother.

"We were younger than you."

"Now we're old."

"So, to give us something to leave behind for our children to inherit when we die, we sold the house."

"I had seventeen children in this house. It was in this very house that our children became men and women . . ."

"Nuns, a priest, farmers . . . a salesman, soldiers."

"Or they died."

"We loved it, this house of ours. When we bought it, it was already old."

"But it got younger because we were young."

"We were young . . . we loved our house."

"We sold it because our children are pretty fond of money."

"And inheritances."

Grandfather looked for matches so he could relight his pipe.

"They turned our house into a pigsty," the old lady muttered.

"But you get used to pigs."

"And you get used to growing old."

"But we haven't finished living yet."

Grandfather stood up. "Either they're going to get rid of their pigs or they'll have to get rid of my cold carcass."

He climbed up on his chair, pulled his shotgun off the wall where it was held by two nails. He opened the window and fired a shot, startling the animals.

"We want to live," said Grandfather.

"What's the good of living?" asked Grandmother.

★   ★   ★   ★

Here comes the procession. Under the polished Sunday shoes the street was quiet. The sun was caught in the monstrance that the Cure held at the level of his head so it seemed to be made of sparkling gold. God was proceeding through the village and his light was gleaming over the silence of the dazzled roofs. The green of the leaves became more intense and the oats bent piously and swayed. Jonas Laliberté and his wife walked behind the Cure, their eyes closed. They were not so lacking in respect as to dare to look at God. Behind them, accompanied by their godfathers and godmothers, followed their twenty-one children. The youngest was closest to the monstrance and the eldest was the farthest away.

Each day that one lives makes one less worthy to be close to God. The wheels of twenty-one wheelbarrows in which the twenty-one children were being transported turned with no sound from the axles, no noise of pebbles under the rims of the wheels. The wheelbarrows floated along in the light that carried them. The children were silent. Arms hung down from each wheelbarrow. Each one was filled not with a body but with a sloppy, spreading formless paste, where a head with lifeless eyes and a blissful smile floated. The big round heads would have tumbled outside the wheelbarrows and dragged the boneless bodies as they fell if they had not been held back by the godmothers' pious hands.

Jonas Laliberté and his wife murmured prayers. They owed much to God, who could have withheld his blessing from their union by giving them only a few children. But God in his wisdom had chosen to give many children to Jonas Laliberté. Jonas and his wife were grateful. They had been chosen to be the protectors of twenty-one little angels, chosen by God in his Heaven to represent his justice and goodness on earth. Jonas and his wife gave fervent thanks. If he had wanted, all-powerful God could have withdrawn the breath of life from these children who had been born as soft as cream, so the Cure had explained, but in the greatness of his divine wisdom, which is incomprehensible to mortals, God had breathed a tenacious life into these little angels whom he had created crippled so that they would receive a greater love. Jonas Laliberté and his wife murmured Hail Mary's to let God know that their gratitude was complete.

In the village street, which the women had swept clean in preparation for the divine visit, following behind God in his monstrance, the godfathers pushed the twenty-one wheelbarrows filled with faccid flesh, with enormous heads, with a tangle of wobbly arms. They carried the children that had come each year to remind Jonas Laliberté that God does not forget his faithful servant, but entrusts to him the most difficult tasks. The god-fathers gripped the handles with great care, if the wheelbarrows had been held less firmly the bodies of liquid flesh would have spilled to the ground like dirty water.

Philibert approached the road, a blade of grass between his teeth. He wanted to watch the procession go by. He wished he could be taken for a ride in a wheelbarrow like those worms with children's heads. But nobody ever took him for a walk. He was condemned always to walk on his own two legs. It wasn't fair that others always had people to take them for walks. He hated those monsters.

After the twenty-one Laliberté children came some hunchbacks, then the ones with clubfeet and those with one leg shorter than the other, followed by the maimed: those who had stopped a circular saw with their bellies, those who had whacked themselves in the knee with an axe, those with the print of a horseshoe on the forehead, those who had had a leg crushed under a tree, those who had frozen a finger during the winter, those who had been cut in the legs by a scythe, those with one bad eye. Finally, walking heavily, but submissive to the will of God, came the widows all in black, walking as though they were tired. All were singing:

Jesus, Jesus, Lord and King,
Jesus who turns the black winter to spring,
Jesus who gives us everything,
Jesus, Jesus, Jesus Lord,
Christ, have pity on me!
Yes, Christ have pity on me!

The rest of the procession dragged on in silence. The old men and women, the mark of death already erasing their features, walked slowly, their bent backs no doubt supporting an invisible burden, their unbearable memories.

Holding himself slightly apart from the others because he did not dare to close up the few steps that separated him from the procession, the child Philibert followed, not praying, and the pebbles pushed along by his foot were not silent. They rippled the silence of the pious ceremony like water.

The cortege followed the path that led to the villages on the plain. The child walked in the field that skirted the road, capering along without letting the distance between him and the others increase too much. He caught grasshoppers, pulled off their legs and threw the impotent little creatures into the oats. The sun, still very high, embraced the earth in its rays. The silence of the cortege was gently transformed into a long plaint, long as the sad wind above the oatfield.

*   *   *   *

Philibert, wearing clothes of his father's that were too big for him, was in a hurry. He was running away. He had already forgotten what he was leaving behind. He had forgotten the effort he expended at every step as he sank to his belly in the snow. He soared like a bird, all his wings offered up to the wind. Everything was erased by the snow. He no longer remembered his father and he had already forgotten his mother. The village was covered in snow. His memory was a white plain that stretched as far as the eye could see and his footprints were the first marks of a new life. His bony adolescent body was too narrow to contain his soul.

At each beat his heart said, "Farther, farther," and all down the length of his veins his blood repeated this word that rose to his mouth like a cry.

*   *   *   *

The truck stopped. Philibert woke up. The big man behind the wheel gave him a push, laughing. Philibert jumped, but there was nothing for his feet to dig into. He was in the middle of a street. The snow was brown. He raised his eyes and it looked to him as though ten villages had been thrown down, piled on top of each other with all their houses and churches and cars and old men. One day it would all collapse; the windows would break, the walls would tumble down, the bricks would rot one by one like apples on a tree. The streets would writhe and the old men would try to escape but they would be run over by the cars. He felt a pitchfork in his belly: hunger.

The walls receded before his eyes as though they were floating. The snow tasted of mud. People were walking behind one another, colliding, their heads pulled down between their shoulders. They were bushy, living overcoats. A door was open in front of him. Would he go in? A bit of warmth caressed his face. He would go in. He didn't dare. Where would this bus take him. anyway? He wouldn't get on it. The bus would take him some place and he would never come back. But it was warm.

"Why don't they build their goddamn cities like villages? Then maybe we wouldn't get lost."

He would not get on the bus. He would retrace his steps, find another truck and go back to where he came from.

"No. *baptême,* I won't go back to the village!"

The driver at the wheel motioned him to get on. He was getting impatient.

Philibert shook his head to indicate that he was not getting on, but he stayed in the doorway. The driver smiled. Philibert guessed that the man did not possess a spark of kindness.

The door closed again. The bus shot forward with Philibert wedged between the two halves of the door, his head inside and his feet, kicking, on the outside. The bus moved on, smug as a cat with a mouse in its jaws.

"Open up, *baptême!* Wherever it is you're going, I don't want to go."

With a broad grin, almost kind, the driver explained, taking his hands off the wheel to make elaborate gestures, 'it's free. There's just the King and the Pope that gets a free ride. And you."

In the bus there were heads sticking out of coats. The faces were broad and they neither smiled nor slept. They simply swayed with the motion of the bus.

"Let me off, *baptême!* I want to walk on my own two feet."

The faces glistened like the dough for the *tourtières* when his mother brushed melted butter over them. The driver's smile had nothing good in it.

"May the good Lord stick a cauliflower up your ass and the devil put cabbage worms in it!"

He burst into tears in the yoke of the two door-halves closed on either side of his neck. His jacket was pulled off his shoulders, but there was no more cold in the Montreal winter.

He hated his clothes with their smell of the stable.

Philibert would be as ruthless as he had to in order to survive.

The doors opened abruptly, the bus came to a stop and Philibert was ejected into the mud. He was on his knees, but he was not praying. He wasn't swearing either. He was hungry. He shook his hands to get rid of the mud and slush. The windows, like the faces all around him, were indifferent. Hunger was devouring him like a voracious rat. He had eaten snow all along the way, but in Montreal the snow was too dirty. If it were summer he would have browsed on the grass. No; there wasn't any grass in Montreal. Philibert saw nothing but walls and streets and a few passers-by bent over in the brown snow.

His feet were floating in a muddy stream.

Montreal smelled of oil. Cars screeched as they drove along. It smelled like a garage.

The houses seemed to be walking in every direction beside him.

*   *   *   *

There was a shovel stuck in the snow. He picked it up, slung it over his shoulder and took off. He ran among the men and women who were walking along with their heads in their scarves. Farther away, much farther, he stopped. He began to clear the sidewalk that led up to one of the houses, heaving big shovelfuls of snow. The snow wasn't muddy here. It was a white powder, where children could slide and roll and go to sleep. They could eat it or hide in it. But Philibert didn't see any children. The snow had a smell that was carried to his face by the wind. It was the smell of ashes. When he had finished digging the passage through the snow he would ask for what he had coming to him and go and find something to eat. There was a strength in his arms that would never have come to him if his father had asked him for help. Each shovelful of snow that he moved from the front of this house was as important as one of his heartbeats.

Then at last the path was cleared. The sidewalk looked nicely grey at the bottom of the trench he had cut through the snow.

He hesitated before the big oak door. But he was hungry.

A light was turned on behind the square of opaque glass. The door was opened part way. Philibert pushed. The round head of a little old man shone in the doorway.

"Shovel your walk for a quarter," said Philibert, holding out his hand.

"No beggars." In English.

He was pushed back by the heavy door. He hadn't understood a word the old man muttered.

"*Vieux Christ!* If you drop dead it won't be me that buries you."

With his shovel and his feet he put back all the snow he had removed from the sidewalk.

How much longer would he have to carry around that fiery stone in his belly?

In front of the neighbouring house he set to once more, attacking the accumulated snow. The sidewalk was long; the house was set back a long way from the street. In summer, when the leaves had not all been devoured by winter, the house must be hidden in whispering green music.

The shovelled walk looked like a very clean rug laid down over the white snow. When he knocked at the door he sensed someone moving behind it, but it wasn't opened. It was as still as a stone wall. He waited some more, then went away without throwing the snow back onto the clean sidewalk.

A little farther on, Philibert dug another path. His jacket was as wet as though it were raining, but his sweat turned to ice and he could feel the cold stiff weight of the wool against his back. He knocked at the door. A dog growled. He waited. No one came and the dog growled again.

Philibert threw his shovel as far as he could. He was hungry. Who would give him something to eat? He would steal, he would rob somebody. But before he did that he would try to earn a few cents. His father used to say, "It's easier to earn the first cent than the first million." Philibert had no desire to be rich. He just wanted to be able to eat. He went back to look for his shovel, stuck in the snow. His boots were filled with water from the snow melting around his icy ankles.

Would he have to clean the snow off all the streets in Montreal before he found something to eat? Philibert pushed his shovel into the snow, lifted the fragile blocks which the wind blew into flakes, and threw them as far as he could. The shovel made a small rough noise as it sank in, then leaped out like an animal that bit at the snow and leaped and bit and leaped along with the sighs that came from Philibert's chest. And then the walk was clean. Philibert rushed to knock at the door. It opened.

"No. No. Sorry." In English again.

The door was shut in his face, like a slap. He wanted to cry. But where could he stop to cry? What could he lean against to let the tears pour out until all the sorrow had been drained from his body?

He was hungry.

In this part of town there wasn't even any garbage lying around. There weren't even any frozen crusts thrown out on the snow for the birds. He looked around for cigarette butts, but these people were very clean and Philibert couldn't put off his hunger by chewing tobacco.

The street stretched out ahead of him; it walked too, just like him. The wall of silent houses appeared on only one side now. On the other side, behind the pillars of some naked trees, a snowy deserted park stretched out. The shovel on his shoulder, Philibert crossed the street where cars moved along very politely. He climbed over the iron fence. The ice in his clothes no longer tormented him. He smiled. For the moment his hunger was asleep in his belly. Playing in the snow like a child he started to write: with a surge of joy, laughing wildly, with a strength that would sear the concrete, Philibert stamped in the snow as hard as he could, spelling out letters, words, a whole sentence that stretched from one end of the park to the other, as though it were a white page. Then he jumped over the fence and into the street.

And behind the shadow of a window, an old lady with a string of pearls around her neck read in the snow words she could not understand. They said: YOU HAVE AN ASSHOLE INSTEAD OF A HEART.

⋆   ⋆   ⋆   ⋆

Suddenly the door in front of him was open. He didn't dare take a step. But the door stayed open. He moved one foot forward, one back. He barely moved at all. The door stayed open and the lady standing in the doorway spoke to him. He didn't understand her.

"If you talked French like everybody else maybe I'd know what you were saying."

"Oh! Poor boy. You don't speak English. . . Are you an Italian?"

And her strange accent made it sound like "an Italienne," an Italian girl. Philibert looked at her, bewildered.

"An Italian girl? *Baptême* no, I ain't an Italian girl. That's the most insulting thing I ever heard." Philibert turned, intending to leave.

The lady put her hand on his arm. He was a dirty, smelly little tramp with drops of ice on his face, but she could not let him go without helping him. His eyes were red and sunk deep in their sockets from exhaustion. He was so pale and his clothes looked so big for him.

God is cruel indeed, thought the lady, if he tosses these poor abandoned dogs into the streets of Montreal. Their parents must be unspeakable if they let their children run away so young instead of making a fuss over them. These children were too young to know life's hardships. This young man, for example: had he eaten today? And he couldn't even speak English. What a pity! These immigrants should learn the language before they set off for Canada. Could he be Yugoslavian, or perhaps Hungarian?

She looked at the young man at her door, pitiful as he was, but she saw only her son. He had been the same age when he left, laughing, his duffle-bag over his shoulder.

"Don't expect me home for supper, Mom! " he had said. He left with the Royal Air Force. He did not come back. But his death had contributed to the liberation of Europe. He had not died in vain.

The lady's eyes, fixed on him, reminded Philibert of his mother's. She had often looked at him with her eyes full of all kinds of things she seemed to see around him.

"Come in!"

As he did not understand she took away his shovel and leaned it against a wall, then, taking his arm, she led him down a long hallway that went into the kitchen. She pushed him towards the table and pointed to a chair. Philibert snatched a bun out of a basket. She poured him some tea. Philibert took another bun and shoved the whole thing into his mouth. The lady burst out laughing.

"You goddamn woman, if you're going to laugh at me I'm taking everything I can eat and getting the hell out. So long!"

The lady held him back with one hand on his shoulder. She said something to him; he could tell from the tone of her voice that she was not making fun of him. He swallowed his cup of tea in one gulp. She poured him another and brought more buns. Philibert enjoyed the sensation of the moist chewy paste in his mouth. The lady laughed as she spoke some more incomprehensible words. He replied "Yes sir," to everything she said. He didn't know any other English words. She laughed, but without making any sound. She only opened her lips. She seemed to be afraid of laughing. Philibert wanted to say something dirty, four or five oaths that would rear up in the kitchen like great bears. But she wouldn't understand them so he kept quiet. Beneath the embroidery of her dressing-gown her large bosom seemed to have been carved from warm stone.

He was still hungry when the basket was empty but the lady did not notice. How could he ask for more buns and make himself understood?

"Yum yum! Yes sir!"

The lady puffed out her cheeks and her eyes sparkled behind

the narrow slit of her eyelids. She poured him some tea which he drank, forgetting that he would have preferred to eat.

"Poor child . . ."

She was saying words he did not understand.

"Yes sir," he replied.

The lady guided him towards another room and opened the door. It was a bathroom like the ones he had seen in the newspaper. Turning the taps at random he felt a rush of cold water on his shoulder. He yelled with surprise. The lady called from the other side of the door. His jacket was all wet and the bathtub was full to the brim. He turned off the tap, undressed, stepped back, sprang forward and jumped in, just the way he used to jump into the Famine River.

The lady was knocking frantically on the other side of the door.

"Don't bust it down, you old bag," shouted Philibert. "Yes sir!"

The lady came in carrying a pile of folded towels under her arm. She put them on the floor one by one to soak up the water, rubbing them around with her feet, but she kept one in her hands. This towel, a blue one, she unfolded and wrapped around Philibert's shoulders. He was enveloped in a gentle fire, spread over his back by a soft hand. Suddenly his sex began to beat its wings. Philibert hunched over, his hands holding back the impatient bird. On her knees by Philibert, the lady dried his back, his chest, with motherly attention. Philibert wanted to hide his nakedness behind a wall. He grabbed the shower curtain, pulled it towards him and draped himself in it. The lady stepped back a few feet and looked at him with such tenderness that he felt something stinging behind his eyelids. He buried his head in the curtain. When he looked up again he saw the lady's hand gently opening her bodice, unbuttoning her dressing-gown all the way, then pulling it off first one shoulder then the other. The bathtub seemed as deep as the sea. At the sight of this woman's body Philibert knew he had nothing more to learn in life.

Between her perfumed, embroidered sheets, where she no longer looked like an old woman, sheets softer than her hands on his body, Philibert wept like a child without knowing why. And when the male strength swelled his body to bursting, he let out a cry like a new-born baby.

Then he went out into the street without looking back. The air had that clear scent that he attributed to the woman of his dreams, before he knew that women sweat when they love.

*   *   *   *

It had snowed during the night. Why did he not notice when he first looked at her that the woman was so beautiful? He decided to go back and clean the walk in front of her house. She would see him, open the door for him and give him tea and buns and perhaps a little money. She had already given him some clothes, but unfortunately her miserly husband hadn't left anything in the pockets. The overcoat wasn't new but it looked as if it had been made for Philibert, who seemed to have his fortune made already. The lady was so rich. He would explain to her that he couldn't spend the rest of his life sleeping in churches, on a bench near the organ. His story would make her sad. No. She wouldn't understand a word of it, but she would invite him into her bed and they would laugh a lot as they ran around the house, her naked as Eve in Paradise, him wearing her husband's pyjamas. He would take his pipe today.

The city shouldn't have been called Montreal. It should have been called Bonheur. Happiness.

He grabbed a shovel that had been left in the snow near the sidewalk.

His shovel on his shoulder, he was happy, dancing as he went off in the direction of the sweet lady's house.

The streets ran right across the city, stretched out, crossed one another, made knots, formed letters that could only be deciphered from the sky, proliferated like jungle vines.

All at once a street had moved imperceptibly, another had twisted, trembling gently, and it seemed to Philibert that the immense hand of the city was closing up. He would be crushed between these streets that looked so much alike, with their names that all sounded the same and their uniform houses.

He had no idea where to find the house of the woman who had changed his life.

*   *   *   *

Their jackets open to the wind that bounced off the buildings, two soldiers were zigzagging along the sidewalk arm in arm, not upsetting anybody because everyone moved aside at the sight of them as though they were kings. The soldiers were yelling rather than singing, yelling a song Philibert wasn't familiar with. They burst out laughing between the words, laughing so hard they could hardly sing. Their words slurred into their laughter and their song was so funny they choked on it. The song was in English. "God Save the King," the soldiers stammered, but Philibert didn't understand. He thought he was listening to a bawdy song. It was time to learn some of those dirty songs and stories they still kept hidden from him in the village.

He followed the soldiers from a distance, but he was determined to hear them. He laughed, came up behind them, spied on them; he laughed with them and without realizing it he imitated the crazy stitchwork of their steps. Then, all at once, he had caught up with them.

"What do you want, little *Christ?*"

"I ain't no little *Christ,*" Philibert replied, "I'm a little *ciboire.*"

The two soldiers, rather taken aback, fell against a wall and laughed. They laughed, all hunched over, and spat and slapped their thighs to punctuate their delight. If they went on laughing Montreal would drown in their joyous saliva.

"What do you want?" one of the soldiers repeated, hiccuping.

"The war," said Philibert.

"When you got a face like a little girl that's never been screwed you don't go looking for no war!"

"The war, that's us! Yes sir!"

"If there ain't no *tabernacle* of a German in Montreal it's because Hitler's told them Lavigueur and Lafortune are in town."

One of the soldiers came closer to the boy to show him a mysterious object. A photograph.

"Hey, kid," he whispered, spitting. "Want to see Hitler's ass?"

"Sure," replied Philibert, suddenly envious of the soldiers.

"If you want to see his ass just look at his face. It's the same thing."

Staggering, the soldier called Lavigueur drew back a little in front of Philibert, then hurled himself forward. His big nailed boot was sticking out in front but Philibert dodged it and Lavigueur fell down in the snow with a splash. Lafortune, choked with laughter, stammered, "You ready to do a left right?"

"Yeah," he repeated, "are you ready to do a left right?"

Lavigueur got up then and stepped smartly onto the street, marching as though he were on the parade-ground, with steel bands in all his joints.

"Yes," said Philibert excitedly, "I'm ready to do a left right!"

Lavigueur and Lafortune hugged him and punched him. They had found a brother.

"Left! Right!"

Lavigueur gave the orders, Lafortune followed, and behind them, in triumph, Philibert went into a tavern, drunk before he had swallowed a drop.

He grimaced at the bitter taste of the first mouthful of beer, but how could he help but be carried away by the shouting and applause and the wild stamping of boots that acclaimed his first success at emptying a glass without putting it down for breath?

He drank.

He drank as much as the others.

He drank as long as his friends.

Glasses piled up along with the bottles that littered the table.

"Make some room," ordered Lavigueur.

Philibert cleared the table with the back of his hand and bottles and glasses shattered and crashed to the floor. But the uproar of broken glass was drowned in laughter.

They were drifting on a river of beer.

⋆　⋆　⋆　⋆

Suddenly Philibert saw people in front of him shivering in the slushy street. Pedestrians were spattered by mud splashed up by the cars. He was wearing a soldier's heavy jacket. Sticking his hands in the pockets he found cigarettes and a wallet.

"Those soldiers are going to come running after me, the *calvaires!* Just let them try and find me."

As fast as his wobbly legs could carry him Philibert took off. He thought he had been running for a long time when he read, in front of his eyes, in big red letters, FORUM. It couldn't be. He came closer to read it again, to check that the big red letters really spelled out that word. They did. It was the FORUM.

"*Baptême!* I'm going to see the Montreal Canadiens in flesh and skates!"

He ran up to the ticket-window. "I'll pay as much as you want but you have to give me a ticket. I want to see the Canadiens."

Inside, he ran up the steps. The crowd was on its feet, roaring and waving their arms. The ice was shining at the bottom of a vast pit. Above it, thousands of open mouths were sparkling, thousands of fists were raised in the air. There was an avalanche of shouts.

The players in their coloured sweaters carved the ice like flaming bolts of lightning. Despite the beer that was bubbling behind his eyes Philibert could read the numbers on the players' backs. And there it was! Number nine, the great Maurice Richard, the man with dynamite in his fists, the rocket-man who sped across the ice like a solitary bird in the vast blue sky.

"*Baptême!* It isn't true! It's real but it isn't true! *Hostie!* I can see Maurice Richard. It can't be! I don't see him!"

Maurice Richard crossed the blue line, then the red line, into the territory of the *maudits Anglais* from Toronto.

"Kill 'em!"

Philibert stood up.

"Kill 'em, Maurice!"

Richard reached the Toronto goal.

"Shoot! Shoot!"

"Come on Montreal, shoot!"

"Shut up, you fucking queer!"

"Shoot straight!"

Feet were fidgeting under the seats. Each foot imagined itself in one of Maurice Richard's skates. Philibert saw a laugh on Richard's face. It was like lightning that smiles before it strikes.

Far behind, the Toronto players were gasping for breath. Maurice Richard was happy. He tensed his fists inside his padded gloves and tensed his biceps under his sweater. Maurice Richard was getting ready to shoot. One of the Leafs came up behind him, stuck out his stick at one of Richard's legs, gave it a twist and Richard tripped. The *maudit Anglais* had hooked Maurice Richard! They couldn't take it when a little French Canadian like Richard was better than them.

Philibert, swearing with all his might, jumped over the boards and ran onto the ice. Not slipping but walking drunkenly, he slid towards the Toronto player, who had his back to him. There was a wall of broad padded shoulders in front of him. Philibert tapped his back. The Leaf turned his head and Philibert's fist landed in his teeth. The player wobbled foolishly, unable to locate the ice under his skates. He teetered and then fell full-length on the ice, crushed by the laughter all around him.

Philibert returned to his seat hastily, leaping over the boards. The crowd applauded, but he heard nothing. He felt friendly hands patting his back and ruffling his hair. He was surrounded by so much warmth and friendship that he wouldn't need to be liked by anyone else as long as he lived.

Because he was watching through tears, Maurice Richard was moving down below with unbearable awkwardness across the ice.

★   ★   ★   ★

Philibert didn't find any more churches. All the temples in Montreal had been obliterated. They had fallen into the centre of the night.

Where would he sleep?

He followed streets as though they were his own footsteps through a forest where he would never again find his way.

Where had he slept the night before? He didn't remember, but his sleep had been soft. Tonight the darkness stuck thorns into his body.

★   ★   ★   ★

Philibert was naked in a big room with red brick walls and no windows, with powerful lamps that gave off a dry light. He was standing up. The floor was so highly polished that he could see in it the reflection of his legs, the black stain that was his sex and his belly. Across from him, far away on the other side of the room, were men dressed in khaki, standing pressed close to one another, very rigid and so much alike they seemed not to have faces.

"He's pretty skinny," said a man dressed in white.

"His feet are as flat as fried eggs," said another man who looked just like the first one.

From the laughter that shook their caps Philibert could tell that the men in khaki had faces — all the same face.

An old soldier with a long white moustache came forward, his medals clinking against his chest. His steel-tipped boots rang across the wooden floor. He ordered Philibert to follow him. Philibert walked behind, infinitely sad, up to the door of a cupboard where he had hung — for ever he thought — the clothes that belonged to the husband of the nice fat woman he loved.

★   ★   ★   ★

An endless staircase clung to the wall, winding like a demented plant in the rain. Philibert turned around towards the bottom, then looked up towards the top. It seemed as though he hadn't climbed a single step; the staircase stretched on eternally and Philibert climbed it, carrying the two cardboard boxes filled with clinking jars of jam.

The steps seemed to be getting farther apart and soon he would need another staircase between the steps, there was so much space between them. "That *Christ* of a staircase," Philibert complained. If Christ had had to carry his cross up that staircase he never would have made it to the end. "That *Christ* of a staircase . . ." Christ would have thrown his cross down to the bottom and it would have soared like a kite over the street. The children would have shouted, "Look at the plane!" The cross would have struck against a wall and rebounded off another. "That *Christ* of a staircase . . ." The cross would have gone sailing into a window and landed in a bowl of soup or on top of a floury rump bouncing up and down on a cackling housewife. "That *Christ* of a staircase!"

Was Philibert to be condemned to carry cartons of groceries up a staircase for the rest of his life?

He threw the two cartons over the rail. With his arms free he raced down the staircase as though he were being pursued by flames.

*　*　*　*

The long snowy season was over. The sun in the sky was as red as the heart in the pictures of the Sacred Heart. Philibert was digging a trench down the middle of Sainte-Catherine Street. His pick and shovel were chewing painfully at the street. He broke through the asphalt covering, threw aside the crushed stone and the dead earth that smelled of oil. The heat of the asphalt burned his eyes and his arms and shoulders rubbed against the rough edges of the hardened earth under Sainte-Catherine Street. The asphalt gave off a bluish smoke, like oil; the street breathed slowly, like a sleeping belly. It would be a long day. The pick knocked off small chunks of earth that were as hard as the frozen ground in winter; but this was warm, this dead city earth. The hole gradually became a ditch and sometimes Philibert looked away, ahead of him. The gash in the street might close back up and Sainte-Catherine Street would come together like the Red Sea. It could swallow up Philibert, who was determined to dig a trench as wide as his shoulders. On either side of his head tires squealed, biting, with a smell of burning rubber. Philibert drew his head back. The wheel aimed at his face and Philibert closed his eyes as he struck at the ground with his pick. The wheel went by without touching him, giving him only a mouthful of smoke that he spat out immediately. Sainte-Catherine Street is long and on either of Philibert's shoulders, bent around his shovel, tires screamed like circular saws. He turned his head aside abruptly, wheels passed by and returned, clattering like whips. Sainte-Catherine Street is long, and a pick is very slow in that earth turned into concrete.

Two well-polished boots sprang into sight. He didn't raise his eyes. A man was speaking to him. Philibert didn't understand the language but the man's words weighed on him, pushed at him. He speeded up his work with the pick until the polished boots had departed.

Sainte-Catherine Street is long. Philibert had never gone all the way to the end of it, but one day he would walk until it stopped somewhere. The ground was pitilessly hard. Philibert would be old when the ditch reached the end of Sainte-Catherine Street. If he never got to the end it would be because a wheel had crushed his head until it looked like a gutted cat lying in its own blood on the pavement, while his body would be stretched out at the bottom of the trench, ready to be buried. Philibert was digging his own grave down the middle of Sainte-Catherine Street.

It was true!

He knew it.

He threw his shovel under a truck that went roaring past.

He jumped out of the trench.

He ran across the street like a child. Without looking.

Then he disappeared into the city, far, far from Sainte-Catherine Street.

*   *   *   *

A brown wall pierced with windows as dark as the brick rose up before Philibert. Very high above his head pulleys were whining in their bearings. He pulled on a cable and his strength, multiplied by the pulley-block, raised the scaffold up into the wind. Was it the platform that was swaying, or the walls? He placed his hand on the brick. Everything stopped moving. The wall was upright, unmoving. He felt the steady weight of the wall in the brick, a tranquil strength.

Philibert's face was as dirty as his brush. He wanted to break the windows, punch a hole in the wall, let the cable slip through his hand, feel the burning of its fibres and then smash like an egg. But he was a man, wearing overalls, and condemned to clean away the black spittle of the Montreal sky.

He tied the cable firmly to make his scaffold fast. The sea of roofs beneath his feet was rough and dark.

An old bearded man had handed him a pamphlet that morning on Craig Street. He opened his overalls to pull it out of his pocket. The wind tried to take it away from him. Holding it tightly in his fingers Philibert read it through. "Men need a reason for living. Life is before us. At the very moment you are reading me, life should be beautiful."

"Life should be beautiful," Philibert repeated. "It's a *Christ* of a madman that wrote that."

He abandoned the printed sheets to the wind.

In front of him bricks were piled on top of bricks, cemented in the soot, extending in a wall from east to west, from ground to sky.

"Life should be beautiful."

Biting his lips Philibert attacked the brick as though he had claws instead of brushes in his hands.

"Life should be beautiful."

*   *   *   *

Machines for making the soles of shoes were chewing at the leather with loud cries. Then they were silent. The floor of the factory stopped vibrating and the workers tried to find their balance in the silence where their eardrums were ready to burst. Without speaking, they took paper bags from under their machines, opening them with caution as though they were afraid now that the sound of crumpling paper would be too loud. They didn't say a word. The knives that gnawed at the leather were still purring inside their ears, screaming insistently. And as he bit into his sandwich Philibert recalled what he had dreamed the night before.

"Hey you guys, want to hear what I dreamed last night? Even if it isn't dirty . . ."

The workers smiled, happy to hear a word above the mute machines; the dusty shadows disappeared from their faces.

"Old-timer," said Philibert to the one with white hair showing all around his greasy cap, "how long you been making boots? Since the war? You mean the first war, don't you? You never did nothing but make boots? And then the others came and they make boots too, and then me, I came and here I am making boots with the rest of you. We could go on making boots for the rest of our life. When we get to the Pearly Gates Saint Peter's going to ask us, What did you do with your lives? and we're going to answer, I made boots, if he's got any brains he'll tell us to go straight to hell, because it's one hell of a serious sin, spending your whole life making boots."

"What about your dream?" asked the old man.

"I always try to have dirty dreams," Philibert answered. "But this time I didn't make it. I dreamed I turned into a boot. Yeah, that's right, a boot. I was a boot and I was taking a stroll along Sainte-Catherine Street like a man. An ordinary boot. Believe it or not. I was a boot but I was thinking like a man. I was living like a man. On Saturday night when I went out to go dancing, instead of shaving my face I gave myself a nice shine. It's crazy. *Christ!* And when I went with a woman I was all nervous and I put myself away under the bed. When I got my pay-cheque I went to the bank. I went to work just like everybody else and I stood up in front of a machine for hours. You know what I did, me, the boot?

No? *Baptême,* I made boots! Then all of a sudden I started feeling uncomfortable. I felt my whole soul being squeezed like a foot in a boot that's too tight. I got sad. I didn't have the energy to get up in the morning. I came to my little square of space in the factory but I didn't go out dancing and I didn't go with women any more. I dragged my heel. I started to rot. I was sad. All of a sudden I heard somebody yelling, Hey, you down there, get to work. You don't get paid for daydreaming. I turned around. I was still a boot. I threw myself like a horseshoe and I landed right in the foreman's ass. I woke up right then. I wasn't a boot, I was a man. But I still smelled of leather.

"This morning when I was getting ready to come to the shop, standing in front of my mirror I couldn't look at myself without thinking that even if I looked like a man I was still a boot. *Hostie!* That's why I feel like booting somebody up the ass."

The old man blew his nose in his fingers.

"You want to boot somebody up the ass? Who?"

"The guy that's responsible," Philibert declared, as though it were perfectly obvious. "The guy that's responsible."

"The guy that's responsible," said the old man, "is the good Lord. He made the world the way he wanted, with rich guys and poor guys, with little guys like us and big guys."

Philibert gave the old man's lunch bag a kick that sent it flying into a pile of leather cuttings.

"The good Lord's like the boss. You don't get to see him too often. He doesn't hang around with people like us, the good Lord. Me, I'm getting out. I don't want to turn into a boot. Tell them to send me my pay."

The street didn't have its usual odour of damp leather and glue. It smelled good.

"Philibert!" somebody called.

He looked up. The old man was waving at him from a window.

Philibert answered his friendly gesture and felt a sudden urge to go back to the factory, because of the old man. What was it about that smelly old man that made him want to go back to his prison?

"Philibert," said the old man, "if your father had brought you up properly you'd be a real diamond in the rough. You could be a Prime Minister."

"I'm not made out of stone, old-timer. I'm not stone, I'm . . . I'm . . ."

The words didn't come to him. He looked at the man with a cane on the other side of the street.

He walked off in the direction of the Gros Jambon Tavern.

He waited for the old man over his beer. He would have liked to drink with him. Then he didn't wait any longer. And he forgot him. Drunk, he was still drunk, so drunk he forgot his whole life.

When he woke up in his little room, he noticed a newspaper open on the floor near his bed. He didn't remember buying it. His aching head felt as though it were being split open with an axe. The news-print formed a grey mass, like a city seen from a distance, a grey city in a black fog, untidy. Each little letter was a house attached to its neighbour, all of them knit together inextricably. It was a city, a real city. It was Montreal.

He heard the old man at the factory saying, "If your father had brought you up properly you'd have the makings of a Prime Minister."

Sorrow weighed on him, as heavy as a city.

*   *   *   *

Standing at the teller's wicket in the bank, Philibert felt as if his hands were paralysed. His fingers were unable to let go of the cheque that he held out to the cashier, his arm could not push his hand forward and his bones were too short or too long for his legs. He wanted to talk but the words turned thick, like molasses, on his lips. His shirt, soaked with sweat from work, smelled rotten under the arms and the filth from the shop was running down his forehead. He was dazzled by the beautiful eyes behind the grille. When the lips on the beautiful face parted gently in a smile, Philibert's lips came back to life at the same instant.

"Cash my cheque for me, gorgeous."

(He spoke loudly to give himself strength.)

"Do you wish to make a deposit, sir?"

"Maybe I do and maybe I don't."

The cashier was impatient.

"If you want to come to the Midway with me to see 'Tarzan and the Man-Eating Tigers' and go dancing afterwards, I won't make a deposit. But if you don't want to go out with me or if you're married you can put it all in the safe."

The cashier glanced professionally at the cheque, then she looked Philibert in the eye. "I'm through at seven."

Walking back to the bank all washed and shaved and perfumed, Philibert was so tall that the buildings drew back to let him pass. He contemplated the Savings Bank like a vegetable in his garden. The little cashier appeared in the revolving door, which at that hour of the day was being pushed frantically by people in a hurry. She was clutching her coat as though she were chilly. She passed in front of the dazed Philibert without seeing him. Then she jumped into a car that went roaring off with its door still open.

"Christ on a bun with onions!"

The car roared impatiently at a red light.

"Taxi!"

A taxi pulled up to the curb.

"Catch up with that yellow Pontiac."

He pulled a two-dollar bill out of his pocket.

"Hold on. This'll give you some speed."

The car shot ahead and Philibert sank back into the seat. Cars were coming from all sides. The taxi wove among the blinding headlights and caught up with the yellow Pontiac.

"What do we do now?"

"Follow them."

The two cars swallowed up streets, jumped across intersections. Red lights twinkled as the two cars sought and fled each other like lost lovers. They made unexpected detours. They squealed and growled like savage animals, weaving in and out of traffic, their wheels clawing at the highway, the bodies seemingly on fire.

The pavement was in an uproar. The two vehicles howled, the yellow Pontiac and the taxi. They barked and hurled insults at each other. They moved along towards the yellow spring that was the sun until the Pontiac seemed to sink into it.

"Stop!" Philibert yelled. "Stop!" he repeated, pounding on the taxi-driver's back.

As he braked the car the road moaned and there was a smell of scorched flesh.

"Stop! Are you deaf? I don't want to get myself wiped out here!"

With difficulty, the taxi reined in. Before it had come to a complete stop Philibert turned his pockets inside out to empty them of money.

"I'm getting out of here."

He jumped out of the car, which was still moving, squealing along the pavement. Ahead of him the Laurentians looked like the muscular arms of men. It was almost winter.

He had to go back to Montreal, back to his new room. Perhaps the landlord had replaced the cardboard in the broken window-panes with glass. Philibert turned his back on the mountain.

Cars punched holes in the air around him.

He leaned against a fence. Cars swam through the night like luminous fish. He wouldn't be happy until he owned a yellow Pontiac.

Philibert saw himself in his long yellow Pontiac, pushing the chrome-plated buttons, the ground rolling by under him at whatever speed he commanded.

★   ★   ★   ★

He tore open the envelope with trembling hands.

How could the letter have come all the way here to this room where the water-pipes rumbled like a hungry belly?

His letter quivered before his eyes like the flame of a little lamp in the window of his childhood. He was sorry that his childhood was so far away. He was sorry that he was so far away. Life back there was waiting for him with the fragrance of fresh bread. Tears came to his eyes. It was too sad, the life of the people he had left behind. It was like a quiet nightmare. Montreal weighed on his shoulders like a stone, but he was free. He was free, but the people in the village were crushed beneath their sky. Through his tears Philibert read the words that had the shape of what he knew best, his village. "My dear boy . . ." (Was it his mother's hand that had trembled? Or was it his own hand, with its black fingernails, clutching the letter?)

"Did you hear in Montreal that your Uncle Fabien got himself ruined by some Montreal robbers, three of them and they only talked English, they said their names but it wasn't their real names so we don't even know who it was that ruined your uncle and he told me that he hasn't seen you for a long time and he'd love to see you and he said you must be a real gentleman by now with a moustache but I said to Fabien Philibert's still young, he's got to earn his living, he won't forget us, he'll come and see us when he can. Your Uncle Fabien had to mortage his land that was all paid for for the simple reason that our late father, your grandfather had sold it to him for ninety-nine cents cash on one condition only that the daughter-in-law, Fabien's wife, had to take care of the old man and our late father couldn't get out of his bed to eat before he died and he used to spill his pea soup on the sheets so the daughter-in-law used to insult poor Fabien till our poor father died and Fabien was working on the land since he was twelve and if any oats grew up in between the rocks it was from Fabien's sweat and because the priest came and blessed his fields with holy water every summer because God's blessing works very well for oats and also anything else a man decides to do, so anyway you could say that Fabien's land belonged to him and even if he was our father's favourite he didn't steal that land because if you ask me he took just as good care of it as our late father. That was his land, Fabien, maybe you remember or maybe you don't but anyway he never said my land's going to give so much oats, he said I'm going to give so much oats and he never said my cow had a calf but I had a calf and he wasn't wrong either. But anyway Fabien lost that land of his. Poor Fabien, it isn't his any more because he mortaged himself. On the train to Québec City, the long one that goes through Valley Junction, he met these three *Anglais* that didn't speak a word of French and they were going to come and build a factory right here in our village. So Fabien mortaged his land and signed a cheque for five thousand three hundred and fifty-two dollars and each one of the three *Anglais* signed one too just like it, they'd been drinking in the train a little but when you're on a trip you're on a trip. So anyway two weeks later the three *Anglais* came to give him a diploma that said he was a vice-president, not the same vice that's in the catechism, but anyway Fabien was going to have a job at the factory he wasn't over the *Anglais* but he was just as important and he had this diploma that had official signatures on it but you couldn't read them. So Fabien managed to sell them the wood they needed for their building and the *Anglais* accepted because he made them a little refund, you can't get something for nothing, and these big trucks came from Montreal, great big red ones if you ever see any, but the *Anglais* weren't driving them it was French Canadians like us and they took the wood in their trucks that looked as if they were going to collapse and Fabien hasn't got his Ford any more and he had to pay for his land just as if our late father hadn't already paid for it so anyway he wanted to get a lawyer to defend him and so he had to mortage his cows and the lawyer sold the cows and afterwards he said the *Anglais* had acted within the law and you couldn't do anything against the law and poor Fabien said the only thing he had left that wasn't mortaged was his dink and at his age . . . So you see you shouldn't get carried away with ambition. Have you got a cold or the piles?

"Your mother who doesn't forget you and who you don't forget and who prays to the good Lord for you."

Philibert could read no more because of the tears that were veiling his eyes.

He opened the vent in the window part way and dropped the little bits of the torn-up letter down among the kleenexes that blew in the wind.

* * * *

The scraps of the letter fluttered and fell for so long that it seemed there was no ground to stop their fall.

In order not to be sad, Philibert had forgotten. He had forgotten, as a traveller gradually abandons his baggage in order to make the route less painful. He did not want his eyelids weighed down with tears that would never flow.

Because he refused to be sad Philibert covered his father in an oblivion that was heavier than the damp earth. He forgot his mother because he did not want to encounter his memories of her at the corner of the street, nor see her face reflected in a window or in the sooty bricks. How could he think of his mother without being too sad to go on living? How could he think of his mother, that frail young girl who didn't dare to smile in the old photograph in the album? How could Philibert keep from weeping at the memory of that young girl he had never known? The beauty had been destroyed by her children as by voracious ants. The children had nested in her belly, distended it and made her breasts sag, swelled the legs that Philibert had glimpsed dark beneath her long skirts. Nights without sleep had taken the colour from her face and the children who had died drifted in the murky water of her eyes. Her fourteen children continued to cling to her breast as though they had never been severed from it.

When Philibert held a young girl's body in his arms he was afraid to break the thin mirror that reflected his joy. A fat old woman might spring out of it.

★   ★   ★   ★

Before he went to work Philibert gulped down a sandwich. His newspaper was open at the financial section. What was the meaning of the long columns of figures, all the fractions and letters running down the page? It was written in French but for all he understood it might as well have been Polish.

"When I think about all the things I don't know . . ."

Someone scratched at his door. Philibert recognized his landlord's manner. The little man with red hair beckoned to Philibert. His wife was waiting for him in the hallway, wearing a black dress as she always did, but today her dress hung to her heels.

"We've found out a lot of things," the obsequious little man whispered.

"So we've decided it's time to teach you some too," the little woman went on.

"Come . . ."

The little man opened a door, the one to the most peaceful room on the ground floor. Philibert thought no one lived in it. The doorway was veiled by a heavy black curtain that the little man raised with a religious hand. Philibert hesitated. What did they want of him? The woman gave him a motherly push. The black curtain smelled like a church. Philibert moved it aside and entered the room. One candle shed a meagre light in the black room. The door closed again. The lock clicked. The woman replaced the curtain. She and the man each took one of Philibert's arms and led him to the flickering candle. There was not enough light to see, but Philibert suspected that the walls were covered with black draperies. They came to a table, covered with a black cloth on which the candle had been placed. Near the candle there was a black shape. A box.

"Now," the little man whispered, "you are going to become a man."

"Now," said the woman, "you are going to learn the only thing a man needs to know."

Because he was uneasy Philibert teased them.

"There's only one thing a man's got to know and lots of girls have showed me before now."

The little man clapped his hand over Philibert's mouth.

"Don't blaspheme on the day of your birth."

He took his hand away and turned towards the candle.

"Come."

His hands, lit by the yellow flame, lifted the cover of the black box. The woman held the flame over it. Philibert started as though a bat had brushed his face with its wings. In the mixture of light and shadow he could see, lying in the box, a little white skeleton with minuscule bones.

"What's that?" he asked, restraining a shriek.

"That is life," said the little man.

"That is life," echoed his wife.

"We do not die."

"We do not die."

The little man replaced the cover, tenderly.

"Kneel," he ordered.

Philibert had no intention of disobeying. The man went to the other side of the table and stood across from Philibert. With a look of infinite hardness, a hardness that Philibert did not know he possessed, the man spread his arms and cried, in a voice that seemed to want to tear the city apart, "We do not die. We do not die. We do not die. We do not die. The body that is placed in the earth is a seed of life. We do not die. We do not die. The seed germinates and another life comes out of it, a human being who is purified of life. We do not die. We do not die. To die is to live. To live. Our child lives!"

Philibert's knees were riveted to the floor. He lacked the strength to get up and leave, to spit out the disgust that was welling in his throat. He heard his tight-pressed lips repeat, "To die is to live."

★   ★   ★   ★

"Goddamn *papier*!"

"It's a *journal*, boss; not a *papier*. It's *Montréal-Matin*."

"Throw away that goddamn paper! *Travaille*. Money."

Big Papatakos, shouting, yanked the newspaper out of Philibert's hands. His fingers, stained brown from garlic and tobacco, made dollar-counting gestures under Philibert's nose.

"Money! Work! That's the life!"

The big hand pushed Philibert down to the cellar. Papatakos had taken away the electric lights, and it was like night down there, as dark as the time before Creation. Electricity isn't cheap.

The Greek had told Philibert, "It's a job you can do with your eyes shut."

So the young man acquiesced to show that he had lots of experience in this kind of work.

"If you can do it with your eyes shut I guess you don't need any lights."

Philibert was condemned to peel potatoes in total darkness. When he went upstairs for his meal the light, made cloudy by the greasy window of the *Chez Papa* Restaurant, scratched his eyes.

Sometimes a burst of laughter would leap at his face like a rat. Rats. He had heard them nibbling along one of the walls, their claws digging into the wood of the boxes that had been abandoned along with their rotting contents. Sometimes he heard them rummaging among the sacks of potatoes. The laughter came from the back of the cellar, from the other side of a wall that his eyes, grown used to the night, could make out in the solid shadow.

On the other side, a woman was laughing. She laughed often, harshly, as though she were a little bit afraid, a little bit amused, he thought. Each time, he gave a start. And now, as her laughter tore the cellar night, Philibert threw a potato at the wall. The projectile bounced back and there was no reply. Philibert went on with his work. The clammy potato peelings wound around his wrist and the potato slipped between his fingers. To forget, he started to think about what he had read in the newspaper.

The Government had built a bridge in a flat pasture where there was neither a river nor a stream. There was no road leading to the bridge; there wasn't even a road to the pasture. The Minister who had ordered it to be built had told the reporters, "Our party has given you a bridge; you can trust us. Soon we'll give you a river to go under it, to say nothing of a road that will lead directly to this magnificent bridge, built on the model of the most modern bridges in America. It's clear proof that our little French

Canadians can be the geniuses of modern technology. Here's what we're going to do. We'll put boats on the river if you like. Our party wants to guarantee that there's work for the French Canadians in Québec. Without taking anything away from the *Anglais*, of course, who are at home here too. We will not tolerate having French Canadians condemned to unemployment here in *la belle province*. We'll build bridges where we want them. That's our absolute, our inalienable right under the Constitution of 1867. Our party builds and creates jobs — thousands of jobs, 100,000 jobs — while the Opposition weeps and moans and claims it isn't a good idea to give work to the heads of good honest Catholic families. No, the Opposition will never stop us from building our bridges. There are two kinds of people who disapprove of this bridge: the Opposition and the Communists. Are you with us or with them?"

Philibert tossed a potato in the air: the Minister's brain. But perhaps he was very intelligent?

Philibert had read another article, hidden away on the page with the birth and death announcements. "Plain Talk from a Psychologist to the People of Québec." Philibert could see the short article as clearly as though he had the printed page before his eyes. "Following investigations and in-depth studies we can now say with certainty that the chief obstacle for the young man from the lower strata of society is his fascination with failure. The young man from these strata of society prefers failure to success. He devotes his whole life to preparing for his failure. This young man has only one basic desire: to punish himself for his deprived childhood. A lifetime of failure, following a modicum of success, is a fair punishment for him, according to statistics from the Michigan Institute of Psychology. In conclusion, we would say that the young man from modest surroundings should be informed of this danger, and quickly. As he travels the road of life the young man must ask himself, Am I preparing for success or for failure?"

In the cellar of the *Chez Papa* Restaurant, in the rotten night that recalled to Philibert the muddy earth his father dug in the spring, he repeated, "Am I preparing for failure?"

Then all the streets of Montreal were leading him to failure. When he had travelled all the roads that lay in wait for him and all the streets that appeared before him, Philibert would drop from exhaustion and he would have to say, "It was all useless." He carried the embryo of failure inside him. It was growing and it would feed on him until it devoured him from within. One day when it was big enough the embryo would tear Philibert apart; it would get out and fall on him, it would crush him like a rock.

There in the night Philibert hurled his knife and heard it sink into the wall. He ran up the stairs into the restaurant as though a dog were after him. He pushed the door and ran right into Papatakos whose greenish face had been invaded by fat smiling jowls.

"*Argent*. Money. It's payday. Here's your money."

The Greek pulled a little bundle of bills, folded in four, out of the pocket of his shirt and held them in his fat fingers, which looked like the pickles on display in his front window. But he didn't give them to Philibert.

"What will you do with all this money? You want to go direct to Heaven?"

The big cheeks, spluttering, came close to Philibert's ear. The whispers changed to little snickers that must have made the cockroaches jump. Philibert laughed a little. Papatakos had moved back to wait for his answer. He gave in. Then Papatakos put his arm around Philibert's shoulder affectionately while with his big hand he replaced the little packet of dollars that Philibert had earned in the pocket of his greasy shirt.

Papatakos led Philibert to a door marked "Out of bounds

Administration." He opened the door and gave Philibert a fatherly push. Philibert's heart beat like the wings of a bird on its way to Heaven, but his feet trembled as they sought the first step leading to the cellar, which was not completely dark. The last step disappeared into a damp curtain that smelled of tobacco. Behind it, he could make out a lighted lamp.

"Come in." said a woman, indifferent.

Philibert pushed aside the curtain which slid along a horizontal track. A woman was stretched out on a bed, wearing a bathrobe. She didn't take her eyes from her magazine to look at him.

"Take off your clothes," the woman ordered, her lips moving around a cigarette.

To show her that he wasn't trembling as he looked at her, and that she wasn't the first woman he had seen in a bed, Philibert undid his fly. But he knew that the woman could guess, as each button slipped through the buttonhole, that a sad clock was striking inside him. His pants dropped to the floor. The woman put down her cigarette without extinguishing it, put her magazine by the pillow and took off her bathrobe. Lying down again, she picked up her magazine and her cigarette.

As he climbed the stairs he felt as if his body had been flayed. He was sad. When the woman was in his arms he had wept because he felt so little joy. He was hungry. He'd given Papatakos his week's wages so he could go to Heaven. But where would he go for a meal?

The Greek saw him come up from the cellar and a greenish smile spread over his coarse features.

"I'm going to peel you some potatoes," said Philibert. "Can I get my pay right away?"

"Go on, go on, young man. Time is money."

There was a grease-spattered photograph hanging near the door to the cellar. Philibert had looked at it many times as he

passed. It was a picture taken at Papatakos' wedding. The inane
smiles radiated joy under the gummy glass. This time though, the
picture held Philibert's attention. He couldn't take his eyes off it.
The woman on Papatakos' arm. younger but quite recognizable,
was the one Philibert had just left in the bed in the cellar.

The cellar's mouldy breath did not relieve Philibert's heart. He
found his potatoes. The knife made a damp little sound under the
peel that slid around his wrist like a long worm.

In this cellar, under the beams, the night seemed like coarse
black earth, stinking and heavy, that had been poured over
Philibert.

Perhaps it was sunny outside in the city, with people coming and going, hurrying and loitering, thousands of feet passing
over his head. Life was not for him. He was buried while others
enjoyed themselves.

On the other side of the night, from behind the. partition, a
coarse laugh exploded. The woman hadn't laughed when she was
with Philibert. Why was she laughing now? He grabbed a handful of potatoes and bombarded a wall with them. He threw his
knife somewhere, shot up the stairs, pushed the door as though he
wanted to tear it off its hinges and went up to Papatakos. Placing
his feet firmly on the floor, puffing out his chest, he announced,
"I'm getting out."

Papatakos didn't understand. He grimaced, but he didn't
laugh. He wiped his hands on his shirt, glistening with oil.

"Papa . . . takos," said Philibert, "I'm going because when I
look at you I don't know if it's your face I see or your wife's rear
end."

Outside, he spat in the face of spring.

$$\star \quad \star \quad \star \quad \star$$

Philibert sold his watch so he could eat that night. He picked at a cold ham omelette that didn't taste very good. He didn't like ham and he didn't like eggs. His fork gave up and clinked against the empty beer bottles in front of him. He talked. He was alone in a corner where the yellow light of the Leonardo da Vinci Pizza Hot Dog turned grey.

"Can anybody prove to me that I was put on this earth just to peel potatoes for Papatakos? It isn't fair. If there was any justice everybody would have to peel potatoes. But then there'd be too many people in the cellar. If you're looking for real justice, everything fair, you'd have to look in Heaven. But you can't find Heaven. It doesn't exist, no more than I've got tits. Papatakos' wife's got nice big tits but that doesn't mean there's a Heaven."

Three faces near his table were listening to him with religious attention, as though his voice were the voice of their own thoughts.

"The *Anglais* made the war because they had factories. They built tanks and machine-guns and rifles. Then they shit gold turds like the priest's servant's holy dog. The French Canadians didn't want the war though. Oh no, they were scared of the war like they're scared of the devil, *hostie*. They didn't have any factories, the French Canadians. No weapons to sell, no boots, no cannons. They didn't want the war because they were afraid they'd lose their arms and their legs and the thing they use to plough their wives. Some day the French Canadians are going to have their own factories and when they do they'll make war on the *maudits Anglais* to make the wheels turn in those factories. And when there isn't a single *maudit Anglais* left the French Canadians will make wars with each other. And then the French Canadians will shit gold nuggets too, *hostie!*"

He emptied another glass.

"I would've liked to go to the war, to get away from things, jump over the wall. I didn't ask to be born. It's like a kick in the ass. I've been wondering why ever since."

Philibert was silent. The beating of his heart resounded in his temples but it was beating for nothing; his hands were calloused from all the painful jobs they had done, for nothing. He breathed for nothing, he had been born for nothing, he got drunk for nothing. And it was for nothing that he had left his village where people died for nothing like dry trees. Those people made children for nothing, and they had spent their lives in fear and poverty for nothing. The long road that had brought Philibert to Montreal had led him to nothing. And it was for nothing that he came back to his miserable little room every evening, the bitter taste of the day's work in his mouth. It was a taste that made him want to vomit as though he had wiped the filthy streets of Montreal with his tongue.

"You live. Then all of a sudden you're dead. If you're rich your soul rots like an old potato. If you're poor you get wiped out by a bus or maybe a truck . . . squashed like a flea. Ah, Christ! What did I want to say? Doesn't matter. Whether I talk or shut up the world's going to stay under my feet and the moon's going to stay up there like an *hostie* of a nun's fat white ass."

*   *   *   *

Philibert was on his knees on the floor of the Leonardo da Vinci Pizza Hot Dog. His pants were wet from the soapy water on the linoleum and his hand had gone to sleep as he pushed the slimy rag back and forth. His shadow followed his motions without becoming completely indistinguishable from the grey linoleum.

Behind the drawn curtains, by the miserable light of the one lamp the Italian allowed him to leave on, Philibert tried to picture women's faces, but it seemed as if the wet rag had wiped out their images too. Philibert's hand wandered under the tables, slid between the legs, under the benches. He murmured names, but the names refused to assume their fleshly forms in this night of his memory. Philibert was alone. He was sad to be so alone and proud to be so sad. In this way he could insult life. Nobody loved him; that didn't wipe him out. Animals in the field don't love each other, why should men?

When he had picked up the cigarette butts and wiped up all the mud and stains, Philibert replaced the chairs; then, folding the newspaper he always carried in his pocket, he sat down in the boss's place in front of the cash-drawer. He lit a cigarette and while the city slept he read how very simple things become inextricably tangled up.

People would go on dying and being born. People had no desire to cure their evil nature.

*   *   *   *

TANCREDE PAPINEAU

The name was printed in big red letters. Philibert had never seen it or heard it before. Tancrède Papineau's face looked insignificant on the enormous poster: a lump of whitish clay that had not been modelled by life. Smooth hair, vacant eyes, thin moustache. "The Man of the Future," according to the poster.

About twenty people were standing in front of the picture, waiting, smoking, stamping their feet. They spoke little. Like Philibert, they were there because of a small advertisement in Montréal-Matin.

A pot-bellied man with tiny hands appeared, fiery as a general.

"You realize that the people are going to elect their leaders tomorrow."

He waved an accusing fist towards Tancrède Papineau's poster. Then he jumped up, ripped it off the wall and tore it furiously to shreds.

"Tancrède, we're going to put you through the meat-grinder. Any questions?"

A few impatient coughs. They had come for a job. not to ask questions.

"Go to room 129. They'll give you some bags with pictures of Tancrède in them. They have to be distributed. All over."

How much do we get paid?" asked a man with a pipe.

"Honestly. We'll count your empty bags. No cheating, now. You have to distribute the pictures one by one, from door to door. Don't stick them in the garbage can. You'll be watched."

"Do we get paid some week with four Thursdays, or today?" asked Philibert.

"Come to the Midnight Café at five o'clock. You'll be paid in cash. And there'll be some women for the men that don't turn up their noses at things like that. Women from the Party."

Like his companions who were going to distribute papers through the neighbourhood, Philibert hung a bag over each shoulder and set off at a run. He got winded climbing stairs, zig-zagged through the streets from one house to another, sticking photographs in letter slots and under doors. Then on to another street. His bags were empty. A car was following him with more bags waiting in the trunk. At the wheel, an eye was observing.

A few hours later every voter had seen the photograph. They laughed. They were scandalized. They were disappointed. Or disgusted.

The photograph showed Tancrède Papineau, naked behind his glasses, in the bed of a young television actress. On the back, Josette Latendresse had written: "Vote for my Tancrède. He knows what to do."

Now no one, assuredly, would vote for the infamous Papineau, that hypocrite, sinner and sex maniac.

The photographs drifted along the streets and into the

schoolyards where they had been sent by the wind. Young boys picked them up, laughing lewdly.

Philibert went back to his room. He was happy because he had been paid.

He would not be voting tomorrow.

"My X on a piece of paper isn't going to change the world. It'll turn whichever way it wants to."

★   ★   ★   ★

Philibert pressed the grease-smeared bell-button.

The door, as it opened, tore through the rancid shadow. He found himself facing a mountain. At the peak, in a cloud of black beard, was a face.

"I . . . I . . . I . . . read your ad in . . . *La Presse*."

"Knock me!" thundered the mountain.

Philibert thought he had misunderstood. The mountain repeated, in strangely-accented French this time, "Hit!"

The mountain got to its knees, the big head coming down to Philibert's level. The breath that came out of it stank like the exhaust fumes of a garbage truck.

"Hit me!"

The bristly hair and beard did not completely conceal the face, stained with blue scars.

"Are you afraid of to hit me?"

Philibert's fist struck at a rock of flesh. He ran to the staircase, afraid of being bashed into crumbs himself. The mountain rolled over behind him. He felt the vast breath in his back, its bitter warmth. Something seized him by the shoulder.

"You know to drive automobile?"

"Yes."

"You are brave. You are now private chauffeur of Boris Rataploffsky, the Ninth Vonder of Vorld."

★   ★   ★   ★

Glowing with pride, the private chauffeur of the Ninth Wonder of the World sat behind the steering wheel of which he would henceforth be in charge. The cab of the truck would not contain his enormous boss; the giant travelled in the back, in a made-to-measure cabin. He had had a plywood box built on the chassis of the truck, the windows in the sides decorated with curtains made heavy by dirt. His throne was composed of two armchairs he had put together, nailed and sewed. The cabin was painted red with big white letters reading, "The Man with the Face of Steel"; smaller letters read, "Boris Rataploffsky"; and in bigger letters, "The Ninth Wonder of the World."

How could Philibert not be proud? The eyes of all Montreal were on his truck. People stopped and turned around to see it drive by. Cars slowed down, braked suddenly and risked collisions to have a look at the truck carrying the Ninth Wonder of the World. It was the first time in his life that Philibert had felt proud.

A small bell rang behind his head. Boris Rataploffsky had given the signal. The truck stopped across from the *Comme Chez Vous* Tavern and Philibert ran to the back to open the doors. The Man with the Face of Steel got out with all the majesty of God the moment after Creation. When the huge foot touched the ground Montreal seemed to sink a little.

Boris Rataploffsky, preceded by Philibert, walked through the tavern. His big belly pitched and heaved above the tables and overturned chairs.

"Set us up!" Philibert ordered, surprised by his own authority.

The old waiter conscientiously brought several trays filled with glasses of beer and arranged them so that they covered the table. Around Philibert and the giant the most animated conversations fell silent.

Boris Rataploffsky, his little finger raised, drank glass after glass, row after row, very carefully, without spilling a drop of beer. He emptied them as though he were inhaling a whiff of air. No one else dared to drink. Life had come to a halt in the *Comme Chez Vous* Tavern. The giant's table was covered with empty glasses where the foam traced fine embroideries.

"Go on, my boy," said the giant.

Philibert adjusted his cap and stood up. "Ladies and gentlemen, mesdames et messieurs. You see before you the one, the only, the brilliant Boris Rataploffsky, the Man with the Face of Steel, the Ninth Wonder of the World, the Queen of England's favourite athlete. He gets a pension from the King of Brazil and the King of Hungary refused to pass over to the other side without seeing Boris Rataploffsky."

The giant coughed. When he was impatient, he coughed. Philibert hurried on.

"Your punches are like flea farts to this giant. Mesdames et messieurs, don't miss this chance to hit a giant. For one dollar you can hit him in the eye or on the mouth. Fifty cents and you can try for his nose and for a quarter you get to hit him anywhere else on the face. Careful! Don't get hurt! Step right up! Pay here. We won't be back. Hit the giant! Pansies, call for your mummies!"

In the cushions of his flesh, Boris Rataploffsky was dreaming.

"Come on, come on! Ladies and gentlemen! The giant won't hurt you. His steel face feels no pain."

A customer came up, taking off his jacket.

"I'm going to wake up that big *ciboire* of a pile of dead meat."

The brave man paid his dollar and, proudly rolling up his sleeves, he walked up to face the Man with the Face of Steel. He caressed his fist with his other hand, stamping like a horse about to kick. He straightened out his fist, clenched it again, tightened it, made it hard and sharp with all his might. All at once he hit the giant. The frightened customer was already far away. The giant slept on.

Philibert's hand was filled with bills and fists fell in an avalanche on the unfeeling mountain. Nothing disturbed the shadows of the face.

The customers hit until they had exhausted themselves. They had less and less strength. They laughed. The giant's thoughts were elsewhere.

Suddenly a little drop of blood was visible in his eyebrow.

"*Baptême!*" Philibert panicked. "It isn't true he's got a face of steel."

He yelled, gesturing broadly, "OK, that's it. All over now."

The Ninth Wonder of the World left the tavern behind Philibert, whose pockets were heavy with the money they had accumulated. Without a word he got into his cabin in the red truck with the flat springs.

Philibert put the take into his outstretched hands. A smile flickered in the beard. Philibert closed the door of the cabin.

*   *   *   *

Philibert broke a dozen eggs, sliced a salami, added onions, red and green peppers and cream, mixed it all up in a saucepan with his hands and then cooked it on the gas-stove, which was no longer sticky since he had cleaned it.

The Ninth Wonder of the World ate the omelette with the enthusiasm of a child. Philibert would never get used to his strength. When the Man with the Face of Steel spoke, Philibert shuddered as the house of his childhood had shuddered in the wind.

"Monsieur Rataploffsky, I've got an idea."

"An idea? Show me it."

Philibert explained: it was a mistake for the Ninth Wonder of the World to display himself in half-empty taverns and miserable restaurants where the neighbours got together for a smoke. Only the great arenas were worthy of an attraction as spectacular as the Man with the Face of Steel. Instead of putting on his show several times a day, Boris Rataploffsky could make more money by exhibiting himself in the big arenas, before delirious crowds.

The giant applauded.

"You're my man. You'll be my manacher."

"OK. And from now on my name is Phil. Monsieur Phil. Mister Phil. Manager! *Baptême!* I can't believe myself."

★   ★   ★   ★

From spring until fall the red truck took the Ninth Wonder of the World from Montreal to Gaspé, from Rouyn to Sherbrooke. Everywhere he was given a royal welcome. On his manager's advice, he wore a gold cape with "The Man with the Face of Steel" embroidered on it. In the cities he was surrounded by children and pimply-faced adolescents and old men. They were all the same age before Boris Rataploffsky, as they pushed and jostled, marvelled and bickered, trying to get a chance to touch the Ninth Wonder of the World. They were ecstatic, doubtful; they argued. If the giant raised his hand they stepped back.

Phil always walked ahead of his boss. He busied himself pretending to chase away the importunate. He told them on every possible occasion that just the night before he had refused to sell the giant for the sum of three thousand dollars to American interests. "We already sold too many of our natural resources to foreigners," he would conclude.

All along the highways linking the arenas, through the poor, interminable forests or the flat infinite plains, the giant sang. Phil didn't understand the words of his strange songs that made the roof of his cabin quiver, but he sensed that they were words of joy.

★   ★   ★   ★

In the middle of the ring, whose ropes had been painted white for the occasion, the Man with the Face of Steel stood motionless under the bombardment of fists. The volcano was sleeping.

"Step right up!" shouted Phil over the loudspeakers. "Here's your chance to hit a bigger man than you are. Right this way!"

All around the ring there were children, pallid labourers, muscular lumberjacks, coughing schoolboys, salesmen with slicked-down hair and distinguished ladies; they grew impatient or startled or placed bets. They climbed into the ring, saluted the crowd, and hit. Joyous applause. Each blow was greeted by a delighted ouburst from the crowd. They paid and began all over again, twice, three times. Their pleasure grew. The distinguished ladies kept their rings on their fierce little hands.

At times a stain would appear on the eyelid of the Face of Steel. An old wound reopening or a badly-healed scab. A little blood would flow. Then the fists would let loose, attacking the Face of Steel on all sides, hitting as though you had to destroy to live, as if the giant's face were a prison wall. Their strength increased with each blow. The giant coughed slightly and the fists persisted as though they were attacking a vanquished fawn.

There were shouts of joy and dancing in the shaking stands. Phil could not pick up all the bills that flew around his head like crazy birds. He was powerless to control the crowd. Like a nation of ants they swarmed into the ring, ready to assault the too kindly giant. There were ten of them hitting without let-up, and without paying.

Phil shouted, "Pay right here! Pay here! It's cheap!"

Suddenly the Ninth Wonder of the World stood up, yelling as though he were spitting fire. Before the shock-waves struck the walls he picked up a big man and threw him among the spectators, where he was crushed like an egg. The giant had already grabbed three other men; these he threw at the ceiling. When the three unfortunates had dropped to the floor the angry mountain fell on them with the force of a landslide.

The crowd was silent.

Women wept.

Lovers let their arms fall from their girlfriends' waists.

The giant came up to Phil, putting a hand as heavy as an ox on the boy's shoulder. Blood was streaming from his mouth.

"You are good boy," he grunted. "Don't forget."

Big tears mingled with his blood.

The Man with the Face of Steel climbed out of the ring and went towards one of the exits. He knocked over everything in his path, crushing it like grass.

The bleachers were on the edge of a gentle lake. The giant walked along the shore and got into a rowboat that sank almost out of sight under the burden of his enormous weight.

Phil called, "Wait for me!"

The giant didn't listen. He rowed, but the submerged boat moved along painfully, an island adrift. The giant put the oars inside the boat. Gently, it came to a stop.

Then very slowly the Ninth Wonder of the World got up and let himself fall into the water. He didn't try to swim. He was no longer a giant but a man.

His body was found by a child swimming in the last rays of the sun.

"Who was Boris Rataploffsky?"

"What country did he come from?"

Phil didn't know. He was too drunk, they said. Phil assured them that he knew nothing of the giant's life.

He replied, "What's the use of being a giant on the earth? What's the use of being an ordinary man?"

They laughed.

Sitting in the water that lapped at the sand, Philibert wept.

★   ★   ★   ★

Real life, the life that set Phil's blood on fire, crackled in the nightclubs on Saint-Laurent Boulevard. His laughter was already famous there, as well as the enthusiastic way he applauded the dancing-girls.

When they left the stage they moved among the customers on the way to their dressing-rooms. Anita the African Tigress ran her claws through Phil's hair. Her caress enflamed him as though he had had too much to drink. He had money in the inside pockets of his jacket, a ring on every finger and alligator shoes. Walking proudly, he followed the fiery serpent that disappeared into her dazzling sequins.

Phil wanted Montreal to clasp him and stifle and drown him. He wanted to be a brick among the other bricks, but alive. He wanted to live.

He liked the warm sidewalks in the slums that gave off an aroma of hot dogs and sausages with onions. He liked the life hidden behind the windows papered with photographs of girls. And he liked the life circulating in the buildings' concrete facades that were closed like impenetrable faces.

In the room with flowered wall-paper, beneath a framed picture of Our Lady, the heart pierced with the Seven Sorrows, Phil sweated, exhausted and out of breath from his efforts to transmit the fire that was in him. The girl under him was a soft living corpse.

He got up, running his fingers through his hair. He rummaged in the pockets of his jacket and pulled out a piece of paper, unfolding it carefully. It was a poster that he held out to the African Tigress. A pout. She was disappointed that it wasn't money. She grimaced at the big photograph of The Man with the Face of Steel.

"It's an ape!"

"Read," he ordered proudly.

He pointed: Mr. Phil, Manager.

He pulled on his clothes, picked up the poster the girl had dropped to the floor and refolded it carefully.

He left Saint-Laurent, wanting to vomit.

Farther away, Montreal looked like a funeral wreath placed on the ground.

★   ★   ★   ★

In the smoky room the night was already brightening.

Phil spoke as though he were reading the words, with difficulty, from a blackboard.

"God made everything. He made our bodies and he planted our minds in them. He made the thunder roar and he bumped off old man Hermenegilde. He made Sister Superior fart and he pulled one hair out of our heads every time we got a little older. One day I realized there's no more God up in Heaven than there's a snake with an electric bell in Quebéc. Heaven, the sky up there, is just a big empty box with a few shiny stones in it."

Ladouceur and Cassidy, cigars between their teeth, smiled. Phil filled his glass and pushed the bottle towards them.

He went on. "No more God, so I was all alone. When I was a kid they planted fears in me that grew as tall and thick as the corn in the garden. There was enough to feed on for the rest of my life. For eternity! Don't laugh, *baptême!* Without God I felt as if I'd been amputated, but I was a man, *hostie!* I could say, God doesn't exist but me, I exist. You haven't been born till you've said those words in the middle of the night, crossing Sainte-Catherine Street, weaving through the cars that whistle past your nose like scythes. Ah, for Christ's sake, listen to me . . . God doesn't exist, but me, I exist. I was breathing. It was *me* that was responsible for my own breathing."

He looked for his lighter, found it, looked for his cigars, chose one and surrounded himself with smoke.

"Sometimes an angel or one of the saints or even God himself used to come and nibble in the corner of my room like rats coming out of the sewer. Sometimes I could feel their little paws running across my chest in a panic when I couldn't get to sleep."

"You said there wasn't any God," the ironic Ted Ladouceur reminded him.

Phil laughed scornfully. He threw the bottle of Scotch at Cassidy who caught it and refilled the glasses.

"Trying to talk philosophy to you," said Phil, "is like trying to put lace underpants on a mare."

Cassidy and Ladouceur folded their stranglers' hands like perfect choir-boys. Heads bowed, in a monastic voice, they murmured, "Amen."

*   *   *   *

The day had to come. Phil's fingers found no more money under the piles of folded clothing in his dresser drawers. He tossed the clothes on the bed, unfolded and shook them and emptied every drawer. Not a single dollar. He had exhausted his savings a long time ago and now he possessed absolutely nothing. His rings? He'd sell them.

The Craig Street Jew offered him a ridiculously low price, an insult. He was a thief. It would be better to be fleeced than go back to work. Ah! Why hadn't he followed Boris Rataploffsky in the rowboat into the water of the beautiful lake at Saint-Benoit-de-Beauce? Montreal was as dry as a stone.

While the old Jew had his nose in the cash-register Philibert picked up a pale blue plastic radio and stuck it in his jacket. He had his revenge.

If he could rob a Jew he wouldn't have to give up hope altogether. Perhaps he would even get rich.

Outside on the sidewalk he pressed the radio against him, being very careful not to look like a thief. The police protected the Jews because the Jews controlled the police and the governments and the businesses. Everybody knew that the Jews even controlled the *Anglais*. Ah, why wasn't he a Jew?

"It wouldn't be as hard as being a lousy stinking French Canadian. The Jews are rich and we haven't got gas ovens in Québec so they've got all the security they want, if we did have gas ovens they'd be the ones that sold them. Ah, those *maudits Juifs!*"

Farther long the street another old Jew in another shop agreed, after much bartering, to buy his radio for two dollars.

The time when life had been generous was closed behind him, like a big door that would never open again.

The Ninth Wonder of the World was dead. The dream was over.

If Phil went on like this he would have to sell his alligator shoes and his blue suit with the pink and green threads.

*   *   *   *

Bulldozers were snoring. Philibert didn't hear them any more than he heard the sound of his own breathing or the intermittent barking of the explosions that shook the bedrock.

Something wet hit him in the face: bird-shit? He looked up but he could see neither sky nor bird. Only the scaffolding crisscrossing over a steel frame. He wiped his face with the back of his hand. It was sticky with blood.

"*Tabernacle!*" yelled the man next to him. "It's skin off a man!"

"Yeah, because women are scarce *en hostie* around here!"

Other men working around them had been hit by bloody droplets too. Shovels were put down, hammers and picks fell to the ground. The workmen wiped their faces, looking around to find the source of the still-living bits of flesh that had spattered them.

The foreman burst out like another explosion.

"Bunch of goddamn lazy buggers, get back to work. You could at least earn enough to pay for the paper your cheques are printed on. I'll cut a quarter hour off your time, *bande de Christ!*"

Philibert bent down to pick up his shovel and held it up by the handle.

"You're a bigger pig than an *hostie* of a pig!"

"I do my job," said the foreman. "When I had to dig, I dug, no crybaby stuff. Now my job is giving you guys shit. I give you shit and you're going to do your work, *bande de Christ!* The Dominion Company isn't going to go broke here because of a *baptême* of a lazy bum like you!"

"Boss! Hey boss," shouted the man from the Beauce, sliding down the ladder. "It's the Portuguese guy. He blew up!"

"I'm telling you cows, *bande de Christ,* if you weren't so lazy maybe you'd be a little more careful and there wouldn't be all these accidents. What's Dominion going to say now?"

When the foreman was nervous he kept taking his cap off and putting it back on his head.

"Boss! Hey boss!" the *Beauceron* repeated. "It is not an accident, he put a stick of dynamite between his teeth and another one between his legs. We were laughing, thought it was a big joke, then he pressed the detonator and we kept on laughing because we thought, it won't go off, but it went off. We didn't see it, it happened too fast, but we didn't laugh any more. There isn't enough of him left to bury now."

"Why did that *Christ* of a DP have to go and do a thing like that? Canada gets too many of these starving Europeans. They come over here and take our jobs and as soon as they've got a full belly they blow themselves up."

"Then we get their crap in our faces," said a welder who was still cleaning himself off.

The foreman took off his cap and put it back on his head. "Why did he do it?"

"Crazy," suggested another welder.

"Crazy," repeated the foreman. "That's the only thing that could account for it."

Philibert threw down his shovel. "Crazy! Boss, we're the crazy ones. We're crazier than the goddamn crazies. If we weren't crazy we'd do like the Portuguese guy and this *baptême* of a pile of scrap iron we're sewing up for the rich guys would be fertilized by a flood of human meat chopped up by dynamite. But we're crazy, by Christ. If the rich guys want a castle, we build them one. That Portuguese guy wasn't crazy. He said, take your castle and shove it up your perfumed ass. Expensive perfume too. I couldn't even afford to put it on my face."

The foreman's hat danced off his head and back but he said nothing. Philibert didn't add a word. He went over to the beam where he had hung his jacket. He didn't pick it up. It was spotted with blood. The police on Sainte-Catherine Street would think he was a murderer.

"You, some day your craziness is going to catch up with you," said the foreman. "One of these days we're going to find *you* with dynamite in your mouth."

"Don't worry, boss. My craziness is taking this bitch of a life with a smile and then saying thank-you for it."

He wandered the streets aimlessly.

He walked.

Night fell.

Alone in his bed, despite his closed eyes and the heavy curtain at the window, Philibert could not erase the image of a chopped-up face, bleeding, whose laugh was a wound. The face was so disfigured he could not be certain that it was his own.

*   *   *   *

How many days had it been since Philibert had seen the springtime sky from the bottom of his grease-pit? He often dreamed of trips he had taken on beautiful sunny days, on highways that took him from the Laurentians to the Appalachians, from the salty Gaspé air to the dry forests of Val d'Or. Now his horizon was restricted by the sticky walls of his grease-pit. Above him there was a sky of muddy tin and rusty pipes that spat out noxious clouds. Philibert coughed and spat. Grey water, grease and oil rained down on him. His coverall and shirt were soaked. No matter how vigorously he scrubbed himself his body left an oily outline on the sheets. The smell of gas and oil followed him; he could smell it everywhere like a stinking cloud from which he could not separate himself.

It was night when he finished work, and the night was invaded by automobiles that slithered along the streets like disgusting illuminated snakes.

One day a letter, stained by greasy hands, fell into Philibert's pit. It had been a long time since he had received a letter. Who could be thinking of him? It came from Morin, Morin, Morin and Morin, barristers and notaries.

"*Baptême!* Now the law's after me. I didn't do anything wrong." He read it with feverish excitement.

Dear Sir:
Will you kindly come to our offices in connection with the death of our client M. Donato Ambrosio, alias Louis Durand, alias Agadad Aglagayan, alias Jean-Baptiste Turcotte, alias Boris Rataploffsky *et alii* whom it appears that you knew by one of these names or another.

Yours very truly,

The signature was illegible.

"*Baptême!* They're going to make me pay for the coffin for the Ninth Wonder of the World. He didn't need a coffin, he needed a steamboat. They'll ruin me, but I don't care, I'll borrow the money. I'll buy flowers too."

★   ★   ★   ★

Philibert had never seen so many books. The house seemed to be built not of bricks or stone but of books.

"Have you read that, *Monsieur le Notaire*?"

The man of law was so clean. No speck of dust, no vulgar word had come near him since his birth.

"No, alas, I have not read everything. One reads, one reads, then one realizes that one learns nothing more. One stops reading. But one continues to haunt the book-shops."

"Jesus, *Monsieur le Notaire,* you wouldn't talk like that if you'd gone to the kick-in-the-pants university."

"One must be determined, young man, and patient, patient. And one must have good will, know when to be quiet. A little luck helps too, of course. But that is something that *you* don't lack for."

"*Baptême, Monsieur le Docteur,* you don't know me very well."

The short bald man smiled—weakly, so as not to disturb the hairs of his moustache.

"Listen."

In a voice accustomed to appearing indifferent to good news and bad, the voice of an obsequious dead man careful not to awaken his neighbours, he began to read, pronouncing words and words and more words. Philibert did not understand a thing, only words piled on words. Suddenly, in the flow of dull verbiage, Philibert made out, "Consequently, Monsieur Phil, my manager, will inherit . . ."

"Not so fast, *Monsieur le Curé!*

The notary looked up from his papers without raising his head. "Monsieur, I lack sufficient holiness to be a *Curé* despite my honesty on which you can most assuredly depend."

"What am I inheriting, *Monsieur le Notaire?* Debts from the Ninth Wonder of the World?"

"Boris Rataploffsky, since that is the name by which you knew him, did not leave you a fortune . . ."

"*Baptême!*" Philibert interrupted. "What *did* he give me?"

"He has left you an interesting sum, a very interesting sum I might say, one that you might profitably invest, following the expert advice of our brokerage office."

Philibert did not understand.

"Only if you wish to do so, of course," the notary specified.

Philibert ran to the door. He couldn't listen to another word.

"I'll be back, doctor. But before I come back I've got to go and get drunk. On credit, but I got to do it.

One last time. When you're rich you get drunk on champagne, but me, I like beer."

★　　★　　★　　★

"I'm an heir!"

Philibert's old '37 Chevrolet was quivering like a child with a new toy. His foot trembled on the accelerator. His hands on the steering-wheel were trembling too, as though he were frightened.

"I'm an heir! An heir!"

He thought he was thinking of a hundred things, but these were the only words that came to his lips.

On the back seat of his car — was that why he was trembling? — he felt the breathing of something enormous, the breath of the Ninth Wonder of the World.

"You're my truly son. You're my boy. Don't forget," the gruff voice murmured very tenderly.

Philibert stopped the Chevrolet. He could not see anything. There were too many tears in his eyes.

"No, *Monsieur le géant,* I won't get drunk after all."

"You are good son," said the voice in the shadow of the Chevrolet.

He was no longer able to drive.

He crossed his arms on the steering-wheel and buried his head there, as though it were a pillow on which he could abandon himself to his sorrow.

Why had the Ninth Wonder of the World left him this inheritance? Was the giant all alone in the world? As alone as Philibert? Why had he ended his life in that ridiculous little rowboat? Why had he gone without a word of explanation to anyone, not even his manager?

"Deep down, you are good boy," said the voice in the back. Although the voice resembled that of the Ninth Wonder of the World, Philibert recognized his father's voice too.

"Father! I'm going to go and see you in the village and you're going to be proud of me. You won't want to boot my ass any more. When you see me you're going to take me in your arms."

He stepped firmly on the starter and drove his beat-up old car in the direction of the notary's office. The car responded like a stubborn mule. He pushed the accelerator to the floor, thinking crazily that he'd like to have a whip to make his car, his old old car, hurry up.

*   *   *   *

Philibert would be a grocer. A little grocery-store as clean as a house, with jars of jam arranged in multicoloured pyramids and dusted every day. A grocery store that smelled good, big with a big front window.

His hands would be clean. He would use a white towel

frequently to wipe them on. He would wear a white shirt and a blue
or red bow-tie. The walls would be white too. The ceiling might be
a bright pink colour. He would swallow his bad language in front of
his customers because he would be a respectable grocer. He would
be polite. After they had done their shopping he would escort the
customers to the door and he would be careful not to pinch their
bums. The store would be called "Boris and Philibert." No. "Boris
and Son"? No. "Rataploffsky and Associate"? No, that sounded too
Jewish. Anyway, the name painted on the front of the store wasn't
very important, the basic truth was written in his soul: he owed his
life to the Ninth Wonder of the World. He would enroll in a night
course to learn English, because English was the language of business, big business and monkey business. If you can't speak English
you can't even take a leak when you want to. He would subscribe
to English magazines like the office workers he'd seen on the bus.
Those magazines told you things. *Baptême!* They had great pictures
of naked women to give you some energy too. Then he would take
a course in accounting because when he went to school they had
taught him how to go to Heaven but not how to go to the bank.
Before he became the manager of the Ninth Wonder of the World
he couldn't even tell a profit from a loss, if he ran the grocery store
well it would grow and prosper. Then later, perhaps he would . . .
He didn't even dare think about it. Go into politics . . . He mustn't
think about it. Politics . . . It was forbidden to think about it: he
might as well dream of having a prick as big as a locomotive. *Baptême!* He might as well dream of having the wings of an angel. But
if he became a big grocer, well, he'd be just as good as a lawyer, and
maybe he could be an MLA . . .

"You, you've got the makings of a Prime Minister," an old man
in a factory had once told him.

He would be a grocer. A nice little grocery store, all clean and
neat and smelling good.

Before he bought his grocery store Philibert would go to the bank to deposit his inheritance. It was a long time since he had gone to the Savings Bank. Not since his unsuccessful rendezvous with the pretty little cashier.

If she was still behind her wicket he would hold out his cheque quite indifferently. She would be uncomfortable because she would remember turning up her nose at Philibert. She would look like a cat that has made a mess on the rug. She wouldn't dare look him in the eye. She would hide her eyes in her statements. She would pretend to have forgotten. Unhappy, she would be even prettier, with a beauty that would make a man happy to be a man and make him want to be good and strong, in love with life. Phil would not be ashamed to look her in the eye. He had nothing to blame himself for. His only fault was having been poor. He would ask her out. She would accept. Her woman's heart would know that Phil was capable of love. She would get into his old Chevrolet as though it were the carriage of a king. Say what you like, what a woman wants most from a man is love. To love . . .

"Ah! To love . . . to love . . . to love . . ."

*   *   *   *

The night was ripped open.

The burning of a whip in the flesh of his back.

A phosphorescent tree sprang into the windshield.

The dark wave of night fell again and the clamour of Montreal, near as it was, did not disturb the silence.

In the depth of the night the '37 Chevrolet had turned over. The wheels were spinning furiously.

*   *   *   *

The phosphorescent Cross of Christ rose up before Philibert like a tree on the road in front of his car. The outstretched arms sparkled like glowing coals and the gaping wound in the side of Christ was as broad as a neon city. He slammed on the brake but the wheels didn't bite the road and the car didn't cling to the pavement. It sank like a sword into the side of Christ and a tide of blood poured down on the windshield. The wipers managed to clear a semi-circle, but it was no use; their mechanism had broken down. Blood soaked the upholstery, flowed onto the seats, stained Phil's suit and trickled into his hair and onto his face. The warm blood ran onto his eyelids and his eyes, and the car was filled with the blood of Christ.

He pushed at the door with his shoulder, trying to get out, but the blood was running like a river and the roof of the car was shining above the red tide. Phil swam towards a shore that must exist somewhere. He had not been swimming since the muddy water of the little Famine River.

At the end of his strength, and heavier than a rock, he got back into the car which was breathed in, swallowed up, by a whirlpool.

His shouts were useless. The night was deserted and the distant windows on the other shore of night were deaf. A strong gust dragged him under the surface of the wave. Phil struggled, waving his arms and legs, and he managed to come up to the red surface. In the sky, stretching as far as he could see, was the gash in the side of Christ. Blood gushed in a torrent that was more tumultuous than Niagara. Blood poured over the mountains, tore up villages, inundated the city. The sea opened great blood-shot eyes.

The blood burned the harvests, carried off trees and rocks, uprooted skyscrapers. Phil could no longer struggle. His efforts had exhausted him. A man alone can do nothing. He closed his eyes, pressed his lips together, stretched his arms out along his body and accepted his own drowning with no anger or regret. He no longer had the strength to refuse.

While he was stretched out there across the blood that had

become as diaphanous as fresh water, he noticed, up high, a man. It was a tight-rope walker, advancing cautiously along a wire stretched out in the sky, above the abyss of the night. The man slid his foot along the wire without lifting it. His arms were outstretched, his body very stiff. The man was staring at a distant point in the night.

"Help!" Philibert called.

At the cry the tight-rope walker turned his head. The wire was shaken, the man tossed over. He lost his footing and fell, a wingless bird.

Phil's head was split open by the impact.

*   *   *   *

Phil opened his lips and a trickle of blood poured down onto his chin. He thought he had uttered the word "LIVE." The night trembled like a contented animal. It was a beautiful word, beautiful like a horse galloping across a field. The walls of night spoke with Phil's voice, repeating the word "LIVE."

His lips were open. Now no sound burst from his mouth. His throat was closed as though a hand were around his neck, strangling him.

*   *   *   *

Through the shattered windshield of his car Phil could see his limbs spread out in the night. A torn-off arm was a red flower. A leg looked like a broken branch and his head was surrounded by the water of a pool.

His body was scattered in the abyss of a dead memory.

*   *   *   *

Steel teeth, wide as doors, forever closed.

The jaws of hell.

When he was a child Philibert used to open the book at the page where they talked about hell and spend hours looking at the drawings of the open-mouthed dragon whose stomach led to Hell.

The jaws of hell.

Philibert used to spend a lot of time looking at the picture, frightening himself. He wanted his soul to be marked by fear, to be deeply scarred by it. The more scared he was the less he would feel like sinning.

The jaws of Hell.

Sometimes Philibert fell asleep on his open book and gently, lovingly, the dragon in the drawing would begin to lick his face.

Here are the jaws of Hell. At the edges of the lips, like spaghetti, but sickeningly slimy, serpents were swimming. The mere sight of them would drive a person mad, but in Hell one does not go mad and one cannot die of fear. Phil gave in to the giant worm's slimy caress as it twined itself around him. The burning of the fire was gentle compared to the serpent's caress. The filthy wetness of its sticky flesh pressed against him and its cold body smelled like vomit. The serpent wound around his ankles, tied itself there, gripped his legs and attacked them, encircled his thighs, his hips, pressed against his abdomen. Phil was no longer able to breathe. The serpent compressed his chest, preventing his lungs from expanding. Phil saw the serpent's face come closer, as though to tear out his eyes. But it rested against his cheek, pressing its cheek against Phil's, drooling. Revoltingly affectionate, the lips with their smell of rotten meat clung to Phil's lips like a bloodsucker. The serpent's tongue uncurled in his mouth and moved there like another serpent, like a maddened viper, sounding the depth of his throat.

Phil choked. The serpent's tongue slid into his throat. He must swallow the horrible living spit. The serpent's snout was now forcing open the ring of his mouth. Little by little the head moved into his mouth and insinuated itself into his throat. The head sank into Phil's chest like a stake, digging its way through the lungs. It dug through the liver, pierced the stomach, rippled through the intestines. Then it hesitated, rested a bit, hiccuped. Its belly growled and Phil thought it was his own. The serpent moved into his rectum. It wriggled through Phil's body as it had in its natal mud. Phil's stomach rotted until it looked like the belly of a dead cow in the wheatfield. The serpent stretched his anus, its head came out and Phil could feel the bumps on its skull, feel the head dangling between his legs like a miscarried foetus. The neck stretched, the head rose and the mouth took hold of Phil's penis. The jaws closed around it. Under his feet and along his thighs the agony of the flames was sweet. He did not feel the pebbles of fire.

All that remained of him was an enormous suffering, a pain that would last through eternity, a pain that would suffer pain, that would prolong its torments longer than it would take the wings of a bird to wear out all the rocks in the world.

"Suffer. Suffer to suffer. Suffer to suffer. Suffer to suffer. Suffer. Suffer."

Phil managed to see through the half-light where the grating voice originated. The shadow did not completely veil a hare-lipped face. The sad features seemed on the verge of tears.

A little snake slid out of the deep-set eye like a tear.

"To be alive is a curse."

The words awakened a snake in its nest. It came out the other socket.

"I never asked to live," said Phil.

A thin pig's head moved on a skeleton whose bones looked like a calcified shrub. The monster threw itself among the burning coals on all four feet, barked, and jostled the serpent like a boisterous pup.

"You are suffering," he said mockingly. "You have always wanted to suffer."

The flames were stirred by the movements of the maddened creatures and the earth decomposed in jagged sparks, but the fire darkened, the flames turning grey. The light was dusty and no longer held back the night, which became entirely black again. The untouchable black vault of the sky hurtled down on Phil, and the weight of that cartload of bricks overturned on him.

★   ★   ★   ★

The night felt warm to him, like a mother. He was alone, but where? In his childhood bed, perhaps; his heart stopped because there was a hand on his chest. His heart was a little berry between big iron fingers.

On the overturned car a wheel that was still alive lost momentum as the blood flowed out. It weighed against the axle, slowed down, hesitated, turned again, barely turned, weakened, moved sluggishly, stopped.

Philibert thought he said, "Is that the sun?"

ROCH CARRIER was born in 1937 in Sainte-Justine-de-Dorchester, Québec. He is the author of more than fifteen novels and numerous children's books, short story collections, poetry collections, and plays. He was director of the Canada Council for the Arts from 1994 to 1997, and he served as the National Librarian of Canada from 1999 to 2004. Carrier is a Fellow of the Royal Society of Canada and an Officer of the Order of Canada. He lives in Montreal.

SHEILA FISCHMAN was born in Moose Jaw, Saskatchewan. She is the translator of more than 150 novels. She has been awarded numerous prizes, including the Governor General's Literary Award for Translation, the Canada Council Translation Prize, and the Molson Prize for the Arts. She is a Member of the Order of Canada and a chevalier of the Ordre national du Québec. She lives in Montreal.

A
LIST

The A List